Praise for the Books of Mary Jane Maffini

"A comedic, murderous romp . . . Maffini is a relaxed, accomplished, and wickedly funny writer."

—*The Montreal Gazette*

"Maffini's new series . . . is off to a brilliant start with this fast-paced mystery!"

—*Romantic Times*

"Mary Jane Maffini provides a first-rate, well-organized whodunit . . . A new series that is fun to read."

—*Midwest Book Review*

"A fast-moving story."

—*Contra Costa Times*

"A great little fun book that has real organizing hints . . ."

—*The Globe and Mail*

"Plenty of twists and turns that kept me turning the pages until the last sentence."

—*Dru's Book Musings*

"There is a place for the clever puzzle plot, and Mary Jane Maffini's series, featuring organizer/sleuth Charlotte Adams, is perfectly at home in it. Devotees of the classic mystery can do no better than this clever mystery."

—*The Globe and Mail*

"Top Pick. 4½ stars."

—*RT Book Reviews*

Books by Mary Jane Maffini

The Charlotte Adams Mysteries

Organize Your Corpses
The Cluttered Corpse
Death Loves a Messy Desk
Closet Confidential
The Busy Woman's Guide to Murder
Death Plans a Perfect Trip

Camilla MacPhee Mysteries

Speak Ill of the Dead
The Icing on the Corpse
Little Boy Blues
The Devil's in the Details
The Dead Don't Get Out Much
Law & Disorder
You Light Up My Death

The Fiona Silk Mysteries

Lament for a Lounge Lizard
Too Hot to Handle

The Book Collector Mysteries
(written as Victoria Abbott with Victoria Maffini)

The Christie Curse
The Sayers Swindle
The Wolfe Widow
The Marsh Madness
The Hammett Hex

Death Plans a Perfect Trip

A Charlotte Adams Mystery

Mary Jane Maffini

Death Plans a Perfect Trip
Mary Jane Maffini

Cover design and illustration by Dar Albert, Wicked Smart Designs

Beyond the Page Books
are published by
Beyond the Page Publishing
www.beyondthepagepub.com

ISBN: 978-1-954717-98-5

Acknowledgments

My sincere thanks to the many Charlotte Adams fans who let me know over the years that they were waiting for more adventures for Charlotte, her friends and her pooches.

One of the best parts of writing fiction is making up restaurants and food shops that I wish existed, and that includes every one of the eateries in this book. Most of them were influenced by happy experiences, except for the sandwich vending machines in Italian railway stations.

I am grateful to Paris for being Paris, Lisbon for being Lisbon, and Italy for being Italy. To the people of Paris, Lisbon, Piedmont and Cinque Terre, thank you for the richness of your heritage and your culture as well as the surprising warmth of your welcome.

I must add a special shout-out to Michael Arno and Mara Taracievicz Arno for a wonderful visit to Vinicola Arno and their home in Piedmont and for useful information about the region. Thanks to Uncle Bill Arno for taste-testing the biscotti and for helpful discussions about Italy.

Over the years, behind-the-scenes chats with Vicki Delany, Barbara Fradkin, Susan Gates, Robin Harlick, Sue Pike and Linda Wiken have kept my spirits high. I am in debt to Linda Wiken (again!) and my daughter, Victoria Maffini, for extra help and support with this manuscript.

Meanwhile on the home front, my husband Giulio provides endless support, information, technical knowledge and even delicious meals. Unfortunately, he does feel the need to look over his shoulder a lot. Penny and Ivy, the latest in a long line of miniature dachshunds in my home, have kept us laughing and inspired many scenes for Truffle and Sweet Marie. Thanks to Canadian Dachshund Rescue for making it possible for them to be in our lives.

I am indebted to Bill Harris of Beyond the Page Publishing for his enthusiasm, support and expertise as well as for being unflappable. Thank you, Bill, for making Beyond the Page a home for Charlotte and her gang. We are very happy here. Further thanks to Tom Colgan and Kim Lionetti for their support bringing the original Charlotte Adams series to print.

Charlotte and I admire the inspirational army of professional organizers who bring hope and order to our lives. Speaking of order, no book, including this one, is really complete without at least one brilliant librarian enriching the plot and the research.

The *Montreal Daily News* doesn't exist, nor do the specific branches of the Bank of Montreal or, for that matter, the numerous underworld figures mentioned. Jean-Claude Dion is fictional but his bravery is inspired by some of the great Quebec crime reporters.

We have used Canadian spellings in the Canadian newspaper excerpts, conversations with Canadians and notes from "Ali," the helpful fictional librarian from McGill. We have used American spellings elsewhere. You may, of course, insert a *u* or subtract from a double consonant from time to time to suit yourselves.

My greatest wish is that you will all have fun on this trip!

The Bus

"You two are going the wrong way." The fat man laughs as we race through the puddles to push onto the next bus. We have already been on two other buses for the longest time. "Don't pay attention. We're going the right way," Mummy says and squeezes my arm. That means I am supposed to stop crying. "You'll see."

The bus is hot and stinky, like old sneakers. The seats feel slippery and there's a lot of gum under mine. Mummy tells me I should sleep now. She says there will be a TV and lots of snacks at our friend Lola's and I can play with her cat. I am trying to look for Lola and her house but we can't even see out the windows because they are foggy. Anyway, it's nighttime.

I am holding on to my new Toy Story *backpack so none of these people can steal it from me, even though I don't like it. I love my Barbie backpack, but it had to get left behind. Mummy says we're perfectly safe but I can tell that she is scared too. She doesn't smile or laugh. She has big dark circles under her eyes. I hate the way Mummy looks now. Why did she cut her beautiful long blonde hair? Short and dark brown is not as pretty. Why did she leave her nice coat behind? This jacket makes her look really fat and she isn't even a little bit fat. Why am I dressed like a boy? I am not a boy. I hate my ugly haircut. I want to be a girl again. Mummy keeps whispering, "Soon soon, Charlie." She calls me Charlie now. That's not my name. I'm supposed to call her Esme. Why did we have to leave everything? Mummy, I mean Esme, says it's just stuff. We are okay. That's what matters. Things will be better at our new home.*

But I miss Buster and his soft fur. Buster's not stuff. Who will take care of him? Mummy, I mean Esme, says some nice people will feed Buster.

Mummy gives me an apple juice box and two chocolate chip cookies. "Don't worry," she says.

I don't want the cookies. My feet are wet and cold. Mummy says I need to go to sleep and they will dry. We can hear people snoring. I don't want to snore. Mummy says, "Lola will fix things for us. Soon."

But what if the bad men find us on this bus? What if there's another fire? I don't even know Lola.

When I wake up, it's time to leave the bus. Now we have to run through the icy cold rain, soaking our clothes and sneakers again. We keep ducking behind houses, keeping out of sight. "Just in case."

Will we ever find Lola?

Chapter 1

The secret to a great trip is great planning.

I jerked awake with a gasp. Instead of bad men grabbing me, two small wiener dogs—one brown and one black—opened their eyes and glared resentfully.

I hate that damned dream.

My sleep shirt was drenched and so was my pillow. The blue and white top sheet lay tangled and damp with sweat. At least my clothes were ready on the chair by the bed. I pulled on jeans and a soft old cashmere hoodie. I slipped on the warm socks and stuck my feet into my sneakers. I reached for my quilted bomber jacket. Mid-April in Woodbridge, New York, can be nippy in the mornings.

Never mind any of my nightmares, Truffle and Sweet Marie, my rescued dachshunds, need to hit the grass first thing in the morning. Because I had been running into some friendly new dog walkers in the neighborhood lately, I brushed my hair and pulled it into a ponytail. I slipped on my sunglasses to hide my bleary eyes. What can I say? The dogs couldn't wait for me to shower, shampoo and do a proper blowout of my hair. And looking presentable at all times is important if your job involves showing people how to live a better life through organizing techniques. This morning, I'd keep my distance and wave. You never know if today's dog walker could be tomorrow's client.

On the way out, I ducked into my tiny perfect kitchen. The dogs scurried back to bed as I took the time to grind beans from my new bag of Kicking Horse coffee. "Get up, you two!" I popped the ground coffee into the coffee maker and pressed the Start button.

I attached their leashes and carried both dogs down the stairs, all three of us grumbling. For eight nights, I'd been having reruns of that old nightmare. Every new day started with walking the dogs, then stuffing the bedding into the washing machine. It was getting old fast.

Truffle and Sweet Marie reacted to the crisp air by racing away. Lucky I had taken those leashes. I nodded at the hand-holding young couple with the boxer, the shy and shambling teenaged boy with the adorable mixed-breed rescue and one of the new people, a burly woman in a ratty trench coat and a mud-colored bucket hat. She had an awkward lumbering walk and was struggling in my direction with a misbehaving corgi. In the past few years while training to become therapy dogs, Truffle and Sweet Marie had learned not to bark at strangers. They were polite to the other dogs. They did bark "hello" to the corgi, a newcomer. The corgi barked back and then broke away from his owner and raced away. I hadn't realized corgis could travel so fast. His owner was quick on her feet too, yelling "Suzie! Suzie!" That did no good at all. With the help of a bearded middle-aged gentleman walking his own small, white, moplike dog, she cornered the wayward Suzie by our next-door neighbor's garage. Suzie snapped and tugged. The woman looked to be losing the battle until the man scooped up Suzie and told her in no uncertain terms to behave. Suzie seemed to settle after that. The romantic in me imagined a love affair developing between a pair of portly middle-aged people with dogs. The helpful man tipped his tweed flat cap to me. The woman was still catching her breath and adjusting her bucket hat.

I grinned at them. Truffle and Sweet Marie wagged their tails.

The moment made me happy. I was blessed in my life here in Woodbridge. People were kind, the scent of spring was in the air and sunny daffodils were popping up in every front yard. There were no bad men chasing me and my mother. That was nothing but a childish dream. Woodbridge was the best place in the world to live and I never wanted to leave again.

As I carted the dogs upstairs, the seductive aroma of coffee wafted out to greet me. I was lucky to be starting the day in the bright and cheerful apartment on the second floor of the yellow Victorian that Jack Reilly, my former best friend and now the man in my life, had inherited from his parents. I had a note in my agenda to put out the beautiful glass hummingbird feeder that Jack had given me for Christmas. He'd had it made for me by an artisan he knew, in shades of red and purple glass. I had already mixed up the sugar water to fill it and Jack had rigged up a way to hang the feeder from a branch that was close enough to the window to reach without anyone (say, me) falling out. Hummingbirds would be migrating through our region soon and I hoped to offer a meal for some and maybe entice others to summer over here in Woodbridge. I'd always loved the tiny creatures.

Truffle and Sweet Marie inhaled their breakfasts. Dinner was good, but breakfast was better, you could tell by those happy tails and the now shiny bowls. Anyone watching would assume they'd been without food for weeks, and at one point they had been. How could anyone have abandoned them? I'll never know how long they were on their own before a trucker stopped for the half-starved and flea-bitten pair stuck on the median on the interstate. Their rescuer knew about WAG'D, the local rescue group that Jack volunteers with. I hoped that whoever ended up with my first dog, Buster, twenty-six years earlier had cared enough to see he found a new home.

I shook myself. Possibly a habit I'd picked up from the pooches. I could have spent my life reliving my nightmares, but I believe you need to seize each morning and squeeze what you can out of it. The washing machine hummed. I sipped my coffee and pondered buying more sheets. Breakfast is not my favorite meal, so I'd settled for coconut yogurt and a banana. The dogs, standing near their shining empty bowls, eyed the yogurt and the banana with interest. Eyeing with interest is one of their best skills. I'm on my guard all the time. "Forget the rough night," I told them, "today will be excellent. I have a presentation at the library and that's always fun and good for business."

But by now they were cleaning their feet. It's really all about them.

• • •

My happy bubble burst when I realized it was Wednesday. Wednesday meant my mother had now missed two of her regular Tuesday "command performance" phone calls.

Two.

Not only that, but she'd been out of sorts lately in the previous calls. I'd put it down to a slipped deadline for the book she was finishing, although that wasn't like her at all. The first missed call had started the nightmares.

I showered and did my hair while stewing about two Tuesdays and no call. I needed to share my worries with Jack. But before the sun was up, he had left for CYCotics, his new cycle shop. Our plans to restore the yellow Victorian house to a family home—for us—were now on the back burner until his business was stable. We had been saving for the reno but needed to know that we had a financial cushion for the first two years. No problem. I had offered to do a business plan for him, including working on his mission and vision statements and, at the very least, to set up spread sheets to track expenses and run projections. His standard response was "maybe next week."

Jack had been my rock for many years and today I needed that rock.

I stopped at Surprise!, the new neighborhood café, to pick up an extra-spicy breakfast burrito for Jack and *caffe lattes* for both of us. Those would help with our heart-to-heart.

The dogs raced through the door of CYCotics and I hurried after them, trying not to inhale the shop smell of oil, rubber and forgotten lunches. I blurted out, "My mother is missing."

Jack looked up from the bicycle he was adjusting and ran his hand through his spiky hair. His brilliant blue eyes twinkled behind the rimless glasses. As usual, I found everything about him irresistible. But this was not a time to get sidetracked by his boyish charm.

"What?" he said.

The lure of a high-end bike has that effect on him. Fills his man-brain and leaves little room for anything else. I know where my competition lies.

"I've been trying to reach my mother for eight days since she missed the first call. I may have mentioned that a hundred times."

Jack quipped, "No more than fifty."

I passed over his burrito and latte and opened the lid of my own drink.

"Not at all funny," I said.

Jack seized the burrito with a gleam in his eye. "Charlotte, remember that your mother is an extremely independent woman."

"Correct. An independent woman who always calls me on Tuesday. Has never missed."

"But she likes to be the center of attention—"

"Exactly."

"—so maybe she just wants a bit more attention."

"She gets tons of attention!"

"I mean from you." He bit into the burrito, meaningfully.

"How exactly would not being in touch lead to more attention from me?"

Of course, I had to wait until he'd swallowed that bite.

"I don't know, but your mother is a world traveler. She's tough as nails and she's dripping in money. She might have taken an impulse trip where she's out of communication range. Maybe an African safari. But she'll have left your contact info if anything happened to her, which it won't have. You have nothing to worry about."

I crossed my arms and glared at him. "Our Tuesday conversations are all about what's going on with her, the parts she wants me to know about anyway. She couldn't resist mentioning a safari or any other glamorous trip."

Jack threw up his hands. "Fine. Be upset if it makes you happy. But let me remind you that you've been worried that she'll visit again. Remember how she made you crazy on her last trip?"

"Yes, but just because it's hard when she visits doesn't mean that I don't care about her."

"I'm not saying that." Jack can be very annoying when he's being calm and reasonable.

"I *am* worried."

"Don't you want to relax and enjoy the lack of drama?"

He had a point. Wherever my mother goes, drama follows.

"Somehow it just feels wrong. *She's* the one who wants the regular calls. She's the one who insists that they be Tuesday."

He polished off the burrito and went back to the bike.

I couldn't just let it go. "Why doesn't she call?"

He gave the wheel a twirl. "Remember, she's a free spirit. Just look at all those husbands. That's without even talking about the boyfriends."

My mother's collection of husbands is not my favorite topic but I had to respond. "You can be a free spirit and still regularly badger your daughter. That's what she has been doing. Also, I don't know that having four husbands makes you free in any way."

"I thought it was five husbands."

"I'm never really sure. And however many of them, her husbands are not the point. Something is going on."

"Guess so."

"It feels weird."

"How old is she?"

"I have no idea now old she is. I would never ever ask her and she wouldn't volunteer the information. She must be around fifty."

A faraway look crossed Jack's face. He was probably remembering his own lovely parents, who hadn't had a shade of vanity. "Have you tried–?"

"I've tried everything! I've called both phones. I've texted her dozens of times. I've tried Messenger, WhatsApp, you name it. I would try a singing telegram if I knew where she was."

Jack stepped away from the precious bike and pulled me into a bear hug. I buried my face in his Hawaiian shirt and clung to him, like I was drowning and he was a floatation device. A few tears escaped and dampened the palm fronds on the shirt. I pulled away and blew my nose. Truffle and Sweet Marie had been racing each other around the shop. Now they shot toward us to get into the clinch.

"Don't worry, Charlotte. She'll turn up."

I gasped. "*Turn up?* I want to know she's safe. Turn up is what they say when a missing person is found and they don't mean it in a good way."

Chapter 2

Keep a flattering work outfit ready to go for when you need it.

Jack said, "Don't hyperventilate, Charlotte! Of course, Esme's not going to turn up in a bad way. She's being inconsiderate again. She'll arrive unannounced expecting everything to revolve around her. Don't forget when she visits, everything becomes a bit—"

"Overwhelming. I am not likely to forget that."

"And difficult."

I sighed.

"But she is your mother. We have to accept our parents the way they are." He put even more energy into the next hug. I held him tight. And not just because he was being sensible.

"Easy for you to say, Jack. You grew up with the two most accepting, loving, cookie-baking, story-reading, pet-providing parents ever."

"True enough. But at least your mother is alive and kicking. That counts for something."

It did.

"It's all in how you look at it," Jack said.

"Right. I am her next of kin and some stranger would have been in touch if she'd vanished from a tour or a cruise or a hot air balloon." Esme was still alive and almost certainly kicking . . . somebody. But where the devil was she?

"Don't take this the wrong way, Charlotte, but have you considered that the events of this past winter may have . . ."

"May have what?" I snapped.

"Made you a bit . . ."

"A bit what?"

"Jumpy."

I made an effort not to jump. "Not jumpy. Worried."

"Try to take your mind off it," Jack said.

I reminded myself that scowling was not my best look and that none of this was Jack's fault. Maybe he was right. My mother was a successful author, famous worldwide for the snappy twists at the end of each novel. She was also a world traveler, diamond bright and tough as steel. Of course, she was all right.

Jack smiled. "You look really nice. Your, um, clothes and all that."

Obviously not my scowling face, but I was pleased that he noticed my appearance as I was not an imported titanium bicycle. I'd chosen my high-heeled cognac suede boots, a swingy black jersey knee-length dress that would be easy to move around in. I'd looped a long silky scarf in black, cognac and red around my neck to give the outfit some oomph and wore my oversize copper hoop earrings. It was my favorite presentation outfit, ready to go at a moment's notice. I topped it with my soft red leather jacket.

"Do you have a consultation?"

"Library workshop. Remember?"

"I forgot. What's the topic again?"

No point in being miffed. In the years since I'd moved back to Woodbridge from New York City, he'd been there for me through way too many murders. That mattered. "Planning a Foolproof Trip."

"Really?"

"What do you mean 'really'?"

"You hate to travel."

"Fair enough, but I have traveled a lot and I know *how* to travel and that's what counts."

"Makes sense. Who do you think will show up midday on Wednesday?"

"It's part of Ramona's information series for seniors. She always gets a great turnout. People get there early because the sessions are popular and she offers refreshments. I am thrilled that she asked me."

He grinned. "Even though the library doesn't pay?"

"She promotes every session and so my name has been on the bulletin board and on posters and in the community papers as well as all over social media. And Ramona really works social media. It's free advertising for my business. I've already had calls."

"Well then, you don't want to be late."

Oh. Fighting words. I am never late. Jack is never on time. And I still had two hours to go. Naturally, I realized he was changing the subject to get my mind off my unavailable mother and to ward off any more inconvenient emotions she might trigger.

"Nice diversionary tactic, I have plenty of time, naturally," I said with a bit of huff. "I just wanted to remind you that you promised to keep Truffle and Sweet Marie while I am doing this presentation."

The dogs had developed a habit of chewing on my decorative pillows when I was out. It was intended to send me a message. Until I found a solution, such as stainless-steel cushions, they could spend some time with Jack.

Truffle and Sweet Marie were racing around checking the potential for mischief in the way that only miniature dachshunds can. Jack's shop is not as comfortable as my apartment, as it is mostly furnished in bike parts. There are no comfy sofas, or beds for small dogs to lounge on or pillows to chew, but Jack always has treats.

Jack looked wounded. "Remind me? I would never forget the pooches."

Truffle and Sweet Marie didn't notice as I left, because their eyes were trained on the container of Greenies on the counter. I guessed they were considering whether a packing box next to a chair might give them access.

"Good luck, Jack."

He grinned that heartwarming grin. "You too."

• • •

I had time. I headed back to the apartment, which was also the home that I had always enjoyed visiting as a child, mainly because of Jack's wonderful parents. There had been hugs and laughter, stories and cookies. Homemade soup too. It had been a refuge for a child of a driven and distracted mother who at that time was trying to write her books.

Although Esme Adams was now a perennial *New York Times* bestselling thriller writer we had been barely holding it together when I first met Jack. We had little money, no stable place to live, no sales of her unpublished manuscripts. We no longer saw Esme's friend, Lola, or Lola's comical tuxedo cat, Pierre. I'd ached for both of them. I'd had school and that was it. My school buddies, Jack, Pepper, Margaret and Sally, had made all the difference in my life. I shook those memories out of my head and turned to the underlying reason why I was worried about Esme. The nightmares had triggered this panic.

At home, I tried again to reach Glenda, Esme's longtime and long-suffering assistant. No luck. I left a phone message (my third) and sent a few texts. Glenda was loyal to a fault and seemed to have no life outside of coping with Esme's needs. She always answered.

I could never resist smiling at the thought of Glenda. Maybe it was the spiky burgundy hair, the green cats-eye frames and the bright red lipstick, currently Dior Metallic Red. Or possibly because she was the last person in the world to be using a cigarette holder. Or it could have been her chirping, whistling, squawking collection of yellow and gray cockatiels. Glenda's style was all her own. She was as bright and colorful as a box of crayons. She laughed with her mouth open—easily and loudly—the opposite of Esme's icy and mysterious elegance. Esme could never have managed her life and career without Glenda's competence. Glenda had helped me when I broke off my engagement with a certain lying cheating swine. "Been there, Charlotte. You are better off without him. But I can always rent a car and run him over if you'd like."

"You haven't left your apartment in twenty years," I'd teased. "You live in your silk pajamas."

"But it might be worth it."

"Hold off for the time being, Glenda. I'm planning to live happily ever after."

So why wasn't Miss Indispensable answering? Was she finally taking a vacation because Esme had gone off the grid? I stiffened my spine and called Esme's agent in New York.

To my surprise, the legendary Sid Greenberg picked up. Before I could say anything, he bellowed, "Where the hell is she?"

I could imagine Sid, his shiny head, the fringe of white hair, his black turtleneck and cashmere jacket, no matter the season, in the office he kept at eighty-five degrees. The office would smell of damp wool and the cigarette that always smouldered near his hand. Sid was like a stick of dynamite with a fast fuse. If you could have a stick of dynamite with thick, black-rimmed glasses and huge, fierce eyes, that is. For some reason, I always found him a reassuring presence. As Sid himself would say, "Go figure."

"Whatever happened to 'Hello, Charlotte'?"

"Yeah, yeah, yeah. *Hello*, Charlotte. Now *what's* going on? Where the *hell* is Esme?"

"I don't know, Sid. That's why I'm calling you."

"What do you mean, you don't know?" Sid was still bellowing. I've never heard him speak at a normal level.

"I've been trying everything and she's not responding."

"Well, I *know* she's not answering, that's why I need to reach her. Where is she?"

I rubbed my temple and held the phone away from my ear as he ranted on. Finally he took a breath. I cut in, "*I* called you, Sid, remember? I thought you might know where she is."

"She needs to deliver that manuscript. Do you hear me? It's way past drop-dead deadline and that's not like her."

All of New York could hear him. "What does Glenda say?"

"Glenda? How would I know? I deal directly with Esme. Glenda does Esme's admin work and the social media and all that."

"Glenda does what seems like the jobs of four people, Sid, and she's always in touch with Esme. Naturally, I've texted her and left phone messages. I haven't heard back."

"That woman is a wing nut. I bet someone in that crazy family of hers died or something," Sid said.

"I thought she was estranged from them, but—"

Sid was back to bellowing. "This stunt Esme's pulling is not good for business."

I found myself choking up. "On the personal side, Sid, I need to reassure myself that, um, she's all right."

"Of course she's all right. Why wouldn't she be all right? What a *ridiculous* thing to say! She's just being a—"

"Sid, this is my mother you are shouting about. It's unlike her not to get in touch with me."

"What are you talking about? It's exactly like Esme. She probably wants everyone to sweat, but this book needs to be done without *drama*."

I couldn't help laughing. "Sid, drama is my mother's middle name. Esme Drama Adams, international bestselling author. Currently unavailable."

Sid sputtered. "I know she loves to play games, but we could end up losing big-time."

"Did you think she's in Europe?" I asked.

"*Europe?* Of course not! The last time we spoke she was in Montreal. Just a flying visit, she called it, a couple of months ago."

"Montreal?" I was unaware of Esme's trip to Montreal. What else had I missed?

"You have to get on her case, Charlotte!"

I imagined the pictures on Sid's walls shaking.

"I've called both her cell phones and everything else," I said.

"What do you mean cell *phones*? There's more than one?"

If Esme hadn't given Sid this information, I didn't plan to. "It's a special one for me and she's not answering. And I have tried messaging her on everything I could think of. When did you hear from her last?"

Sid was puffing. With hot clothes, hot office, cigarettes, self-inflicted stress and temper tantrums, I hoped he wasn't heading for another heart attack.

"Last time, we talked about modifications to this contract. Everything seemed fine, although she was being . . . *whimsical*. You know."

"Maybe I should go into the city and check her condo, although . . ."

Sid grumbled. "I checked it out. There's no sign of her and the doorman says she hasn't been seen for a couple of weeks. Apparently I'm not the only person looking for her."

"What?"

"Maybe it's a *man*. I thought she might be tiring of the last toy boy, but she hasn't mentioned anyone new."

I brightened. Perhaps it *was* nothing more than a new man. That would be great news. A picture flashed through my mind of my beautiful, glamorous and impossible mother arm in arm with some Greek shipping magnate or a rising European film star or even a Lithuanian mob boss. I was smiling when Sid slammed down the phone, still furious at his best client, as he had been for nearly twenty years.

So. Sid hadn't heard from Esme in far too long, despite her practically being in breach of contract. I'd had no word for fifteen days. Was she head over heels or playing games?

After all, the famous Esme Adams likes nothing more than a surprise twist.

Chapter 3

Keep a small suitcase packed with essential clothes, snacks, cash, medication, ID and key documents in case you have to leave home in an emergency.

Next I checked for recent posts on Esme's Facebook and Instagram. Her face is always slightly obscured on social media in an appealingly mysterious way, and Glenda is a savvy promoter of all things Esme. There was nothing new.

Not a word about her trip to Montreal either. What was that about? Esme had always refused to go to Canada and I'd had no clue that anything had changed. I've always wanted to visit Montreal. I could have gone with her.

I tried Twitter.

There is always something there from Esme through her invisible assistant, about new or forthcoming books, and Esme had a new hardcover about to launch. Again. Nothing doing. Where there was usually an array of shots of Esme looking glam, behind her trademark sunglasses, hats, scarves, shadows and so on, there was nothing doing. Not the slightest hint a new toy boy.

I turned to her website. Perhaps I'd find an event coming soon. She could be the guest of honor at a conference. But wouldn't those things be all over social media? Surely Sid would have known. The website had a comprehensive list of events where eager readers could expect to catch a glimpse of the glamorous Esme Adams. The International Writers' Symposium was scheduled in two weeks in the UK. I had a vague memory of Esme telling me she was one of the guests of honor.

Of course. She must be on her way to England. If history was to be a guide, she'd swan through Harrods and Harvey Nichols and drop a bundle. Perhaps that would be followed by martinis at the Groucho Club. Then she'd make an entrance at the Savoy dripping with shopping bags and have a luxurious nap before heading to dinner at Le Gavroche. The three-month wait for reservations wouldn't apply to her. London was the only place where Esme played the glamor card. Everywhere else she enjoyed anonymity.

Funny that she hadn't mentioned the symposium on her social media. That wasn't like Esme or Glenda.

The knot in my stomach grew out of my frightening and disrupted childhood. Even my talk Planning a Foolproof Trip had roots back in the day.

Esme and I each kept a small suitcase tucked away in an easy-to-access location. Always. The suitcases were packed with necessary clothes, medication and key documents. Cash and credit cards too. Cash had often been hard to come by, but there was always a roll in my mother's suitcase, no matter how broke we were. We might have needed cash for tickets, food on the road, other necessities. My mother told me that sometimes you had to pay someone "a little something" just to keep your location secret. We even tucked snacks and drinks in the cases, refreshing them every few weeks. As a child I kept a favorite toy too, because you just never know.

I'd been clutching a small *Toy Story* backpack when Esme and I first splashed through the dark streets of Woodbridge more than twenty years earlier, looking for Lola. Now I realized that Esme needed a town close to New York City, large enough to allow us some anonymity and small enough to be able to afford.

I never wanted to be reminded of the nightmare trip so Esme got rid of the backpack and bought me a new Hello Kitty rolling case as soon as she could. She said it was much better than the old Barbie one we left behind. We kept the Hello Kitty case hidden and packed throughout my childhood. I still store the Hello Kitty roller inside my regular travel bag. In its hidden compartment, there was a roll of bills in various denominations, credit cards, a passport and documents I wouldn't want to admit to, plus a pay-as-you-go phone. I didn't think I'd ever need it but Esme had instilled enough anxiety in me that I couldn't bring myself to get rid of it. Once I've packed for a normal trip, Hello Kitty stays home.

I felt quite twitchy and it still wasn't time to leave for the library.

I asked myself why I hadn't waited to drop off Truffle and Sweet Marie. I could have used their company and snuggles.

Perhaps Ben and Jerry's New York Super Fudge Chunk would provide the best distraction. I headed for the freezer. Minutes later I was staring at the bottom of the empty container. Some people take tranquilizers or meditate, other people eat ice cream. I checked the full-length mirror in the entry to see if this might be the day my Ben and Jerry's habit would finally catch up with me. No splotches on the clothing and no popped buttons, but who knew where those calories had gone.

"I ate it all. So what? Nobody's perfect," I said to my mother, wherever she was.

Time to go.

• • •

I learned early from Esme that no matter what you fear, panic is your greatest enemy.

Nothing to panic about, remember?

I double-checked my materials in the car. Presentation outline and handouts. Brochures. It was all there in the passenger side of my new Mazda MX-5, the replacement for my beloved Miata that hadn't survived an encounter with a killer. Never mind that. Today everything was ready for the workshop. This time, I'd tucked my materials into my practical carry-on case, to illustrate packing tips to make the best possible trip with the least amount of luggage. Obviously, I hadn't included the fake passport, cash and credit cards.

I had just turned onto a pretty, tree-lined side street, when a siren's whoop erupted behind me.

Red and blue lights flashed in my rearview mirror.

My heart pounded.

What if the police were here to tell me that my mother had "turned up"?

An officer exited the cruiser, looking like he was the inventor of swagger. I opened my window. He leaned in and grinned.

"Hello, Charlie."

Damn. Nick Monahan, aka Nick the Stick. "Nick, you scared me."

"Just saying hi."

"Don't say hi. You know how Pepper feels about that." Pepper Monahan, former close friend and now rising star detective on the Woodbridge force, had a tangled history with me and a jealous streak, not that I had any interest in her hunky, useless husband.

By now the scent of Nick's aftershave had filled the car. Or maybe it was the aftereffects of his hair gel or shower soap. I knew that Pepper had recently stocked him up on every product in BOSS Bottled, wishful thinking on her part, of course.

"You're white as a ghost, Charlie. Something wrong?"

Nick Monahan is the most self-absorbed person I know. If he'd noticed I was upset, it must be glaringly obvious.

"Nothing wrong, Nick."

"You don't look good. I mean you look *good*, but you don't look well, Charlie."

"I hate being called Charlie."

"I forgot. But you—"

"I'm just a bit worried about my mother. She hasn't been answering my calls and messages."

He shrugged. "Old ladies. You know, things happen."

That was jaw-dropping even for Nick Monahan. What was worse: being cavalier about "things happening" or calling Esme Adams an old lady? What did Pepper ever see in this jackass?

"Thanks for the reassurance, Nick."

"Hey, no problem." He pulled his hand away fast as the window whipped closed and I drove off. In the passenger seat, the little carry-on bag seemed to taunt me. *Remember that trip on the bus, when you were Charlie?*

Who could forget?

Chapter 4

Make a photocopy of your key travel documents: passport, ticket, insurance and ID just in case. Leave a copy with someone you trust at home and keep one with you.

The carry-on case is an inanimate object, I reminded myself. It is not heckling you from the passenger seat. The bad old days are gone.

I cast a quick glance at the case. It did seem to be sneering. I was definitely losing my marbles. Stress, for sure, but even so.

"That was then. This is now," I said out loud. "I am ready for any emergency trip because I am organized, not because I might have to climb out a bedroom window with my mother to avoid some nameless and faceless danger."

The familiar panic washed over me. I'd never shared those fears with anyone. No one, not even Jack, knew the full story of my early life.

• • •

As always, my favorite reference librarian, Ramona, was resplendent in blue. Her spiked silver hair went perfectly with her vintage silver jewelry. The attendees were in their chairs waiting, although I'd arrived a half hour ahead of schedule. Ramona doesn't believe in latecomers, so I suppose they were just playing it safe.

I glanced at the community bulletin board jammed with flyers for the usual church events, concerts, used furniture, services and a surprising number of newly missing dogs. The dogs were all starting to look alike. I hoped that most of them had been found by now.

The room smelled nicely of coffee and homemade brownies, I made a mental note to be an hour early the next time so I wouldn't have to set up with everyone watching and munching.

I rolled my carry-on suitcase up to the table and accepted Ramona's gracious offer of coffee. A white-haired patron presented it with a flourish. I felt like visiting royalty.

She said, "We can't wait for you to set us straight about how we prepare for trips. Ramona says you have a system."

I produced a smile. Have I mentioned I detest travel? Perhaps because I'd been dragged on dozens of trips by Esme or maybe because I really love being at home. But everything's not about me. Most people need better systems for planning and packing for their own trips. I pride myself on offering organizing principles that help.

A regal woman with gold-tipped cornrows, ebony skin and a form-fitting crimson dress made an entrance and surveyed the group with a smile. All eyes turned to watch. She gave Ramona a nod before leaving. Vanessa Vallerin, the new head of public services, was Ramona's boss, although it was hard to imagine anyone bossing Ramona.

Once my table display was set, Ramona strode to the front, silver earring shooting sparks.

"Welcome to our first program of the spring session of You Learn Something New Every Day: Making the Best of Your Retirement," she said. "It is my great pleasure to welcome back one of our most popular library presenters and my friend, personal organizer extraordinaire, Charlotte Adams. Charlotte is giving her time today at no charge to the library to show her support for our services."

Correct. And just try saying no to Ramona.

The applause was deafening. I felt a frisson of fear. But I am used to managing negative messages that rise from anxiety. I told myself it would be fine and if it was not, no one would die. Plus, it would take my mind off my mother.

"Thank you for taking time to come today, everyone, and thank you, Ramona, for making it happen. Ramona is passing around my brochures in case anyone would like to consult with me on any of my services: travel planning, time management, decluttering, downsizing, home, office and personal organizing. See me after my talk or get in touch if you want my help now or in the future. So, it's time to take a trip! Who is planning to travel soon?"

Half the hands went up.

"And who is imagining future trips?"

A few more people raised their hands, mostly single women. Two of the men stared at the ceiling, examining the acoustic tiles. Oh well, maybe I'd learn what they wanted during the presentation.

"One final question: what do you hope to get out of this session?"

A grim-faced woman in the front said, "I want to pack efficiently to avoid baggage fees."

"We can help you with that."

In the second row, a hand shot up. "I'd like some tips for making an overseas flight bearable."

I smiled at the questioner, a pleasant man somewhere in his seventies. His wife was nodding enthusiastically.

She said, "If he's bored or uncomfortable, poor me! So that's my question too."

He ruffled her hair playfully and I started to relax.

Off to the side, a plump woman with near-burgundy hair slashed with honey highlights piped up, "I am looking for wardrobe tips and your suggestions for a capsule wardrobe to take on a two-week European trip that involves evenings out and sightseeing during the day." I was distracted by her fantastic hair. It took my eyes away from her triple chin and tiny dark eyes.

Excellent. "I have a great handout on capsule wardrobes. Please help yourself later."

She curled a lipsticky smile. I sensed a potential customer for the type of expertise I provide. I tried to figure out why she seemed familiar.

A grinning fellow near the door called out, "I just came for the brownies and sugar cookies."

"And who can blame you," I said. "Our thanks to Sue, the kind volunteer who made these treats for you to enjoy." Like me, Sue is a person who can't say no to Ramona. There are many of us.

I enjoyed the session, explaining with visuals how rolling clothing tightly can save space and prevent wrinkles. They laughed when I offered tips on packing small items in shoes. The women nodded when I talked about using beautiful scarves to change up a look. Too bad that reminded me of Esme and her Hermès collection. I felt the knot in my stomach.

As I was packing up, the woman who wanted the wardrobe tips swanned up to the front. She stuck out her hand. "I'm Harriet Oberon. I really enjoyed your presentation. It answered many—but not all—of my questions. Do you do follow-up sessions?"

I blinked, perhaps blinded by the impressive emerald ring on her finger. "I could give you an individual session at my regular rate if you think that would help."

"Oh, I do! That would be wonderful."

"You have my brochure?"

"Indeed."

"My contact information is all there. If you call or text, we can set up an appointment."

The session was over and things were already looking promising.

As I walked out with Ramona, I glanced at the bulletin board again.

"I didn't know you had a French book club, Ramona."

"Not me. Vanessa Vallerin, the new boss. She's a dynamo."

Ramona calling someone else a dynamo? That was funny.

Ramona said, "She alternates the French group with a Spanish book club. She speaks three languages that I know of. Her mother was Dominican and her father Haitian, or the other way around. She grew up in Montreal, got her library degree there. She's shaking things up here, runs a World Politics and a Social Justice discussion group. Wait a minute. Didn't you once tell me you had a Montreal connection?"

"It's unclear." I wished to nip any talk of Montreal in the bud.

Ramona gave me an uncharacteristically kind pat on the shoulder as I headed out the door.

"Are you okay, Charlotte?"

"Of course. I think most people liked the session. There are always a few complainers who think the room is too hot or the room is too cold or—" I avoided her steely blue eyes.

"Excellent session, but you don't seem to be yourself today. Is something wrong?"

I wanted to snap that the only thing wrong was people not believing that nothing is wrong but I knew better than to try to fool Ramona. "I am struggling with a bit of a personal problem."

"I'm here if you need me."

"Thanks, Ramona." I knew deep down that there was nothing Ramona or anyone else in Woodbridge could do about Esme. What I needed to know wasn't in any book or database or on any bulletin board.

Chapter 5

Pack shoes in small plastic bags. That will protect clothes and other items.

I drove home in a daze, something I don't recommend.

For the second time that day, I heard the whoop of a siren behind me. Had I blown through a stop sign? Or was Nick being stupid again? Was there a traffic safety blitz on? How embarrassing to get caught up in that. Would they make my name public? My enemies in the media would love that.

My heart raced when Pepper stepped out of a large black SUV. She sauntered toward me looking slim and fit, with her blonde hair in a fresh blowout, wearing a fitted black leather jacket that looked as soft as a glove, a gray wool dress and kick-ass boots with four-inch heels. I got a whiff of her signature scent, J'adore by Christian Dior, as she leaned toward me. Pepper O'Day Monahan was once again the star she'd been before her maternity leave. She was also my oldest friend, one of the five of us "misfits" back in the day. Jack, Margaret Tang, Sally, Pepper and I had made each other's lives bearable. Now that Pepper was married to Nick "the Stick" Monahan and mother to Little Nick, she has become my sometime friend and frequent enemy, the enemy bit triggered by Nick's big mouth. If only Nick didn't talk about "Charlie" quite so enthusiastically, things might have been better between Pepper and me. I wouldn't have had Nick Monahan on a bet, but common sense told me not to share that opinion with his wife.

"Hey, Charlotte."

"Hey, Pepper," I said with a shaky smile.

"Nick tells me he stopped you this afternoon."

"Yes, it was nothing."

"Nick doesn't think it was nothing."

What had he told her? That I was flirting with him? The truth has never been important to Nick.

"Really? I don't see–"

"I owe you, Charlotte. You know why."

True. I had done my best for Pepper and Nick despite both their best efforts in a recent series of dangerous encounters. But did that mean Pepper had to take time from her detective job to badger me?

I opened my mouth to protest. Pepper held up her hand to silence me.

"This is you all over," she said. "You can never admit that something might be wrong in your perfect life."

"There's nothing wrong—"

"Oh, no? Nick said your mother died."

"What?"

"When did she die?"

"She didn't!"

"Don't shout. So then, why did Nick—"

Because he is an idiot. "I just told him that she's not answering my calls and messages."

"Oh."

"That's a bit different, right?"

"Especially since you're not that close."

I opened my mouth again and then snapped it shut.

"Well, if you're worried and you want to talk, I'm home tonight, with lots of salty snacks and chilled white wine. Nick will be bowling. Come over. Unless you're afraid of a little frank conversation."

"See you tonight," I said with a grin.

Pepper would be the perfect person to advise me.

• • •

Jack was napping with the dogs when I arrived home. He woke up, stretched and headed downstairs to do some urgent bike thing and I walked the pooches. I always love that, especially since lately there were more friendly dog walkers than ever. You can always chat with dog walkers. They're not like other strangers. You don't introduce yourself or ask their names, but dog names can be exchanged. I smiled at a man in a denim jacket. He reminded me of Humpty Dumpty with a ponytail and was struggling to control yet another small moplike dog that didn't want to be controlled. It wasn't quite the moment to exchange pets' names so we hurried home before Truffle and Sweet Marie picked up some bad habits.

After fixing a quick bite of dinner for Truffle and Sweet Marie, I made my decision. I would take my small lifeline suitcase to Pepper's and use it to try to explain my worries. I'd share a bit about my murky background without revealing everything. I'd make it sound like running from an abusive spouse. She'd be ticked off that I'd never told her when I was growing up, but it would be worth it to get some clarity. Pepper knew enough about toxic households to understand why a woman would need to flee with a small child.

I made a peanut butter and banana sandwich for me and wrapped two to leave for Jack, who had dashed back to CYCotics. Pepper had a small child, a fool for a husband and a serious job. She didn't need me showing up expecting dinner on top of all that.

• • •

I have found that most children like miniature dachshunds. Truffle and Sweet Marie, with their therapy dog training and their experience with Sally's four kids, would be okay with Little Nick. It might make the whole visit a bit more fun.

As I was working to recover my public image, I stuffed the Hello Kitty case into my largest work tote and slung that over my shoulder.

I popped the pooches into the car, slipped the heavy tote onto the floor and waved at Humpty Dumpty, still struggling with the stubborn moplike pooch.

We spun off to Pepper's.

Every intuition I had told me Esme was in trouble. But when I tried to interpret why, I couldn't make sense of it. But I believed it was time to face my past.

Pepper knew about my mother's physical and emotional absences. She knew about Esme's strange and secretive behavior. She'd been well aware that from time to time I'd been dumped with Jack's parents for days or weeks and that St. Jude's school wasn't supposed to know. Still, my family situation—while weird and even worrisome—was nowhere near as bad as Pepper's. I didn't have to hide bruises under long sleeves, for instance. As Pepper's dad was a cop at the time, she had no way out.

We settled in. Pepper had an oversize wineglass glittering with a pricy sauvignon blanc. I had some sparkling cranberry juice in a wineglass. Little Nick was a surprisingly happy toddler. He loved chasing the dogs and Truffle and Sweet Marie enjoyed running away. They all raced in circles as we relaxed and watched. I made sure the dogs didn't get too close or too agitated. Eventually, the three of them collapsed on a blanket for a much-needed snooze. The dogs cuddled up to the beautiful sleeping toddler, his hair damp from exertion, and for a flicker, I questioned my single and childless status. Then I remembered the Nick part of the equation and regained my sanity. I switched my thoughts to Esme.

"She's in between husbands and I imagine she's just visiting her favorite places in Europe. She's been in touch regularly every Tuesday night for the last few years, so things have been good between us."

"Never kid a kidder," Pepper said.

"Tolerable then."

"So what are you so worked up about?"

"Because she's not responding to anything. Nick kicked it up a notch and decided that because she's—and I quote—old that she might be . . . you know."

Pepper rolled her eyes. "She's what? Fifty? OMG. That fool!"

"I don't actually know, but too young to be expiring from old age."

Pepper chuckled. "Are you just being Charlotte and getting in a state over things that may not happen?"

Considering their marriage and the life-threatening situations I'd bailed Pepper and her husband out of, that seemed unfair. "I have a bad feeling. We've been talking but she hasn't mentioned where she is. I can hardly traipse around the globe hunting for her."

"The cold hand of anxiety touching your spine?"

"Very poetic. Maybe she just has a new man. It's been a while since the French IT wizard and the English poet."

"Did you bond with either of them?"

"Never even met them. But I'm not sure it's just a new relationship."

Pepper took a long, speculative sip of her wine. "Would be good if that's all it is."

I reached into the bowl of crinkle chips. But of course, the ambitious detective just couldn't let it go. "Does she have any friends you could get in touch with?"

"I've been in touch with her agent. Esme's assistant, Glenda, seems to be AWOL and Sid, the agent, is apoplectic. She doesn't really have friends."

"Huh. Okay, would she visit the ex-husbands or boyfriends?"

I crunched a handful of chips and thought about it. "I doubt it."

"Might they know where she is?"

"Hard to say. She never talked about them once she kicked them to the curb."

"So you're worried sick but not willing to try to track her down."

I bit my lip. I hate doing that and I really hated having done it. "You're right. I have a problem but you're wrong that I haven't tried. The trouble is that I've hit a wall."

"You contacted her home?"

"She's not in New York. Sid actually went over to the building. She hasn't been there for weeks. I don't know where she is."

"But you talk every week."

"Not about where she's staying, apparently. Not on this trip anyway."

"Cell phone?"

"Both of them. No answer. Straight to message."

"You left messages?"

"Of course I left messages!"

"So where else? Canada?'

"Actually, Sid said she visited Montreal recently."

"Montreal? And wasn't your father from there?"

"I don't really know anything about him. And the little I do know I heard from Esme and her talent is fiction."

"You don't remember him at all?"

I shook my head. "I still dream about him. He's always laughing in the dreams and he's always with my mother and his friends. I can't tell what's a dream and what's a memory."

"Right. So is there anyone else on his side? No aunts, uncles, cousins?"

"Apparently not."

"I suppose a grandma or grandpa would be out of the question?"

"In this case, yes."

"Fine. Esme must have family."

"She would only say they were estranged. It was always just the two of us, as far as I can remember." That wasn't entirely true but the memories of our time before Woodbridge were blurred and confusing.

"Think about her colleagues. All you need is one weak link and you've got her. Try that Sid again."

"Actually, he makes me look calm."

"And think about Europe. She's a cosmopolitan type."

"There are more than forty countries in Europe."

Pepper snorted. "You know I chase down criminals for a living."

"She's hardly a criminal!"

"Of course not. But, like a criminal, she doesn't seem to want to be found."

I swallowed.

Pepper waited until I could speak. Finally, I was able to say, "What if she can't be found because something happened to her?"

She reached over and patted my hand, an emotional tsunami by Pepper's standards. "You know her patterns. You have to follow them. If I remember correctly, Esme Adams can afford to be self-indulgent."

"True. She enjoys her creature comforts."

"Exactly. She's probably somewhere that she likes. Somewhere classy and sophisticated."

"Unless something happened to her."

"Start with what you know: How she travels. Where she stays. Where she eats. Didn't you used to travel with her?"

Tough one. "Yes, until I finished college. I didn't have a choice. Esme held the purse strings. These past few years, she kept asking me to join her. But she knows I hate to travel so she's sort of backed off that. Except for Paris last year."

"Where all did you go?"

"Actually, the usual tourist high spots for once: the Louvre, the Musée D'Orsay, boat trips on the Seine, Versailles Palace, the fantastic gardens and even the Moulin Rouge for old time's sake."

"Lucky you. Wish I could have had all those opportunities."

"Yes. I know I was fortunate to do all that travel. I think she was trying to make up for my strange childhood, but . . ."

"Did she have any favorites?"

"She did. I'd say Paris, Lisbon and Northern Italy. And London, of course."

"Do you have access to any of her bank or credit card information?"

"You must be kidding."

"Well, in my world, one contact leads to another which leads to another.

You should try that route. Identify someone who can help."

"Normally, Esme's personal assistant, Glenda, would be that person. I can't reach her."

"Aren't you quite close to this Glenda?" Pepper asked.

"Yes. I've known her for many years and she's always been a big help. But she's very loyal to my mother, so I'm beginning to think Esme told her to keep a low profile so Glenda couldn't be badgered into giving out any information."

"Keep me posted. I always found Esme fascinating. She was fearless. The opposite of my mom."

I had seen Esme when she was anything but fearless and I'd been traumatized by that. A shiver ran down my spine. I smiled weakly and stood up to leave. "Thank you."

It turned out that I wasn't quite ready to share the story of the Hello Kitty suitcase with Pepper after all. As she'd said, she chased criminals. What if Esme had been involved in something criminal? Better Pepper didn't know.

I was a tornado of anxiety by this time, but Pepper leaned back, apparently prepared to chat away. "Like I said, keep me in the loop, but I'm sure you have nothing to worry about."

I couldn't tell her that I had a thundering heart or why. And I would keep my nightmares to myself.

My phone vibrated. Jack. I'd be home in ten minutes and we'd catch up then.

I said, "It was really good to spend time together—"

Pepper's phone rang. "Hold that thought. It's Jack," she said.

I said, "But he just texted me." Normally Jack would just leave a message. Pepper handed the phone to me.

"Jack?"

"Charlotte, you'd better come home."

I forced myself to remain calm. "Is it Esme?"

"No. But you *really* need to come home."

Chapter 6

Shop for travel sized toiletries, over-the-counter medications and small refillable containers until you can fill a travel kit.

The sight of my home usually makes me smile, but tonight I worried that Jack had some bad news about Esme and I needed to hear it in private.

A police car was parked on the street. Jack had left the front door open and that did not make me smile. Even in safe little Woodbridge there's no point in asking for trouble. Jack doesn't see the world the same way.

He was waiting at the top of the stairs, leaning against the wall, phone in one hand, talking to someone. He ran his free hand through his hair, spiking it more. I glanced into his unit as I picked up the dogs. For some reason it looked more chaotic than usual.

"Doesn't matter," I told myself. "We each have our own space. Life is about compromise."

My door was wide open. As I approached, I said, "Jack?"

He seemed to be having trouble speaking.

"I'm so sorry, Charlotte."

"For what?" I said before I looked past him into my home. My brain couldn't make sense of the scene in front of me. Was it another nightmare?

Had Jack lost his mind and started the reno?

But Jack would never overturn my sofa or slice open my new decorative blue-and-white down-filled cushions. Feathers were everywhere, some still drifting through the air. I was so stunned I barely noticed the crunch of glass under my boots. Glass? The glass shards were jagged, shiny, reflective.

Jack leaned forward and took the dogs from me. "Don't want them to dash in and cut their paws."

I'd been too overwhelmed to even imagine the danger to their little paws.

I stared at the foyer wall. The stylish black-framed mirror was gone, smashed to pieces on the floor. Had I been careless with the hanger when I'd proudly placed it on that wall to expand the space? But that wouldn't explain the rest. The contents of my armoire were scattered. Jackets, scarves, boots and gloves mixed randomly with the broken mirror and what looked like dog kibble. The armoire doors had been wrenched off.

"Charlotte?" A police officer emerged from the bedroom.

Dean Oliver, a bright spark in the Woodbridge Police Service, was wearing blue disposable booties and white gloves.

I tore my gaze away from the overturned bookcase and the shattered vases and my favorite books that had been hurled at the walls.

Apparently Dean was sorry too.

"Any idea who did this?" he said.

I stepped past Jack and the dogs and closed the door. It didn't stay closed because it had been kicked in. The latch must have been damaged.

"Thank God you took the dogs with you to Pepper's," Jack said. "What if they'd been here?"

"Can you take them downstairs, please? I'm worried about all this broken glass."

Jack wrestled the struggling pooches down to safety.

I followed Dean into the bedroom. Clothing spilled out of my closet and dresser drawers and onto the floor. My mattress had been upended and slashed. My pillows had been reduced to flying feathers. My clean bedding had been tossed aside and trampled. I could see the muddy footprints on my duvet cover. Truffle and Sweet Marie's cute little dog beds had been cut to bits. I tripped over my own carry-on case, with its lining now hanging in ribbons. My workshop materials were spread randomly around the room. Everything I owned was on the floor, slashed or broken or ruined.

I peered into the bathroom, inhaling competing scents of the shampoo, conditioner, and shower gel that had been splashed around and mixed with the shards of the medicine cabinet mirror. The toilet tank had been smashed too, along with tiles in the shower. Why not?

I wondered if anyone had had the presence of mind to turn off the water.

I had to maintain my composure in front of Dean Oliver.

"The kitchen?"

He shook his head sadly.

First, I gaped at my fridge, which was tipped over with the contents lying on the floor. The flour and sugar cannisters lay overturned. The scattered flour gave everything a ghostly look and the sugar crunched underfoot. The new Kicking Horse coffee beans had been thrown to the ground and walked on. Nothing remained in the cupboards or drawers. The heap of pots, cans, my smashed butter dish and my English breakfast tea caddy taunted me. The teapot was too broken to taunt.

I stared at two containers of Ben and Jerry's New York Super Fudge Chunk, now melted over my only two cookbooks. I don't have many spices but the sight and scent of them was everywhere. The place smelled like a rogue fruitcake. I thought I saw a coating of cinnamon on the light fixture.

I turned over one of the chairs from my little breakfast set and collapsed on its ripped seat.

Dean patted my shoulder, although I'm sure they don't teach that at Police Academy. "This is probably worse for you than for other people because you are, um, a little . . ."

"Obsessive?"

"I was going to say particular."

That was kind.

Jack appeared behind Dean, minus the dogs. They were raising a ruckus downstairs.

Dean scanned the room and glanced out to the foyer. He nodded to Jack and then met my eyes. He cleared his throat. "You know, this all seems very personal."

Jack said, "Personal?"

I butted in. "It feels really personal. I mean, they let all of the Ben and Jerry's melt. Why would anyone do that? Who would destroy my home? Why?"

Jack shrugged his Hawaiian shoulders. "Burglars."

Dean shook his head. "I think this is more than a simple burglary."

"Yes." I glanced back into the living room. "My smart TV looks like someone put their foot through it. Why wouldn't they take it and sell it? It's practically brand-new."

"Exactly," Dean said. "Burglars like things easy. In and out in minutes if they can, snatching whatever they can fence easily. They don't leave new TV sets."

Jack said, "Don't some burglars vandalize too?"

Dean was on familiar territory there. "Sure they do, just to thumb their noses. You don't even want to know some of the stuff they do."

"Like what?" Jack said.

I interrupted. "I don't want to hear what else."

Jack ran his hands through his hair again. "But who would do it?"

"Not sure. But I'll tell you this. Wrecking Charlotte's home took time," Dean said. "And thought."

"And energy," I added. "But, Dean, why are you here?"

"Jack called it in as a break-in. I took the call. I knew it was your place and I owe you."

Jack said, "Yeah. Front door kicked in."

Dean said, "That's what usually happens. Ninety percent of break-ins are right through the front door. Kicking it in or breaking the glass and unlocking it from the inside or using a jimmy if that seems easier. That's what I'm telling you, break-in artists are all about the path of least resistance."

"So it's typical in that way," Jack muttered.

Dean said, "But not the time of day. It's early evening. Most burglaries are between nine in the morning and three p.m. Folks are at work. Kids are at school. Easy. Ring the doorbell. Duck out of sight. If someone answers, move a couple of doors down. It's straightforward to figure out if someone's home. Television flickering. Kids crying. Cars in the driveway. This time of day people are having dinner, kids are doing homework, avoiding chores or on TikTok. This doesn't follow the usual patterns. That troubles me, Charlotte."

Jack straightened up. "Me too." He's never liked Dean. We have a bit of history and that might explain it.

Dean said, "We agree. It seems personal."

Downstairs the dogs set up another commotion.

I had started to shake. "My home is almost completely destroyed. I don't think I can salvage any of my furniture or décor. Did you see that my books have their spines broken? The lamps are shattered. I don't even have shampoo. Who would want to do that to me?"

We whirled at the crunch of glass behind us.

Pepper stood in the door, taking in the scene.

"Well, whoever did *this* meant business."

"Could it have been kids?" I couldn't quite manage to keep those shakes out of my voice.

Pepper rolled her eyes. "Kids? Doesn't seem like anything I've ever seen kids do. But in this line of work, you learn something new every day."

Pepper stalked back to the living room and into the bedroom and then the bathroom, assessing. You could practically see her detective brain working, recording details, making observations. She crossed her arms and narrowed her eyes. "As far as I can see, they left nothing untouched. Nothing. So the thing you have to ask yourself, Charlotte, is what were they looking for?"

I stared from Pepper to Jack to Dean. "I have no idea."

"And then," she added, "could they have found it?"

"But everything I own is here."

She shrugged. "Do you have a safe-deposit box?"

I shook my head.

"Where did you keep your passport? Is it still here?"

"My passport?"

"Yes. Passports are always in demand with the sleaze crowd. Easy money."

"But why break everything?"

"Hard to say what the motivation was. Lot of criminals can have a low frustration threshold."

"I had my passport with me. They couldn't have found it."

"You always carry your passport?"

"'Course not. It's a long story. But this was your night at home, Pepper. Where is Little Nick?"

"When Jack told me what happened I called our neighbor to take care of him. She's happy about it and so is he."

"But why me? Jack's place is just downstairs."

"It's not as fancy as this," Jack said. "Pretty basic really."

"There are lots of high-value bike parts there," I blurted out. "And entire bikes. Are they all there, Jack?"

"I didn't look. When I saw the door had been kicked in, I ran up to see what had happened. I was floored by the damage. Maybe I should check downstairs." Jack bounded down the stairs to inspect his place that—to tell the truth—always looked like it had just been tossed. Truffle and Sweet Marie set up a welcoming racket. I tried to pull myself together while we waited. Dean and Pepper spent the time examining the disaster that had been my home.

Jack was back in five minutes. "There are a few things out of place but nothing taken that I can see."

"How could you tell?" Pepper likes to tease Jack.

"Laugh if you want. I know what's there and where everything is. I think they just turned a few things over to make it look like they were after something."

The dogs had started howling downstairs. I stepped away and phoned my sometime assistant, Lilith Carisse. There's no one better than Lilith in an emergency. She lives with our elderly friend, Rose Skipowski, and takes care of things in return for a roof over her head.

"I've had a nasty break-in and Truffle and Sweet Marie need to stay someplace calm and cuddly tonight. I wonder if Rose and you would be okay with a visit from them?"

Lilith checked with Rose and reported back. "Very happy to cuddle them here as long as you need us. Schopenhauer agrees. Dogs have to stick together."

That done, I returned to the conversation. Jack was saying, "They broke one of my photos, but they didn't find my passport and it wasn't particularly well hidden. It was tucked into some papers in a drawer." He pulled a passport from his pocket, waved it and then stuffed it back in. He added, "I had a bit of emergency cash in the corner of the same drawer, along with euros and a couple of credit cards and other ID. But everything is untouched. Safe." He patted his pocket.

I doubted that Jack's passport, cards and cash would be safe for all that long in his pocket, but I managed not to point that out. After all, Jack has been all over Europe without incident. Unlike me, he loves to travel. Don't let the shorts and the Hawaiian shirt throw you off. He was "this close" to his PhD in Philosophy when he decided to take another path. Before that he'd visited the major universities, spent time in the great libraries and just rambled around Europe's art treasures, plazas and historic communities while I was nose to the grindstone in New York City with the absolute wrong man.

My passport was current because I might need it in emergency, but Jack kept his passport up to date in case something fun came up.

Pepper pivoted to face me. "I suppose they got your cash, Charlotte?"

I shook my head. "I didn't have any." My money, along with my passports and the VISA and Mastercard I rarely used, was hidden in my Hello Kitty stash.

For some reason, I couldn't bring myself to mention that. The old fears were creeping back into my life, spawning secrecy and the need for caution. I felt weirdly relieved that I hadn't showed the bag to Pepper and shared its history. Of course, I also knew that didn't make sense. Pepper's a highly intelligent and trained detective and no one was better placed to investigate. Still.

I said, "Do you think you'll find who did this?"

Pepper made a face. "Maybe if they pull the same stunt elsewhere and they get careless."

Dean said, "We haven't had anything similar reported recently."

I felt certain whoever trashed my place hadn't started a rampage in Woodbridge.

Pepper said, "This is targeting Charlotte and it worries me. We'll get a team over here to gather evidence." Pepper has always had first-class instincts except when it came to her own husband.

I looked out the window to try to calm myself and spotted a bit of good news. "On the other hand, at least they didn't destroy my new hummingbird feeder."

Pepper ignored that. "Charlotte, you can't stay here tonight."

I wasn't sure I could sleep anywhere ever again but, Pepper had it spot on, I would definitely not be sleeping in my own home.

I knew this was about me. And I was betting it was also about my mother.

What's the good of having nightmares if they don't prepare you for things to go very wrong?

Chapter 7

Always carry an emergency first aid kit: bandages, painkillers, burn ointment, antibiotic cream, Epsom salt, baking soda, and blister patches.

Our choices were limited. I could stay in Jack's place, although the front door had been kicked in and there was the danger of having my body perforated by random bike parts. Pepper had reluctantly offered the pull-out bed in her family room but I'd have preferred to sleep on my glass-encrusted floor rather than share a night under Nick's roof. Our friend Sally offered her extra bed, although with her four kids that didn't strike me as a plan. While I spoke to my home insurance company to arrange for cleanup and I hoped compensation, Jack called Margaret Tang. I refused to do that as she and her unlikely new husband, Frank D'Angelo, were still practically on their honeymoon.

"They're away," Jack hung up and announced with a grin. "Out of town for the week. Margaret has offered us her place."

"We don't have a key."

"There's a coded entry. We have the code."

"But–"

"Accept it, Charlotte," Pepper said sternly.

Jack said, "Only thing is that there's no parking in the area and no room in their parking garage for the Mini or the Mazda."

Good thing Rose and Lilith were happy to pick up Truffle and Sweet Marie and keep them as long as necessary. I could imagine the sharp-clawed and entitled little dachshunds making themselves at home on Margaret's new leather sofa or on her eight-hundred-thread-count sheets. I already had enough insurance troubles. As Pepper and Dean crunched around a bit more making notes, I headed downstairs to liberate the dogs and take them for a walk. The night was growing cool and I shivered. Woodsmoke swirled through the neighborhood and, except for us, people got happy and cozy. It seemed that even the cheerful yellow daffs were mocking me: *So you thought we were safe here.*

When we returned from our tour around the block, Suzie, the uncooperative corgi, was taking her time peeing on the grass while her flustered owner paced awkwardly in front of my car.

"Oh, boy. Sorry about your lawn," she said. "When that girl finally has to go, she really has to go."

"Not a problem." I wasn't in the mood to chat even with friendly dog owners. I knew the presence of Dean Oliver's marked police car behind my Mazda would have her wondering.

"Is everything all right?" She tilted her bucket hat toward the cruiser.

I shook my head. "I had a break-in."

"Oh, no! Did you lose anything?"

I struggled to keep my voice steady. "I think I just lost everything."

"I'm so sorry."

"You walk here with Suzie. Did you happen to notice anything unusual going on? Suspicious characters?"

She blinked.

I couldn't help a small chuckle. "Right. Silly of me. What do suspicious characters look like? Are they wearing *I'm the Best Burglar* T-shirts?"

She managed a fake smile at my pathetic joke. "I noticed teenagers around, but Suzie and I have just moved in and I don't know who's who in the neighborhood yet."

"The police will probably want to talk to you," I said.

"Sure thing." At that moment, Suzie bolted and raced along the sidewalk and shot into a neighbor's yard, her owner lumbering after her. The bucket-hatted woman tripped over a hose and grabbed on to a garden gnome to save herself from a face plant. I was heading over to help her when the man with the silly moplike dog joined in the chase. At least, I was off the hook. Suzie would be safe and I didn't have to worry about Truffle and Sweet Marie making the situation worse.

I felt guilty but I had my own troubles and some people are not meant to have dogs. Eventually Suzie's owner, her bucket hat askew, staggered back in our direction, wheezing in a worrying way and again dragging a reluctant Suzie. Truffle and Sweet Marie managed not to bark.

The guy with the moplike dog had made it back, holding his pooch, and staring at me, in the light of the streetlamp. I probably had a track of mascara down my cheeks.

"We see the police are still here."

"I had a break-in, a lot of damage. It was just stuff, as they say."

He said, "Is everything all right?"

"We'll get it cleaned up. Been through worse." Would everything ever be all right? I decided it was well past time to figure out what was going on and how it connected with Esme and our history.

I didn't bother the dog walkers with my issues. They had enough troubles with their misbehaving pooches.

• • •

A half hour later, Lilith pulled up in Rose's ancient Grand LeMans and I waved her into the backyard, where no one could see what was going on. I deposited Truffle and Sweet Marie into the backseat and got my tote bag from the Mazda. Then I climbed in with them. Jack got in the front seat.

"I really appreciate this, Lilith," I said.

"I'm late for work, or I'd stay to help," she said.

"It's okay. We need to have the insurance adjuster assess the damage before we do anything. Not that there's much more they can do to us, but we left the lights on timers anyway."

Jack said, "We're both grateful, Lilith. We know how busy you are."

Lilith was juggling three jobs (Rose didn't count as a job) to work her way through college. She'd lived on the street and worked with troubled youth. I'd be glad to get her opinion on the kind of person who would do that damage. We decided that the dogs would stay with her and Rose until Jack and I were settled again. No rush, I was told.

Jack kept lookout from the passenger seat. Lilith and I stopped at Hannaford so we could get a new supply of Ben and Jerry's. Luckily Hannaford is open until ten p.m. because I had no idea what Margaret and Frank would have in their fridge. I couldn't imagine either of them cooking. The dogs yipped in the car as we headed in to get supplies.

As we were leaving Hannaford with an impressive array of ice cream containers, Jack decided that we needed sandwiches. Hannaford had a good deli. I wasn't sure I could eat anything except ice cream because it had such a seductive way of sliding down the throat, but Jack would take care of any sandwiches I left behind.

I waited for him by the door, pacing with the ice cream. I turned my attention to the community notice board. Missing pets seemed to be on the increase. I couldn't imagine losing Truffle and Sweet Marie. I checked the heartbreaking posters from panicked families. Several cats. A parrot. There was even a lost corgi! I stared at Daisy, the beautiful missing pooch, who grinned wickedly from the notice with its fringe of phone numbers on the bottom. Daisy had been missing from her yard on Tulip Street for three days.

The hair on the back of my neck stood up.

Was that Suzie?

Unless all corgis looked alike?

I knew that they did not. I have no trouble telling one dachshund from another. They may all be long with short legs and pointy snouts but they are all distinct too. No question that this was Suzie. The expression said it all.

Jack barreled out with the sandwiches. I didn't bother to ask who would eat four sandwiches, especially large ones on Kaiser buns.

I pointed to Daisy. "Have you seen this corgi, Jack?"

Jack shook his head. "Nope."

"Oh." Disappointing. Was I losing my marbles?

Jack said something.

"I can't hear you with your mouth full," I grumbled.

He swallowed and inclined his head toward another leaflet. "But I've seen this pooch on our street."

I stared at a small and mysterious white moplike dog. You couldn't see her eyes. Annabella had not been found for three days.

But I had seen Daisy and Annabella not an hour earlier in front of my own plundered home with two new and neighborly dog walkers.

What the hell?

Chapter 8

Always keep some cash on hand in case you need to travel in a hurry.

"That must be it," I said, snatching a phone number from the bottom of each flyer. "Someone stole those dogs. That explains why Suzie won't do what her owner says. That's why she runs away. Annabella seems terrified."

"What are you talking about, Charlotte?" The half-eaten sandwich hovered around Jack's mouth.

"Two people are walking stolen dogs in our neighborhood, parading up and down the sidewalk, every day. Multiple times a day. I should have realized that they weren't walking their own dogs."

"That's not the first thing that would occur to most people."

Jack eyed his sandwich but exerted a bit of control. My stomach was in knots. If I never saw another giant Genoa salami, provolone, lettuce, tomato and pepperoni sandwich it would be too soon.

"I think they were casing our house."

"Casing our–?"

"Watching so they'd know when we were coming and going. No one pays any attention to dog owners. It's only the dogs we look at. The two beige people blended right into the environment. I couldn't even describe them except for their clothes and their shapes and I've seen them both a half dozen times. But I'd know those dogs anywhere. They may still be on the street, biding their time. Maybe these slimeballs will go back in to finish the job."

Jack blinked. "Why would they do that, Charlotte?"

"I don't know. But it has something to do with Esme and me."

"Let's let the families know we've seen the dogs. Then we'll call Pepper and tell her. Or maybe Dean Oliver. After that, we'll check out the street. Or should we . . . ?"

We decided to parallel process. I called the numbers I'd torn from the notices and told the families that their dogs might have been on our street that day. I described the walkers. I suggested they search the area and talk to residents.

Just as I finished, my insurance agent called back and agreed to liaise with the police. Luckily, I had photos of my apartment and its contents in the cloud where it was safe. I shuddered at the thought of going back and trying to reclaim my home.

Pepper's phone went to message. Of course. It was nearly ten and she was the working mother of a toddler. She'd be home again, most likely conked out on top of the bed with her clothes still on. I called the police department and asked to have Dean Oliver contact me, adding that it was urgent.

My phone buzzed two minutes later and I filled Dean in on what I'd seen on the notice board and how it fit with what had been going on in front of my house.

"I'll go by and have a look," he said. "We talked to your neighbors but we didn't ask them about dog walkers. You're saying they have been there for days?"

"At least two days. I thought I was getting to know new neighbors and all along they were just waiting for the chance to break into my place in broad daylight. It doesn't make sense they would be coincidentally walking stolen dogs past my front door."

"Agreed. We'll check again with your neighbors."

I said in a small voice, "Can you keep me posted? We'll be staying at Margaret and Frank D'Angelo's place tonight but I'll keep my phone on."

"I'll take an unmarked car and watch for them. And Charlotte?"

"Yes."

"Since you may be the target here, don't go home without someone from the police, like me. Make sure no one follows you."

"We've been careful."

"Good. I'll let Pepper know."

Good luck with that, I thought. "You may run into the families whose pets were stolen. I called them. These dogs need to be rescued from whoever stole them."

After Dean rang off, I said to Lilith, "We'd better take a complicated route."

"Great! I know all the back alleys. That'll be fun," she said.

Our one-mile trip to Margaret's condo took about twenty minutes because we zipped through back alleys, drove the wrong way on one-way streets and I believe right through a park, although I had my hands over my eyes.

"You're supposed to be watching for a tail," Jack said.

• • •

There were no other cars in view as we approached the controlled-access garage at Margaret and Frank's condo. Lilith had truly enjoyed ditching any possible tail. I had to grin. The day had been without any lightness and this helped. My grin turned into a laugh and I relaxed a bit as we let ourselves in using Margaret's code. The condo was a modern and surprisingly spacious unit overlooking the Hudson and, as a bonus, on the top floor of a secure building with an elevator and plenty of cameras. There was a rooftop patio off the living room. I couldn't see any way for somebody to get at us from outside.

Unlike Pepper, Margaret didn't care much about stuff, except for her leather sofas, silky sheets and court suits. Oh, and bath products. She cared about her career, her friends, and now Frank, the tall, dark and very good-looking new husband. Her home was austere and spotless. No knickknacks. Nothing to clutter the mind. Unlike Sally and Pepper, Margaret's plans didn't include children. Frank's three kids were grown-up and gone. Frank's décor style was more tired detective, let me doze in this old leather recliner next to the bar cart. Surprisingly their two approaches blended. Some glass and metal, all very minimalist, and a battered footstool plus a few sport magazines tossed around. I spotted a pair of slippers. I liked this. For one thing, I was pretty edgy and I didn't want to feel nervous in Margaret's new home. I decided to unwind in Frank's old leather recliner but Jack beat me to it.

I tucked our ice cream into the sleek European freezer and popped the remaining sandwiches into the French-door fridge.

The time had come.

No more beating around the bush. Through the wide living room window, the Hudson glittered in the moonlight. In my memories, Esme said moonlight was bad. Made you easier to spot. I turned off the lights.

"How about that ice cream?" Jack said, looking hopeful. "Could be romantic here in the dark."

"Better wait until after you hear what I have to tell you. We'll both really need the New York Super Fudge Chunk then."

I lifted the Hello Kitty rolling case out of my oversize tote bag. I made myself comfortable in the streamlined gray felt Scandinavian design accent chair that must have been Margaret's. I turned it to face Jack.

"Jack."

He seemed miles away.

"Earth to Jack Reilly!"

He started. "Sorry. I have a lot on my mind. I got distracted by a new business opportunity that came up today and now everything that's happened at home."

"I have a lot on my mind too."

"'Course you do. The place being trashed. All your things ruined."

I sighed. "Yes, I was shocked at the effort and the intensity that went into ransacking it. But you know what?"

"What?" Jack said. He always does.

"It's only stuff."

Jack blinked. "But you love stuff."

"Yeah, I do. But it's replaceable. If something happens, I can get new stuff. Or not, depending on what we want."

"Are you saying you're not upset?"

"Not about my possessions. I am inconvenienced and it will be a lot of work to fix everything, but that's what I do. I bring order to other people's homes. Now I'll just be doing it for my own home."

"Okay, then. So . . ."

"No. Not upset about the stuff, but I am really disturbed by the violence they showed in trashing the place. Somebody was sending me a message. Everything they did was to make it personal. They wanted me to freak out."

Jack leaned forward to squeeze my hand. "I let you down and if I'd been there—"

"It's not at all your fault, Jack. Not mine either. Something else is going on. It's time I told you a few things about me."

Jack threw back his head and laughed. "What don't I know about you? We've been friends since kindergarten."

I felt a bit huffy. What woman wants to be an open book?

"Believe it or not, Jack, this goes back before that." I opened the Hello Kitty bag. Jack stared at the contents. A travel toiletry bag. Small first aid kit and a vial of painkillers, another one with antibiotics. Energy bars. Drinks. Dark clothing, rolled. A week's worth of clean underwear. Black socks and sneakers. Plastic rain cape. A couple of very different hats.

"That's a kid's bag, but it's packed so tightly, it must weigh a ton. Why is all that stuff in there?"

"It's all part of the story you don't know."

He chuckled. "I can deal with whatever you dish out."

"Don't be too sure."

"You dropped something. A candy case?"

I stooped quickly to get it but not before Jack opened it.

"Give me that, please."

"Sorry, didn't mean to upset you over some ancient candy. Oh. It's something else." A pair of earrings slipped into his hand.

I fought back tears.

"Earrings. Little ruby-throated hummingbirds. They're so you, Charlotte. Why are you hiding them?"

"They were Esme's," I croaked.

"And . . . ?"

"And I stole them."

"From your mother? I can't believe that."

"She threw them in the garbage. I loved those earrings and I dug them out and hid them. She never knew."

"They look like the real deal."

"Yes. I think they are real rubies set in gold. My father gave them to her."

"But she threw them away. Why would she care if you took them?"

"There's more."

"Fair enough. That ice cream is calling and, after all, how bad can your story be?"

"Worse than you can imagine, Jack. For starters, I'm not who you think I am."

He laughed. "Never kid a kidder."

I felt like I was swimming in sorrow. "Really. You don't know who I am."

He ran both hands through his hair, which now seemed to stand up in alarm. "Okay. All right. If you're not Charlotte Adams, who I have known for twenty-six years, who are you?"

I worried that the words wouldn't come out.

"That's the thing, Jack. I have no idea who I am."

Chapter 9

Practice folding and rolling your clothing. It will keep wrinkles down and save space.

Jack said nothing, probably a good thing.

"Sometime before you met me—"

"At five years old."

"Before I came to Woodbridge my mother and I were on the run."

"On the run? You were just a little kid!"

"Yes."

Jack said, "I remember when you first came to school. You were so tiny. So serious."

"I had things on my mind. And now I am *trying* to tell you about them."

"Sorry, it's hard to take in."

"I get that."

"Maybe it's not true. Did Esme tell you that? Her business is churning out far-fetched fiction."

"Esme didn't talk about it. She said our lives started when we got to Woodbridge and I had to forget everything else."

"To forget everything else," Jack repeated, shaking his head.

"Of course, I couldn't forget my little dog, Buster. I never found out what happened to him when we sneaked down the back staircase that night. We walked down twenty flights of stairs with our packs. We slipped into the dark outside and started running until Daddy picked us up around the corner. Then he took us to a bus station. Esme was crying and I was so afraid. Before he left, he told her everything would be okay if we kept going and didn't panic."

Jack sputtered, "How could a five-year-old child deal with that?"

I shrugged. "I just dealt with it. We were safe here in Woodbridge."

"Safe."

"At least, it seemed that way. But Esme said I had to keep my bag ready all the time just in case. Hers was ready too. We had a false panel in the back of my closet and we kept our emergency cases behind that panel in case we needed to get out in a hurry. It had a hidden latch that Esme rigged up. No one else would spot it. In our first apartment in Woodbridge we would have gone out the bathroom window and onto the roof of the back porch. There was a trellis that Esme bought and she planted roses to make the place look nice. But it was really there so that I could climb down. We moved a few times but we always lived in a place with an exit that wasn't obvious."

"Charlotte, what were you running from?"

"I don't *know*. Dangerous people. Esme was really scared and so was I."

"My God. What a burden for a child." Jack loves kids and he was worried for the little me I had been.

"I was all right, Jack. We got here or near here on the bus. On a lot of buses. Going in different directions. I was dressed as a boy and not too happy about it."

"You were?"

"My hair was cut like a boy's and I had boy's clothes. I hated it. It's okay if you laugh. I need a bit of levity. I am having trouble talking about all this."

"Okay, dressed as a boy."

"And Esme changed her look completely. Cut her beautiful blonde hair. Dyed it dull brown. She even spoke differently, with an accent. Then when we finally found her friend, Lola, things got better. Lola dyed Esme's hair red and she gave me a pixie cut. I was a girl again. That helped."

Jack said, "This explains so much about you."

"It does. You've noticed I rarely run if I don't absolutely have to."

"I put that down to your love of high heels. But it explains why you crave stability. Order. A nice home. But I'm surprised that you didn't want a dog at first when I tried to interest you in Truffle and Sweet Marie."

Tears stung my eyes. I'd been doing so well holding them back. It took a while for me to pull myself together. Finally, I blew my nose and said, "I never knew what happened to poor Buster. It was the hardest part, harder than being afraid, harder than hiding. But I am glad you persevered. Truffle and Sweet Marie have made all the difference for me. What if I hadn't taken them with me to Pepper's? What if they'd been home during the break-in?"

"You did take them with you and it turned out okay. But why do you have this suitcase? Was there a hidden panel in the apartment? Wouldn't I have known about that?"

"There wasn't. It was just in the closet. I didn't feel that anyone would be after me now. Or Esme."

"So, back to the suitcase, why didn't they find it?"

"I had it in the car in my large tote. I took it to Pepper's to try to explain the–"

"You were going to show it to Pepper? Not me?"

"You were so distracted with your business opportunities and I tried to talk to you about Esme and you kept reassuring me that everything was all right and I was overreacting."

Jack hung his head. "I should never have done that."

I still felt a bit betrayed by Jack's lack of interest in Esme's disappearance, but I had to admit that no one could have expected this crazy story. "You couldn't have known how upset Esme's lack of contact made me. I thought that Pepper, being a cop, could help me."

"And did she?"

"No, I decided against it just before you called and told me to come home. I think these people were looking for information about Esme and wanting to shake me up, but at least they didn't find my emergency kit."

Jack reached over and squeezed my hand. "Have you had any indication that someone from your past was hunting for you?"

I shook my head.

"Then why now? After all this time?"

"I've been trying to explain, there's something going on with Esme. You know she's stopped calling me and Sid too."

"Face it, your mom isn't the most–how should I put it?–diligent."

"Sure, but even when there were new husbands, or new lovers, or big book deals or whatever, she called on Tuesday night or whatever schedule we'd agreed on."

"Always?"

"Yes. That's why I was having nightmares. My subconscious must have been telling me . . ."

Jack leaned toward me, his forehead creased. "I don't understand. Telling you what?"

"I think that my mother is running for her life again."

Jack blinked.

"She's gone silent because she doesn't want me to be involved in whatever's going on."

"Well," Jack said. "Looks like you're involved now."

He leaned back and said nothing for several long minutes. His face was in shadow and it was hard to read his expression.

Finally he said, "Okay, so even if someone from your past—whatever that may have been—tracked you down here after all this time, there's nothing in that suitcase except perfectly rolled clothing, snacks and hats. And money, of course, but you said yourself they weren't after money. Are you telling me they wanted your chocolate protein bars?"

I carefully peeled back the lining that Esme had made for the cute little suitcase.

I reached in and pulled out my passport, a tight roll of bills, a couple of credit cards and a debit card for a bank I normally wouldn't use. The name on the cards was Caroline Adamitz. But Jack didn't seem to notice that. Or the burner phone. There were a few clippings and faded photos. Also sharp scissors, hair dye and black-rimmed glasses, but Jack stared at the roll of bills.

"Yowza. How much cash is there, Charlotte?"

"Five thousand."

He stared at me. "But why would you keep that amount of money in this little bag? Instead of the bank?"

"Might need it in an emergency. I replace items from time to time and update the cards and passport when needed."

"But it's only an ATM away. You could have easy access twenty-four-seven."

"Sometimes your ATM and your credit cards can give away your location."

"Give away your—?"

Jack leaned forward and stared intently.

I pointed to the hair dye and glasses. "As you can see, I can be someone else very quickly if I need to be."

Jack said, "It's a lot to get my head around."

"Yup."

I picked up the old photos and flicked through them. The first one was Esme and me in a fenced backyard with dappled sunlight glowing through the trees. We were smiling at whoever was behind the camera, but I could see the wariness that never really left Esme.

Jack reached for the photo. "Where was this? Before you came to Woodbridge?"

"No. Did I mention she was blonde in our old life? You can see she is already a redhead when this was taken, but her hair's still quite short. We were just starting our life here in Woodbridge."

"You look like you did when I first met you. Who took this photo?"

"Our friend Lola. This was my birthday party in her backyard, so late August, just the three of us and Pierre, the cat. She made me a fantastic castle cake." I thought back to Lola's gravelly voice, her husky laugh. I'd loved her wild and kinky blonde hair and her brilliant blue eyes. Her nails had always matched her lipstick. Who could forget Lola?

"Why did you keep the photos hidden?"

"They're not really hidden. I just didn't want to lose them if we had to vanish again. Except for the hummingbird earrings, I have nothing from our life before these photos were taken so I just left them with my kit. I looked through the prints. "I wish I had one of Lola herself. She was the person who saved us."

"And who exactly is she?" Jack asked, reasonably enough.

"I don't remember her last name. I think she was from our old life. She was already here when we arrived and she got us set up in an apartment, and then after a while Esme's career started to blossom and we lost touch."

"Who did she save you from? Was Esme running from . . . her husband?"

"You mean my father. No, in my foggy memory, he took us to the bus station. We hugged him. Esme was crying because we had to go. She didn't want to leave him. I don't have any bad feelings about him and I don't believe Esme did. But she was definitely afraid of somebody."

"Maybe your parents' marriage was over and you were unaware."

I shook my head. "I would have known."

"But can't you remember where you came from?"

"A big city, I think. We had an apartment twenty stories up with a balcony that looked over the park. Esme called it a penthouse."

"Who lived with you?"

"Just my mother and father. A lady named Celine came in to clean. She spoke French."

"French?"

"And my father would speak French to her but English to me and my mother. He taught me quite a bit, but the sort of vocabulary that a child would need."

"Not much to go on."

"Actually, I think it couldn't have been all that far from here. We were on buses for hours and one overnight, but not days and days."

Jack unbent slowly out of his chair and slouched over to the window. "So somewhere in Quebec."

"Yes," I said. "It must have been Montreal."

Jack's lanky form was silhouetted against the window. I joined him as he stared out at the glittering Hudson below. I leaned into his body, enjoying the warmth.

He said, "Wouldn't someone have reported you and Esme missing? A woman and a small child? Wouldn't that have made the news?"

"It might have made the news in Montreal or wherever we started out but we were already in another country."

"But you would have needed passports to cross the border. And she would have needed documentation to take you with her."

"I think she had it all. I have a vague memory of Esme showing passports. Mine had my 'boy's' name in it. Looking back, I think it must have been a planned escape and my father would have been part of that plan."

Jack said, "The passports would have had to match your appearances and you were both in disguise. How could that be?"

"I'm asking myself the same question. Illegal passports would not be easy to get, especially—and I think it was—in a hurry."

"Unless . . ."

"Right. Criminal connections. There's more."

"I want to hear everything, but let's finish this part first. You are obviously a girl. So wouldn't Esme need your birth certificate to send you to school?"

"I have a birth certificate. We had it before I got to school. How do you think Charlotte Adams got a Social Security number and a passport?"

"You mean you had forged documents for that?" Jack ran his fingers through his hair again.

"Too risky. I assume that somewhere back in the day, a mother and a young child died, most likely in an accident. Or maybe the mother died after giving birth and the baby died soon after but lived long enough for the birth to be registered. And almost certainly this happened in another state."

Jack stared at me.

"But the names—"

"It wouldn't have mattered what the names were. If they were available and there was no competition from their previous owners, they would do."

"But what if some relative came across—"

"Adams is a common name. And so is Charlotte. I am far from alone. But it's unlikely another mother and daughter would have those birth dates. She would have taken her time to make sure of that."

"Esme isn't a common name."

"Oh, that. Esme is the name my mother took on when she started to write. The name on the birth certificate she used was and is Esther Marie Adams, but she called herself Esme."

Jack hadn't stopped shaking his head. It was a lot to take in.

I said, "She reinvented herself and me. She got braces and a bit of plastic surgery. I was never supposed to mention that. With the red hair and her various changes, I don't think anyone from her old life would even recognize her. But you have probably noticed that she never really shows her face on anything, social media, book covers."

Jack paused and thought. "That's true, but the whole thing is so hard to believe."

"I lived it and it's still hard to believe. Partly because Esme and I always pretended that it hadn't happened."

"But this whole deception, the identities, the fake birth certificates—"

"They weren't fake. My mother just applied for them. They are completely genuine. It's just that the people on our birth certificates didn't happen to be us."

"This would take expertise. The internet wasn't what it is now."

"Esme is pretty smart. You know that. But I believe Lola helped her. We came to Woodbridge because Lola was already here and she could fix things for us."

I could see Jack was puzzled even in the dark room. "But did you know her before? She must have had some criminal connections too."

"I think so, and now you probably understand why I had second thoughts about showing my secret suitcase to Pepper. She wouldn't be able to just let all this fraudulent behavior go. I don't know what I was thinking. The situation with Esme was messing with my head."

"Fair enough. Should we be trying to find the original Charlotte Adams and her mother?"

"What good would that do? It won't tell us who I am or who my mother was. Or who we were fleeing from. Or who has found us after all this time and still wants something."

Jack wrapped me tightly in his arms. "You know what?"

"What?" My voice was muffled because I had buried my head in the pineapples on his Hawaiian shirt.

"Whoever you are and whatever your reason for being on the run, I am here for you."

I looked up to meet his blue eyes. For once, they looked serious. "I never doubted you, Jack."

"We'll get through this."

"We will." I hoped that *we* included my mother.

"No question. In the meantime, would some New York Super Fudge Chunk help?"

"It couldn't hurt."

We made ourselves comfortable on the leather sofa and watched the night sky. It sounds better than it was.

"Aside from fearing for Esme's life and having my home wrecked, the worst part is that I don't know who I am, Jack. That's what I find so hard to cope with."

The lights from the patio glittered in Jack's glasses. "I know who you are. I know how you think and what you do and how you care passionately about the people in your life."

I said, "But you don't—"

"I don't need to know who you were. Charlotte Adams, no matter what other names you've had, you're the person I love."

Well. You can't whine about your worries when someone uses the *L* word. That is something Jack and I rarely do.

Finally I pulled away from him. My deepest fear was that the before part would turn out to matter.

"Thanks, Jack." I kept my lip from wobbling. "Now we have to get to the bottom of my mother's disappearance."

"You said she's not missing. She's running for her life."

"No question. And now that you know something of our murky history you have an idea of why she might be hiding."

"Let's recap what I think I know now, reconstructed from what you've said and what's happened. Twenty-six years ago you and your mother fled, most likely from Montreal, in the middle of the night, in disguise, probably with the help of your father, to get away from dangerous people."

"Accurate so far."

"In advance of this, she had a plan, disguises and fake documents with new identities."

I nodded.

"You traveled on buses for quite a while."

"Right."

"You probably left from Canada and you were pretending to be a boy."

"Esme was pretending I was a boy."

"You made your way to Woodbridge and someone named Lola was able to help you."

I found myself rocking back and forth. Jack put a soothing hand on my shoulder. I said, "And from that time until today, no one from before ever showed up. Except in my nightmares."

"To continue the recap, you had as normal a life as you could with a mom like Esme. Then for some reason, this week, people showed up outside our house, using pilfered dogs as a ploy—really that's almost the hardest thing to believe about this—and cased the place. They or their accomplices broke in and trashed the apartment that you love, looking for something."

"Yes."

The phone rang and I jumped.

Margaret said, "Just checking in. I hope you and Jack are comfortable. There's a bottle of red wine on the sideboard that might be just what the doctor ordered after the day you've had."

"Thank you."

"I know you're probably missing essentials. In the bathroom, there's a basket for guests, not that we ever have any, but you'll find the necessities: toothbrushes and toothpaste, bath salts, bubble bath, bath oil, Epsom salts, handmade soap, skin cream. There are two extra terry-cloth robes hanging in the closet. Help yourself. A nice long soak helps with most situations."

Margaret had never been allowed baths. It was considered a waste of time in her family. She was making up for years of missed luxurious baths. Jack opened the wine and poured us each a jumbo glass. I understand red wine is supposed to breathe, but really, who cared?

I sipped and said, “The suitcase would have been there if I hadn’t taken it to Pepper’s place.”

“Maybe they wanted to destroy your peace of mind. They want you to panic.”

“They succeeded.”

“Not really. You are nervous, maybe even jittery, but you’re holding it together.”

“Well, I can’t panic, can I? What if they want me to lead them to Esme? I might have done that if they hadn’t jumped the gun and destroyed . . .”

“Not everything,” he said, squeezing my hand.

“You’re right. Esme always says, ‘You can’t replace the people you care about.’”

We stared at each other. My lips twitched first and Jack said, “Except for husbands and lovers.”

I joined in laughing. That felt better than any sedative.

I tucked the little case out of sight under the sofa and capped off the end of the longest Wednesday ever with a luxurious soak in the tub. I was wrapped in one of the ultra-soft terry-cloth robes when I curled up on the sofa again with Jack.

The last thing I remember is Jack carrying me into the bedroom whispering, “Sleepy time.”

Chapter 10

It's a good idea to boost your security whenever you're away.

The phone blasted me awake. Why was Dean Oliver calling after midnight?

I listened. Jack hovered, bleary-eyed.

"A fire?" My voice shook. I put Dean on speaker phone. I could hear the anger in his voice.

"I've been keeping an eye on your place tonight. I saw your lights go off."

"They're on timers."

"Good idea. I guess they wanted to wait until you were asleep. I had this gut feeling and I doubled back. I heard a window break and saw a flash. I think it was a Molotov cocktail. Good thing you weren't home."

I stared at Jack. "They didn't know we weren't home. I think they meant business."

"They meant business all right," Dean said grimly.

"We have to get over there." Jack jumped up, ready to go.

"Better not," Dean warned. "If they did know you weren't here, they'll be waiting for you to return after the fire. And if they didn't know, they'll figure it out and you could be followed. Let us handle it. I'll keep you posted."

I held my breath. "Is the house . . . destroyed?"

"That's one bit of good news. I called it in immediately and the fire department was there in minutes. They did a great job. Your windows are broken and there's probably a ton of smoke damage, but the flames didn't get near the roof. I think you'll be able to save your home."

Jack sat there, shocked. I knew he was imagining his parents' home, the best place in the world, in flames.

Who were these people? And what would stop them?

I heard voices and then Pepper came on Dean's phone. "Do *not*," she said grimly, "go anywhere without letting me know. Neither one of you is safe. No snooping. Do you hear me?"

We did.

It took the rest of the wine and the ice cream before we finally conked out again.

• • •

By the time I pried my eyes open in the morning, Jack had already left a note and departed for the condo gym to work off his restless energy. That was good. I needed quiet to wake up and think. While I was thinking, I decided in future to have smaller wineglasses or fewer of them. I chugged down a tumblerful of orange juice. I wasn't much in the mood for breakfast but coffee was essential. Margaret and Frank had a high-end coffee machine and always keep Medaglia d'Oro Classico on hand. I made myself a mug and hunted for something to eat. The kitchen was spotless and that meant Jack hadn't made himself anything yet. Our bag of bagels looked promising. I waited until my body could cope. I wracked my brain about where my mother could be hiding in Europe but my mind came up empty. But I did ask myself how these people—whoever they were—had found me. We'd been told to stay at Margaret's with no snooping around town for me, despite the fact I was the one who needed to know what was going on. But something Sid had said was now flickering in the back of my mind. I was reminded that Esme's doorman had mentioned that Sid wasn't the only person looking for her. At the time, I hadn't realized the possible implications.

I knew Regis, the doorman, well. He'd helped me many times when I lived in the city and visited Esme for our Tuesday encounters. I'd used his pleasant services when I needed to send something to Esme. I had his number in my contacts. I figured I'd find him at the front desk of the building, where he kept an eye on everyone and everything.

"Regis? It's Charlotte Adams."

Regis, a highly dignified Englishman in his sixties, sounded like he might have stepped out of the pages of a Victorian novel. He always smelled elegant too with the Taylor of Old Bond Street cologne Esme gave him twice a year. I waited until he finished his effusive greeting. "Your mother is not here, Miss Charlotte."

"I didn't realize she was planning a trip."

"She was arranging for some redecorating and small renovations while she was away. Then she needed to depart in a hurry and she asked me to cancel the appointments with the tradespeople."

"Oh."

"Naturally, I was more than happy to do so."

I knew that Esme valued Regis's services and she was generous with her tips. "Did she say where she was going?"

"She did not. Mr. Greenberg asked me the identical question. I hope everything is all right, Miss Charlotte."

"I'm sure it is," I said untruthfully. "But I am trying to track her down."

"You certainly aren't the only one."

"What do you mean?"

"Some of your mother's old friends have shown up looking for her."

"Old friends?" Esme had no old friends, aside from Lola. Colleagues, staff people, that was about it. Esme did not inspire closeness. In fact, Regis and Sid and Glenda probably knew her better than anyone. "What old friends?"

"Two very nice ladies, both carrying spectacular bouquets of flowers."

"Who were they?"

"They didn't give me their names, now that you mention it. But they were asking for Esme. They wanted me to call up. They said it was a surprise."

The skin on my arms prickled. "And did you let them in?"

Regis chortled. "My dear Miss Charlotte, that would be more than my life is worth."

My brain felt like an excited popcorn maker popping questions rather than kernels. "What happened then?"

"Both ladies tried to persuade me, very charmingly and indeed with monetary enticement, but my job is to deal with situations like this. They wanted to know when your mother would return so they could show up again to surprise her. Naturally, I was noncommittal. Did you hear from them?"

"No. How would they know about me?"

"They were old friends, from Montreal days, they said. I assumed they would know about you."

Montreal days.

"What did they look like?"

"Two ladies of a certain age both very nicely dressed and a bit on the, um, portly side. Perhaps sisters? Nothing much to distinguish them. They both had brown hair, but one had what I believe the ladies call highlights. Oh dear, did I detect in your tone that I may have put my foot in it?"

"Not at all, but did you give them my address?"

"Most assuredly not, but I did say that Esme might be visiting her daughter in Woodbridge. Perhaps that was an error on my part. Do you not think they were actually old friends?"

"Listen, Regis, could they have been caught on your security cameras?"

Regis went quiet.

"What is it?" I asked.

"Now that I recall, they kept their faces turned away from the security camera at the desk."

"But is that the only place where they could have been caught on camera?"

"No flies on you, Miss Charlotte. There are two other cameras disguised as lamps for that very purpose."

"Would you have their images on that?"

"Possibly, but I am mortified that I slipped up in this way."

"Don't worry about it, Regis." I wasn't at all sure that Esme would have agreed. "Please check those other cameras for me. If they're there, do you have a way to transmit the images?"

"I will certainly find a way."

"Thanks, Regis. Text them to this number and call if you think of anything else relevant."

"Certainly and a thousand apologies for my lapse, I—"

"It's already forgotten, but there is something else."

"Anything."

"Did my mother get anything from the vault?" For some reason, Esme didn't trust banks for safe-deposit boxes, but one of the features of her building was a locked room with individual secure boxes. She kept her valuables there—discreet, convenient and available twenty-four-seven.

"Ah. Perhaps I shouldn't—"

"You definitely should, Regis."

"She did retrieve something shortly after she arrived back from Montreal."

"And it was?"

"A carry-on suitcase."

And so it begins again, I thought. Esme would have had her passport with her and U.S. and Canadian cash and credit cards hidden in the apartment, but she needed her emergency bag and at least one other identity. I knew she was on the run, but where was she going? More to the point, how did she know there would be danger?

"Regis," I said, with a wobble in my voice. "Please be careful. Something is going on and it's not good."

• • •

Next, I really needed to let my clients know that all plans would be on hold. I managed to reach most of the people I had appointments with for the following three weeks. I estimated it would take at least that long to sort things out and get the office back in shape. I held it together as I explained that my home and office had had a fire and that I would need to reschedule. The people I reached were sympathetic. I left messages for the others and hoped for the best.

Next, sipping the fragrant and bracing coffee, I tried to reach Glenda yet again. No luck with phone, email, text or social media accounts, as Glenda ran all of Esme's behind the scenes. As Glenda once took a call from me while she was in Emerg having fourteen stitches, I suspected Esme had sworn her to secrecy. Attempting to keep my mind off Esme's disappearance, I searched for items about a mother and child vanishing in Montreal in the year we came to Woodbridge. I broadened my search to Quebec, then Ontario. I found many heartbreaking stories about missing women and abducted children, but nothing that could have been about us. A lot of papers and documents from that era hadn't yet been digitized so that might account for it. Plus, most of the Quebec media was French. Could a missing mother and daughter story have been covered in the French papers but not the English ones? Unlikely but not impossible. I decided to check in with Ramona, who is a genius at ferreting out information. I thought she might already be at the library. And now she had a French-speaking connection with her boss, Vanessa. As I started the call, Jack burst through the door. "Lola!" he shouted.

"Charlotte," I said.

"Very funny. Lola's the only person besides Esme who knows the story behind your identity. We need to find her and get to the bottom of it. Are those bagels for me?"

"Already toasted. I found cream cheese and fig jam in the fridge."

"That coffee smells great too. I guess being on the run isn't all bad."

I joined Jack at the glossy granite-topped breakfast bar between the kitchen and living area. We had a nice view of the river in the daytime through the huge living room window. Even though I felt safe in our borrowed cocoon, we desperately needed a plan to go forward.

A text pinged and I snatched up my phone.

Regis had sent an image along with a wordy explanation.

I stared at the slightly blurred images from the hidden cameras. No question about it. One of the visitors was the bucket-hatted dognapping woman from in front of my own house. She looked much more affluent now with her chin-length bob an attractive light shade. Her well-cut black suit and statement jewelry gave her an in-charge look that had been absent when she was walking poor Suzie. I have previously established that the bucket hat is rarely a friend to the wearer. And, of course, she had stolen that dog. Suzie was a better judge of character than I was. The second person was more of a surprise: Harriet Oberon, the woman who'd engaged my services at my library presentation was smiling like a serpent.

Regis stood his ground with his usual magnificent and barrel-chested dignity. Although the image was in black and white, Harriet's salon highlights were clearly visible, as was the large emerald ring on her finger. They had to be sisters: they shared tiny ball-bearing eyes and the extra chins. I felt no obligation to think kind thoughts about them. No wonder they had been able to find me! A search for "Adams" and "Woodbridge" would have brought up plenty of information about me, including my photo and the date of my presentation at the library. Not too difficult to get my address after that. Then they would have staked out our home under the pretense of walking their pilfered dogs. What would have happened if I had met with Harriet alone? Now I hoped I would never come face-to-face with her, no matter how angry I was about the trashing of my house.

I picked up a bagel before they all disappeared. "Jack, you have to see this."

He turned away from his breakfast, reluctantly. He stared at the image that Regis had sent. "I have seen her on our street."

"Yes. And the other one was at my library session. They put a lot of thought into this, Jack. They know where Esme lives in New York and they found out where we are."

I dropped my bagel. "Wait a minute! How did they find Esme?"

"Wouldn't that be pretty easy?" Jack eyed the fallen bagel with interest.

"No one knows where Esme lives."

"You do."

"Yes, and I'd never dare let anyone else know. For instance, I am closer to you than anyone else in the world, but did you know?"

"I was going to suggest ex-husbands."

"Nah. I don't know that any of them would have ever got past Regis."

"Yet, these dangerous people were there."

"And I wasn't, so they didn't follow me."

"What about Sid?"

"I bet that's it. He got in a panic and went to Esme's place. They must have been watching him. I need to talk to him. And he needs to try harder to track down Glenda."

"We'll figure it out. You want any of these bagels?"

Eventually, Sid barked into his phone. "Well? Where is she?"

"No idea, but people have been trying to get into Esme's apartment. I think they must have followed you."

"Ridiculous," he blustered. "The only way to reach Esme is through Glenda."

"Sid, I am one hundred percent sure you have Glenda's address. I need you to go there, find out where Esme is and get back to me for everyone's sake. Thank you." I hung up and exhaled.

Jack said, "Whoa. You were channeling your mother. That was magnificent and a bit frightening."

"Uh-huh." I picked up the bagel and bit into it with a certain ruthlessness.

"Well, we can't proceed on those lines until Sid gets back in touch. What else do we have to go on?"

"We can dig into our Montreal connection. Esme went there recently. That's something."

Jack and I needed to conjure up solutions to a problem we didn't understand. I stared out the window at the Hudson below and he polished off the rest of the bagels. Eventually he said, "At this stage, we don't know where Esme is and you have exhausted all avenues."

My head snapped. "I wouldn't say exhausted all avenues. I just did the logical stuff. Agent. Social media. Assistant. Glenda's part of the problem, keeping Esme's secret. She'd absolutely do that. Sid had better succeed in finding her. You know what the other problem is?"

Jack said, "Lost your home? Remembered your traumatic childhood? Missing your dogs?"

"Exactly. We should call and see how they are."

"After that, how about putting Find Lola on your list? She helped and you liked her and trusted her."

"Yes, we trusted her. But they drifted apart after that first summer. Esme had created a new life for us. She was starting to write books and I was making new friends like you. When I asked about Lola, Esme told me we had to look to the future. What kind of thing is that to say to a five-year-old who'd lost everything?"

"Lola knew all about you both, your background and Esme's intentions for the future."

I thought back to Esme and Lola, their two beautiful heads together, laughter, whispers, plans and Lola consoling Esme about our state of affairs. "Yes, I think Lola knew everything."

Jack located some artisan crackers in the cupboard. He was having trouble being stuck in someone else's home with no bike parts and no remaining ice cream or bagels. Restlessness always made him hungry. "Aren't you going stir-crazy, Charlotte?"

"No. I'm going worry-crazy."

"And we're kind of trapped here."

"Actually I feel completely safe in Margaret and Frank's place. Unless, of course, we clear out the entire contents of their fridge, freezer and cupboards."

"Back to my suggestion." Jack took a plate from the open shelf and dumped some crackers on it.

"What?"

"If we track down Lola, we'll find some answers." He added a slice of cheese to each cracker.

Jack was right. I wasn't sure why I felt reluctant. We hadn't heard from Lola for over twenty-five years and I realized that was a sad thing. "I think that there may have been a falling-out. Or maybe they decided it was better not to associate in case someone from the past showed up in Lola's life and that led to Esme and me."

Jack shrugged and went back to pacing.

I found myself staring out the window again. The sky was brilliant azure today, scudding white clouds, happy sun shining brightly. The very image of a child's painting. "I wonder."

Jack stopped pacing. "Wonder what?"

"Maybe we can find a clue to her location in that photo of my birthday party in Lola's backyard."

"Yeah, wasn't that just you and Esme in a nice yard? But nothing of Lola. Only her shadow."

I rummaged through the contents of the bag and came up with the photograph.

"She had an old-fashioned house. She always had Cheez Whiz and crackers. And Cherry Kool-Aid. I loved that. And she had Pierre, the tuxedo cat. She took the picture carefully, I imagine, so no one could learn anything about us or her if they found it."

Jack said, "Are you sure that all you can remember was the cat, the Cheez Whiz and the sugary drinks?"

"Let's see what we can figure out. That is a two-story house maybe from the early twentieth century and I remember Lola told me that the fancy wooden trim was called gingerbread. I was a little kid so that made me laugh. It was an old house and she had fixed it up and she did a lot of work herself, but she said she wanted to keep the original look of it. The house was a pretty blue. I've always liked blue houses. Check out that fence, Jack. See the color of the wood? Not at all weathered and not yet painted. Does that fence look new to you?"

He blinked. "I guess. So we're looking for the backyard of a blue two-story house that was renovated twenty-five years ago and could be anywhere."

"Not anywhere. Lola said she was a city girl and used to going on foot. She said she needed to stretch her legs or she'd seize up. She loved to walk. She'd take me with her. I rode my tricycle. We checked out everyone's front garden. Lola had always wanted a garden. And she planted some trees because they would remind her of home."

Jack had a soft spot for trees. "What kind?"

"I didn't know the names of many trees but I remember she planted a maple tree and made a big deal about it. I do recall we were close enough to walk to Tang's Convenience and sometimes we'd get chips there. It was before I met Margaret at school."

"She didn't have a car?"

"Brilliant, Jack! She did."

"What kind?"

"I remember it was blue and the roof came off."

Jack whooped. "Honda del Sol!"

How did he know these things? "Little blue beauty. Of course, I doubt if it's still on the road after twenty-five years."

"Woodbridge isn't that big. We can drive around the older streets and see if anything strikes you as familiar. At least we'll be doing something useful."

"Agreed. We have nothing to lose either, but we should also ask Ramona to search for the story of the missing mother and daughter in Montreal."

Jack nodded. His mouth was full. Again.

Ramona wasn't in until ten, it turned out. "Why not look for Lola's now and then go to the library. But we can't just go around looking like ourselves. They'll be watching for us at home and at CYCotics."

"I thought of that. While you were snoring away, I called Jorge and told him I had an emergency. He'll cover the shifts until I'm free again. He has a useful supply of brothers and cousins who can help if he has classes."

"I'm glad you won't be at the shop. I hope you didn't tell Jorge or anyone else where we are staying."

"Nope. And he didn't ask. So since we don't want them to see us, should we look like someone else?"

"Good thinking, Jack. How about Margaret and Frank?"

"Oh, I don't know–"

"They told us to make ourselves at home. Take anything we want. Anything. Let's hit the closets."

Chapter 11

Use scarves, jewelry and other accessories to maximize your travel wardrobe.

There weren't a lot of disguise options in Margaret's closet, but I was happy to have a change of clothes. I picked the oldest-looking navy pantsuit from a row of ten similar suits hanging neatly. Half the suits were navy and half were black. Margaret apparently didn't own skirt suits. Two suits still had the price tags attached. Margaret had a selection of identical classic top-quality white cotton blouses and a few in more adventurous medium blue. I spotted two silk ones with tie collars. I had my emergency sewing kit in my tote and while Jack played—there was no other word because he was having fun—in Frank's closet, I did a quick and very imperfect temporary hem of the pants and the sleeves of the suit. When you hover around five feet tall, you can practically hem in your sleep. I took one of the cotton shirts and rolled the sleeves. I used a belt to keep the pants from falling down and left the jacket open so it seemed like the trendy "boyfriend" style. Margaret's jewelry ran on the conservative side and she never wore scarves. I took a red and gold one from my own emergency travel kit and arranged it to brighten the look. Margaret's feet are two sizes larger, so I kept my own boots. Margaret owned a small collection of hats, so I borrowed a navy beret and tucked my hair up under it. If the hems didn't fall down, I might possibly look all right from a distance.

Jack borrowed some of Frank's golfing clothes. Although Frank was heavier than Jack, they were about the same height. Jack shopped the back of the closet and found an older pair of chinos and a salmon-pink golf shirt. He accessorized his look with a ball cap and a pair of white sneakers.

We headed out to search for Lola. Jack was full of bagels, cheese and optimism. I was full of apprehension.

• • •

As we were already the guests from hell, we borrowed Margaret's Kia. She and Frank had taken his vehicle on their getaway.

Jack eased out of the controlled-access underground parking and inched onto the street. He said, "It might look more normal if you didn't keep peering around like that."

I calmed myself and we cruised Uptown to check out the nearby older neighborhoods. I took Margaret's map from the glove compartment and assigned myself the task of checking off streets. There are worse things than taking a slow drive through established streets on a spring day when the trees were just starting to leaf out.

On every block, Jack would pull over and I would scan up and down, looking for what had been Lola's house.

"She probably moved on long ago," I said.

"A neighbor might know where."

"Not if she's anything like Esme."

"Right, her old partner in crime."

I bristled at the words. "Hardly crime," I snapped.

But those words whirled in my head. Had Lola and Esme been partners in crime? How else had two young women survived on their own without working? I wasn't sure I wanted to know the answer.

"The gingerbread might have been taken down in a later reno," Jack said. "People kept telling my parents to get rid of it at our place to modernize the look."

"I'm glad they didn't listen. And I hope it wasn't destroyed in the fire."

Jack's hands tightened on the steering wheel. "If it was, we will find a way to replace it."

"Lola's place might be a different color by now. I'm trying to remember the shape of it. A lot of these old houses have been made into separate apartments too, like yours."

We were running out of steam when I saw the house. "This is it!"

Jack squinted. "It's not that large."

"Yeah, much smaller than I remember, but I was just a little kid then."

"And it's not blue."

"Not anymore. I like the dark gray."

A man with white hair and garden shears was puttering around his bulb garden. You could smell the hyacinths from across the street. He peered at us suspiciously over half-glasses. A battered three-wheel bike was parked by the side door.

I conjured up a smile. "Hello. I am hoping to connect with an old family friend, Lola. I think she used to live in this house." I pointed next door.

He shook his head. "Nope."

"Oh, but I was sure–"

"No Lola there."

"But she may have moved."

"The McCarthys have been there for fifty years."

My face must have fallen. Lola was nearly our last hope. He turned away but I couldn't help but notice a small smirk. A screen door banged behind him and a round, smiling woman bustled toward us.

"Hello!"

"They were just leaving," Mr. Grumpy said with a scowl.

Her smile vanished. No doubt, living with someone like him, you'd be glad of a fresh face from time to time. I said, "We were looking for my old friend Lola. I thought she lived next door to you."

"Sorry, dear. No Lola ever lived next door to me."

"That's too bad. I remembered the blue house with the gingerbread trim and her blue Honda del Sol parked in front like it was yesterday."

"Guess your memory's wrong," he muttered, with obvious enjoyment.

"Honda del Sol?" she said. "I remember that car! And the house. But it wasn't this one, dear. It was just around the corner. There was a pretty woman with curly strawberry-blonde hair and freckles who lived there and, later, a man that we never saw. I think he died a few years ago. They kept to themselves. The car is gone, but I've seen her working in the garden recently. The house is white now and the porch is gone. She had to renovate it to make a ramp for his wheelchair.

Of course. We'd already driven by that house but the ramp must have made it seem different. "Is it the house with all the trees?"

"Yes, those gorgeous red maples."

"Thank you."

"My pleasure. Glad to help." She beamed at us.

Jack beamed back. He reached into his pocket and pulled a business card from his wallet. "Call me in a couple of weeks and I'll tune up that bike for you. On the house."

Minutes later, we hustled up the long ramp to the front door of the white house and knocked. The door was glossy and black with a brass lion's head knocker. A pair of cast-iron urns bursting with yellow pansies and pussy willows stood guard on each side.

No answer.

We tried again.

Jack knocked extra hard the third time.

In case she was in the garden, we followed the path on the side of the house past a bed full of exuberant daffodils, the double-faced kind.

The backyard was private, thanks to a tall fence painted deep blue. There was a small sunporch in the rear of the house and a still-covered swimming pool with a curved flagstone patio around it. The dark green PVC lounger had a woolen shawl draped over it and an ashtray with a smoldering cigarette on a small metal table. By the fence, a handsome tuxedo cat twitched its tail ominously at us. It couldn't have been Pierre. That was too long ago.

"Someone was just here."

"You can smell the perfume, even over the smoke. What is that scent?"

"I don't know but Lola wore that!"

We should have kept an eye out rather than sniffing the air. We whirled at a sound behind us. Lola emerged from the sunporch looking like she always had, except for even more freckles and a few deeper lines. She still wore vivid coral lipstick as I remembered and had a fresh manicure to match. I imagined that behind the mirrored sunglasses her blue eyes were flinty. It would have been great to see her except for that gun in her hand.

I know little about guns except that they can make holes in people.

Jack said, "Whoa!"

I said, "Lola?"

"Get the hell out of here." I could still detect a hint of a French accent behind the gravelly voice.

"It's me, Charlotte. Esme's daughter. Do you remember me?"

"Charlotte." Her glance flicked toward Jack.

"And this is Jack, my friend since kindergarten and now my partner—"

She lowered the gun but didn't smile. "You can't be here, Charlotte."

"Don't you remember the good times we had? You used to make birthday cakes and Kool-Aid and Cheez Whiz—"

"You have to go now."

"I missed you after we lost touch."

"It was for the best. You were too young to understand. Esme and I made a decision."

"I need help to find Esme."

Lola placed the gun on a cedar planter and lit a fresh cigarette. It gave me a chance to study her. She was still very attractive, her kinky hair faded, and shorter, but still flattering.

"You are better off not knowing. And you shouldn't have come. You may have led . . . people . . . to me."

"We've been very careful! Lola, someone trashed my home. They were watching it, disguised as dog walkers. Last night they set fire to it."

Lola inhaled. "That's very bad."

Jack said, "We are aware of that."

"It means they know who you are."

"They? Who are *they*? How could they find out about me?"

"Maybe one question at a time, Charlotte?" Jack suggested.

Lola shrugged.

Chills raced down my spine.

"These people mean business. If they take you, they could use that as leverage against Esme."

"What people? What do you mean 'if they take me'?"

Jack interjected. "We are already making ourselves scarce. As you can see, we're in disguise."

Lola couldn't suppress a snort. There's no hope of disguising Jack. And I looked like a character in a high school play without a proper costume director.

The tuxedo cat was obviously bored with the chat. He jumped on the lounger and stared at the little table.

Lola said, "You'd better get out of town until things die down. If they find you, they'll use you to find her."

"But I don't know where Esme is."

"They'll never believe that." Lola exhaled a long stream of smoke. "I wouldn't want to be up against any of them."

"Any of whom?"

"People from Esme's past. People you don't want to know."

"But why did they show up now?"

"I can't help you."

"You did help us when we were on the run. Did you help Esme disappear?"

"And I'm still trying to help you, sugar. Get as far away and stay as far away for as long as you can. Don't worry about Esme. She is a survivor."

"I'm a survivor too."

She shook her head. "You have no idea who you are dealing with."

"Who am I dealing with?"

"The less you know the better." She turned her head to include Jack in all this.

"But why wouldn't she have contacted me?"

Lola drew deeply on the new cigarette, exhaled and said, "I guess you better sit down."

Jack stretched out on the lounger. Lola and I took the chairs at the bistro table.

"What happened with my mother?"

"Sugar, what happened to your mother was she married the wrong man."

"More than once," Jack said, languidly staring at the pool.

"It's not a pretty story." The cat batted the ashtray onto the patio stones. "*Méchant*, Pierre!" Lola scolded. I guessed this new Pierre was just as wicked as the original. Lola picked up the cat, hustled over to the sunporch and popped him inside. She took the gun with her.

Jack sat up straight. "Was Esme running from domestic violence?"

Lola returned and sat down again. "Don't be ridiculous. Sean would never have laid a hand on her. He was crazy about her from the first time he saw her."

"Sean? Was that . . . my father?"

"'Course. Those two never could keep their hands off each other." Lola waved the smoke away and said, "Oh, didn't she tell you, sugar?"

I shook my head. "I don't know anything about him."

"Just as well."

"Was he from Montreal?"

"They met in Montreal at Le Club, a bar in the west end. That's where I met her too. She was stunning. He fell hard. *Un fou amoureux*, they say. She was a fool for love too. He was a handsome little guy, smart, cocky and charismatic and she couldn't resist. After a while, you came along and they wanted to get out of that life. But they needed one last big job to disappear. Sean took a lot of chances and he got on the wrong side of some very bad people. Evelyn's snooty parents weren't any help. They cut her off when you came along."

There was so much to respond to. That life. Evelyn. Being cut off. Very bad people.

"I just intended to stay in this area until things calmed down and I could go home again. But that wasn't to be."

"Why couldn't you go home again?"

"The less you know the better, sugar."

"Just tell me where Esme is and we'll get out of your hair."

"No idea and I wouldn't tell you if I did know."

"Has she been in touch with you?"

Lola shook her head. "Not a word. That's for the best."

"But . . ."

"Look, if you care about Esme—"

"*If* I care about her? She's my mother!"

"Then, *since* you care about her, you should leave her alone."

"But she could be in danger."

"Esme is cunning, like a fox. If she knows that someone is after her, she'll go to ground, probably someplace she feels comfortable, where no one will think to look for her. You will just complicate things."

I whispered, "Who is looking for her?"

"Dangerous people."

"What is Sean's last name?"

She stood up and gestured toward the path. "Hit the road, sugar. I've said more than I should have."

"But I need to know where she is."

Lola used the gun to point the way out.

• • •

"I guess it's better than nothing," Jack said as we drove toward the corner.

"It's way more than nothing! I learned my father's first name."

"Do you think Lola would have shot us?" Jack kept his eyes straight ahead. Personally, I would have chosen to check to the left before pulling onto Long March Road.

Jack added, "I'm wondering if she had something to do with Esme's disappearance."

"Sorry. I should have realized that the gun might have—Wait a minute!" A large black SUV was crawling along Long March, its occupants obviously on the lookout for something. The driver had mean little eyes and a triple chin. I recognized the two women as well.

Jack slammed on the brake.

"No, don't stop. We need to go after them!" I shrieked.

"What is wrong with you? You sound like a freight train."

"I saw them!"

"Who?"

"The dognappers. The house trashers. The people who tried to get into Esme's apartment. And they saw us. They're in that black SUV. Jack! It's a Ford Explorer. They've made a U-turn! They're after us!"

"They're chasing *us*? But shouldn't we go after them? Fight instead of flight?"

Jack had a point. "Yes. Turn around. I don't want them to know how much they scared us."

Jack made an impressive U-ey. "We don't know whether they're armed or how dangerous they are, but . . . look at that!" The SUV raced toward us with two people visible in the front seat and one in the back. "I'll get a photo for the cops."

The SUV loomed closer and I got a shot of it and the plate. "Okay, get out of here!"

"Flight it is," Jack said, putting pedal to the metal. We flew past them. Jack made a surprise one-eighty at the intersection. There was a screech of brakes but we were halfway down the next street. Jack shot into a half-hidden alleyway and parked behind a dumpster. Seconds later they sped by. As soon as they turned the next corner, we rocketed out of our hiding place and raced back the way we came.

"We lost them, but I'd like to get off the roads."

My hands shook as I called Pepper to tell her we'd spotted the dognappers and suspected house trashers and told her a large black Ford SUV was pursuing us on Long March Road. I blurted out the plate number. "I've texted the photo and you can see the people in the front."

"Did I not tell you two to lie low?" she complained. "I'll get the word out and we'll trace that vehicle and keep an eye out for it. Get back to Margaret's."

"We are lying low. We're just going to the library."

"The library's nowhere near Long March Road."

Did she ever stop detecting? "We were getting stir crazy. We thought it would be fun to go for a spin in Margaret's car."

"And now these people have seen you."

"A man was driving and there was a woman in the passenger seat. I saw another woman in the backseat, but that won't show in the photo. These people are dangerous."

After the call, I turned to Jack. Before I could say a word, he said, "You didn't tell Pepper about Lola."

"Um, no."

Jack said nothing. A bad sign.

"Look, Jack. About Lola and her gun. I am so sorry. She's obviously in fear of someone. But you've been shot before, so I should have been a bit more sensitive to how that would have felt."

"It's not your fault. You were hot on the trail of your personal history. But I don't ever want to get shot again."

"Agreed. Now, boot it to the library before they spot us. They've seen our faces and seen this car so that's not good."

"It's not, but we'll find a way out of it."

• • •

At Woodbridge Public Library, Jack whipped the Kia around to the staff parking in the rear of the building, tucking it out of sight beside a bookmobile. We hopped out and went in the rear entrance. Inside the reference department, Ramona was in full swing. She looked up at me and blinked. I guess it was my outfit.

"Emergency," I mouthed.

Ramona picked up her blue suede bag and directed us into the small meeting room off the front foyer.

"I'll fill you in," I said.

She nodded. "I understand that there was a fire and a break-in at your home last night. That's serious business. What's going on?"

Ramona watched without emotion as I told my tale, going lightly on some of the details. I knew I could trust Ramona. As I finished up with the latest bit of bad news, she said, “What can I do to help, Charlotte?”

“Well, I’ve been looking for information about a woman in her twenties and her child who went missing in Montreal twenty-six years ago. I don’t have much but I have the name Sean and something called Le Club. And a woman called Evelyn.”

“Could be that the terms you’re using are a bit off. Or possibly the information is in a for-fee-service database.”

“Or maybe it would have been in the French papers. Or . . . who knows. Any point in searching for ‘very bad people’?”

Ramona grinned.

“Anyway, I came up empty.”

Ramona picked up on the backstory. “I’m sorry for your troubles, Charlotte, but I’m going to love this project.” She flashed an even white smile at me.

“Do you read French?”

“*Comme ci, comme ça*, but Vanessa is fluent, as you know. She still has lots of contacts in Montreal: she got her library degree at McGill. We’ll get her on the team.”

“You think she’ll help?”

“Are you kidding? We’re librarians. We live to dig.”

“Great. Please don’t tell anyone about this, except Vanessa if you have to.”

Ramona’s nostrils flared dangerously. “Your privacy will be respected here. We take that seriously.”

“Of course but—”

“Vanessa doesn’t need to know the whole story.”

Jack said, “While we’re at it, do you think we could borrow your car? The people who trashed our place spotted us, um, on the way over. We were driving Margaret’s Kia, but they got a good look at our faces. Maybe we could leave hers for you and switch again later.”

Ramona didn’t even blink at the outrageous request. She merely took the keys from her blue suede bag and handed them to me.

“You are awesome, Ramona.”

Jack said, “They saw our faces, so I don’t know if just changing cars will be enough.”

“You’re such a princess, Jack,” Ramona said. “I’ve been hiking on the weekends and there's still gear in the trunk that might change you up a bit. Plus, I think a couple of Library Squad ball caps and extra sunglasses in the glove compartment."

Problem solved. "I owe you big-time."

Jack handed over Margaret's key fob.

Ramona grinned. "Full-service library here."

• • •

The matching Library Squad ball caps changed us just enough that we felt confident to drive around. Jack wore his backward. He also took a blue nylon jacket that was just a bit tight on the shoulders. I helped myself to a jean jacket because they can still look good if they're oversize.

Usually I'm a glass-half-full person but I felt despondent as we left the library parking lot in Ramona's Volvo. She loved the dark powder blue because it went with everything in her wardrobe. We peered through our sunglasses as Jack drove, watching for the black Ford Explorer and its vile occupants.

"Don't worry," Jack said. "With their research skills, Ramona and Vanessa are bound to find some useful information."

"Not sure that will help us here. Face it, Jack, we have no home, we're wearing borrowed clothes and we can't even drive Margaret's car anymore and—"

"And you're missing your dogs."

"At least they're safe with Rose and Lilith and Schopie."

"Uh-huh. Why don't I pull over and we can do a video call?"

"Because they're dogs?" I muttered.

But Jack was right. Seeing Truffle and Sweet Marie chasing an obliging Schopie was just what I needed. I swear the huge mutt even pretended to be intimidated as a small black torpedo and a small brown missile hurtled after him. Lilith followed their antics with the phone, then picked up the two dachshunds and put them on Rose's sofa for a "face" chat. "Are you getting lots of treats?" I asked.

They cocked their heads. *Treats* is a favorite word. But then when no treat came through the receiver they dashed off to trap Schopie under the table. Busy busy.

Rose took the phone and said, "They can stay as long as they want. Lilith loves walking them and I adore them. I am baking homemade dog biscuits for them. But as of today, the toilet paper is under lock and key."

"Oops. I guess I should have mentioned that."

I thanked Lilith and Rose profusely. Jack had nailed it. The video visit with my pets made me feel a bit better.

"See, Charlotte, they may never want to come home."

"Thanks a lot. Our home is . . ."

After a long pause, Jack said, "Is what?"

"A place they love. That reminds me of Esme. She'll be somewhere she loves, almost certainly somewhere in Europe."

"And? I'm not sure what—"

"This means *I* should be able to figure out where that place is."

"But you and Esme aren't all that close, Charlotte. And she obviously has secrets from you."

"We're as close as we need to be," I snapped. "We may have an unusual relationship but we communicate, and we've traveled together. I need to figure out where she feels comfortable. And safe."

"Maybe you shouldn't try to find her. You could be leading someone to her."

"Don't even suggest that. I'll make sure I don't."

"We'll make sure we don't," Jack said. "Are you starving? Feels like time for lunch. I can almost taste fries."

Chapter 12

Invest in an inexpensive pay-as-you-go phone when you travel overseas. You can avoid local connection and roaming charges.

Fifteen minutes later we were tucked in a corner booth at Betty's Diner. Betty's is hidden away on the outskirts of town. There are rarely any strangers and the food choices are firmly stuck in the past. I wasn't hungry, but I had a couple of ideas that were slowly taking shape. I picked the old-fashioned chicken sandwich. I figured that Jack would eat at least half of it. Jack scoffed his double cheeseburger and fries. I nibbled on the edges of the sandwich. In the laid-back atmosphere of Betty's, I was able to calm down and think.

"We need to visit Lola again," I said after a while.

Jack swallowed. "Maybe we should wait until she calms down. Remember that weapon?"

"You can stay in the car if you want. I'm pretty sure she won't shoot *me*."

Jack said, "Very funny. Let me remind you that Lola was talking about very bad people. She's connected to them."

"And the good news is that we now have a photo of the people we suspect of trashing the house and kidnapping the dogs. They are dangerous and likely deranged."

"Since when are dangerous and deranged good news?"

"The photo, Jack. We can show Lola the photo and she might be relieved to learn that the police are looking for these people and, better yet, she may be able to tell us who they are."

"Unless she's involved with them."

Patsy Magliaro, one of Woodbridge's most recognizable hippie residents, sashayed over, tie-dyed skirt swinging, Birkenstocks slapping the floor. As usual, a marijuana mist surrounded her. She brought fresh coffee and a slightly unfocused smile.

I smiled back as Patsy filled my cup. Jack grinned at her.

"I'll be back with refills," she said. "Might be able to scare up a piece of fresh lemon meringue pie for you, Jack. Charlotte, you want dessert? You haven't even made a dent out of that sandwich."

"I'll have the devil's food cake. I should have skipped the sandwich and gone straight for it."

"One devil's food cake coming up. You want whipped cream with that?"

"I believe I do."

"A lot of people like that," Patsy said. "You think they'd put it on the menu."

Jack turned his attention to me. "I guess it *would* make sense to see Lola in that case. Do you think she'd tell you who they are?"

I shrugged. "Worth a try."

"Guess so. And what do you think she meant by 'very bad people'? Thugs? Drug dealers?" Jack asked. "I got the impression she was genuinely frightened."

"She was. And scared for Esme too. I think she means the kind of people who do much worse than steal dogs and trash houses."

"Blackmailers? Extortionists?"

"We won't know until we talk to Lola."

"Bank robbers? Murderers?"

"Definitely arsonists, but beyond that there's no point in speculating. It all gives me a better idea of why we changed our names and Esme altered her appearance."

"It didn't sound like your dad was one of the bad people." He paused and looked straight at me. "Or did it?"

I glanced away. "I'd like to think not. I don't believe Esme and I were running from him. But I don't remember him being around much, although I think it was fun when he was."

"But he must be connected to these people somehow."

"Esme never talked about him after. She just said he was gone. I realize that she was protecting me."

"That makes sense."

"But also to protect herself. The less I knew, the less I would blab. You know what kids are like."

"Right. You might have tried to investigate as you got older."

Patsy arrived back with Jack's lemon meringue and my cake. She pointed to my plate. "You going to finish that sandwich? You only took two bites."

Jack suggested a doggie bag for the sandwich. Probably to have as a dessert after his dessert.

"So where does this leave us?" he said, picking up his fork and aiming for the meringue.

"Firmly in the dark." I stared at the reassuring vinyl and Formica interior of Betty's. It didn't help much. "I don't know what to do next."

Finally Jack said, "You'll be happier if you have a plan."

"But it's hard to plan when you don't know what you're planning for."

"First priority should be staying alive."

"No arguments here. But they know where we live."

"As long as Margaret and Frank are away, we are probably safe coming and going from their place. We can use that time to figure out what to do without panicking. We can rent a car and get better disguises."

"Or keep Ramona's hats and jackets."

"We need to ask Pepper if they tracked down the people in the SUV." He started in on the pie.

"Good thinking, Jack. You call her. I never know when I'm going to set her off."

Jack pointed at his plate with his fork, indicated his full mouth with the same fork, and then pointed it in the direction of his phone.

"Fine, Jack, but I say we show Lola the photo of the piggy-eyed perps."

• • •

As we got close to Lola's, fire trucks wailed past and police cars raced by, sirens blaring, roof lights flashing.

"Looks like we're not the only people with troubles," Jack said.

"Ummm," I said.

"Everything we lost can be replaced, except maybe our peace of mind. Our house didn't burn to the ground. No one was hurt. We were already planning to renovate and do a new kitchen."

"Right." I didn't want to whine about my treasured belongings and the utter disorder that had replaced my comfortable life.

Jack grinned at me. "And we can concentrate on finding Esme."

"Don't worry. I won't be a Debbie Downer. You know what? I'll call Pepper."

As usual the Pepper call didn't bring much joy.

I put her on speaker and asked if she had any word on the people in the

Ford Explorer.

"Yes. That vehicle is a rental."

"That's great," I chirped. "You can get their names."

"Uh-huh. Except the ID on the rental agreement seems to belong to a guy who didn't rent that Ford Explorer."

"So he says."

"He's in the hospital trauma unit after a hit to the head with a blunt object. Been there for days. Lost his ID in the process. We have confirmation."

I got the shivers again. "These people are vicious."

"Yup. But we're tracking the vehicle. We'll get them. In the meantime, I need to know where you are."

"We're driving."

"You're supposed to stay put."

"After the library, we were desperate for fresh air. We're not used to being cooped up in a condo, alone for hours. We drove to Betty's."

Pepper snorted. "Sometimes I'd give anything to be alone for a few hours."

"I imagine. The condo is lovely but we don't have any of our stuff or the dogs."

"I need to know that you haven't gone anywhere near your home or Jack's shop to get any of that stuff or to Rose's to see the dogs."

"Nope. Just wanted to know if you found out anything about the SUV people."

"Just their victim. Wait. I am getting called in on another incident. Gotta go."

• • •

As we rounded the corner onto Lola's street, Jack stood on the brake. Police cars blocked access both ways, three fire trucks were angled in front of Lola's house and an ambulance idled. Powerful streams of water bombarded the house. Plumes of smoke streaked the sky. We pulled over, next to neighbors rubbernecking on the sidewalk. We scrambled out and edged toward the action. I broke into a run, choking on the acrid smoke. Jack loped ahead of me.

I raced up to a fireman. "My friend Lola was in the house." He turned and stared down at me. "And there was a cat. A tuxedo cat," I babbled. "Pierre."

"Step back, please," he said, gesturing for us to make space. A police officer shouted at the crowd to stay well back.

A murmur rose from the crowd as the EMTs emerged with a gurney. A sheet covered the body lying on it. My knees buckled. Jack caught me.

"Lola!"

"Very bad people," Jack said again as he half carried me back to Ramona's blue Volvo. We got there just before Pepper pulled in, roof lights flashing and siren blaring as the cops let her into the scene.

I put my head between my knees. "They killed her and it's my fault."

"Nothing is your fault. You could never have known this would happen. And if it helps, that fireman has a live tuxedo cat in his arms."

"But Lola's on her way to the morgue."

• • •

At least we had a secret hideout. After a furtive stop to pick up our favorite food and lots of it, we made it to Margaret's without any sign of a tail. When we finally flopped onto the smooth leather sofa in the condo, I blurted out what I had been worrying about as we fled.

"That was no accident."

Always the philosopher, Jack said, "Well, it was an old house and fires happen. Lola was a smoker. It might have nothing to do with you looking up the woman who helped you and your mother flee from danger twenty-five years ago."

"Twenty-six."

"That cat could have knocked over a candle. Or an ashtray with a burning cigarette."

"Don't be ridiculous, Jack. It wasn't Pierre! You know perfectly well it had to be the people in the Explorer. They saw us turn out from Lola's street. They must have figured out where she lived."

Jack ran his fingers through his already spiky hair. "How?"

I resisted the urge to pat down the spikes. "The same way we did. By coming up with a cover story and asking people until someone told them. And I led them to her. And the police have nothing but a license number for a rental that these thugs got under false pretenses and will probably ditch."

"Charlotte, you—"

"But I remembered something, Jack! It could help. I'll call Pepper again and then we can continue arguing about my guilt or lack of it."

To my surprise, Pepper picked up. "Pepper," I blurted. "Fingerprints!"

"You are in such troub—what do you mean, fingerprints?"

"The woman in the bucket hat! The dog thief. She tripped and touched the garden gnome by my neighbor's house when she was chasing her stolen dog."

"What are you . . . ?"

"You might be able to identify her from her fingerprints."

"If she's in the system."

"Think about what she's done: Trashing homes? Kidnapping dogs? Attacking people, stealing rentals? Setting fires. She'll have a history. That kind of behavior doesn't come out of nowhere."

"That's good. But you know what's bad?"

"What?"

Pepper used her cold, hard cop voice. "You and Jack were seen in the vicinity of what appears to be a case of arson and most likely murder this afternoon."

"What? Arson and murder?" My heart thundered. I sank onto the bar stool, nearly missing the seat.

"Don't play innocent with me. You called from that neighborhood and you have been identified as being there."

I summoned up some outrage. "Pepper, do you honestly think Jack and I set that fire?"

Jack stared.

"Fatal fire, Charlotte."

I swallowed. "You couldn't believe that we would be in any way responsible for—"

"Did I mention that you were seen leaving the property?"

"Fair enough. We went to talk to an old friend of Esme's. Her name is Lola. But there was no fire when we were there. The people in the Ford Explorer must have done it. Check those fingerprints and you will learn that woman has been involved in other crimes."

"And you returned to the scene of the crime."

"We saw a body being taken out. Is Lola dead?"

"I can't tell you that. The homeowner may have been one of the bodies. We will need to interview you."

"What do you mean, 'one of the bodies'?"

Without a touch of irony, Pepper said, "Don't leave town."

• • •

"We need to leave town," I said as soon as she was gone.

"But we just got all this great food."

"You will have time to eat but we have to make our plans and bookings fast. That's only if you want to come with me."

He blinked. "Where?"

"Wherever I need to find my mother. You have a lot of business to take care of this week. I'll be fine if you choose to stay here."

"What are you talking about? Of course I'm coming with you. The shop can wait. But I'm not sure we should be going anywhere before we talk to Pepper."

"If we talk to Pepper, we definitely won't be getting to Europe in time."

"We're going to Europe?"

"Yes, and that reminds me." I pulled out my emergency case from its hiding place under the sofa, located the burner phone and copied the contacts from my regular phone.

Jack said, "But . . ."

"But nothing. We'll leave our phones here in the apartment in case Pepper wants to trace our whereabouts. Give me yours and I'll copy your contacts on this."

Jack's forehead furrowed. "A touch of paranoia today, Charlotte?"

"She suggested we were implicated in arson and murder! I bet she could get a warrant for our phone records. That would give her our location as well. If you're sure you're coming, I'll use the burner and the credit card in my other name to book our tickets and shuttle. But first I'd better find out if Sid has tracked down Glenda."

Jack nodded. "Wait, what do you mean, credit card in your other name?"

"It's part of our escape strategy. Remember?"

Sid's phone rang on and on. Just as I was about to hang up, he bellowed with more than his usual fury. "Well, where is she? I'm out of patience."

"Hold your fire, Sid. Esme's not only missing but in danger and I need to ask you some questions."

"What do you mean, in danger? She'll be in danger from me if she doesn't get in touch by morning."

"Tell the publisher that it's a medical emergency. Do whatever you need to keep them happy. But for now, listen: some very bad people are after Esme. Has anyone has been asking where she could be found?"

"Aside from her apoplectic publisher and you, no, not really."

"Did you get to Glenda's place?"

"I'm a busy man!"

I gritted my teeth. "Has some stranger inquired about where Esme likes to go in Europe?"

"Do you think I was born yesterday?"

Far from it, I thought. "Where are you? In the city?"

"Visiting a friend on Long Island. I'll be back in the office tomorrow . . . Wait, you know what? There was a photographer from *Vitality!* who was trying to find Esme for a shoot involving a designer who wouldn't be named."

My heart clenched. "What did you tell him?"

"Her. Nothing. Esme would have my guts for garters if I gave anything away about her."

"Did you see this woman?"

"No. I was in a rush to catch the train to Long Island when she called. I just told her I was in a meeting and I'd get back to her. I sent Esme messages on everything and tried to call her. I wasn't sure how she'd react to a fashion photo shoot. You never know with Esme."

"She'd wear sunglasses and a big hat. So this person doesn't know how to find you?"

"What is going on, Charlotte?" It sounded like Sid had begun to grind his teeth.

"Bear with me, Sid. People disguised as dog walkers trashed our home and then they set fire to it. We believe that they were looking for information about Esme. They're not just joking or expressing annoyance. She is in danger."

Sid paused before speaking. "I had a break-in too, just after I left. The door was kicked in and files thrown around. Nothing stolen but my security service reported that they made a mess."

"It had to be the same people."

"You know what? The photographer said she was right outside my office. She was really pushy. I told her I was leaving."

"Did she actually see you leave?"

"I ducked out the service entrance. I have a deal with the super when awkward moments arise. I hate pushy people."

Never mind that Sid is the pushiest of the pushy. "It's a weird thing for a photographer to do, show up at an agent's office. You were lucky you didn't run into her. Can you check with *Vitality!* tomorrow to see if they actually sent a photographer? And ask security if they got a look at her."

"You think she's behind the break-in?"

"If she is, she and the other people she's involved with are dangerous. Better stay with your friends on Long Island until we, um, sort this out. And actually check on Glenda. Ask your friends to come with you. And be careful in case you're followed. Promise me that, Sid."

"Yeah, yeah, sure. What else do you want from me? My life?"

"Let's hope it doesn't come to that."

After I disconnected, I noticed Jack leaning back and peering out the window without being seen.

"It's worse than I thought, Jack. They broke into Sid's office. I am very worried about Glenda, especially after Lola. I hope Sid will actually check her place."

"How would they have found Sid's office?"

"That part would be easy. In every book, Esme effusively thanks Sid as her agent and Glenda as her indispensable assistant. It's easy to find the agency address online. I bet they found Esme's New York address in Sid's office, somewhere. Glenda knows everything about Esme's movements. I hope they didn't find her address too when they broke into Sid's office."

"You have to keep yourself safe too, Charlotte."

"Sure thing. But finding Esme is nonnegotiable."

Jack stared out the window into the darkness. "Not trying to negotiate, just saying we have to be careful. We don't know who is out there and what they want."

I said, "I do know the chances are Esme's in Europe. That's where she goes to get away and she feels very comfortable there. That's where I'll start."

"That's where *we'll* start," Jack said with a faraway look in his eye. "Europe will be great."

"Our trip won't be a vacation and it will cost a bomb to get last-minute tickets and accommodations. Think twice, Jack."

"I've thought. I'm up for anything."

"It will mean postponing our renovation because of the costs."

"We agreed that we need to do this, Charlotte."

"Right."

"So where exactly are we going?" said Jack, probably wondering what the food would be like.

"I'm trying to figure that out so I can book the tickets. But first I had an idea."

"What?"

"After talking to Lola about Esme and my father, I think the connection is definitely through Montreal."

"Right."

"So, there's a good chance these monsters are from Montreal too. So, their fingerprints may not be in our system at all. I need to bring Pepper up to speed without letting her know too much about Esme's and my background."

I texted Pepper and suggested she check with the Canadian authorities when she had the fingerprints, mentioning that the piggy-eyed perps had the slightest suggestion of French-Canadian accents.

"That'll keep her busy," I said smugly. "Next a communication plan."

"What sort of communication plan?"

"We'll need to stay in touch with Ramona and Lilith and Sid without attracting Pepper's attention. She's smart enough to check their phones too. If we use the burner, she'll spot that number soon enough too. We'll need to use another medium. How about WhatsApp?"

"I use WhatsApp quite a bit with bike contacts in Europe and South America. Maybe we both should use fake names though. If Pepper would check their phones, she could check WhatsApp messages too."

"I knew I could count on you, Jack."

"Sure thing. I'll be Damien and you'll be Dolly. I'll arrange with Lilith. You set it up with Ramona. We'll need to be in touch with both of them.

• • •

A half hour later, our Pepper-proof communication was a go. Plus, I'd worked out a plan of sorts to find Esme. I felt good. Plans have that effect on me. Esme would be hiding out somewhere familiar, safe and comfortable, somewhere she would fit in, also somewhere inconvenient for any pursuers. I listed the special places we'd been together and where she seemed happiest. She'd pick a city, with access to an airport, taxis, car rentals. She'd want good roads and not a scenic village where she would stick out. That left a few choices: There was Paris, of course, where Esme wandered the cheese shops, the dress boutiques, the markets and the parks, as carefree and chic as any Parisienne. Free and unrecognized. That was my first choice. Plus, Esme owned an apartment in the Batignolles neighborhood. Not in her own name, of course, that would be too normal. Very few people knew about that. So my plan was to fly in, hunt down Esme, find out what exactly was going on and, of course, keep her safe by whatever means. Nice and neat. But I dithered about other possibilities. I didn't want to make a mistake with a pricey overseas trip.

I took a break from trying to decide without all the information I needed and tidied up the signs of our visit. I wrote a thank-you note to Margaret and Frank for the use of their beautiful condo and their clothing. I promised to be in touch and to replace whatever needed replacing. I didn't want to speak directly to Margaret because she would only offer me logical, well-thought-out legal advice, probably including "better not leave town." And I had already decided to ignore whatever advice she would offer.

"Pack up, Jack," I said. "We'll be out of here soon."

"Where are we going?"

Back to the dreaded decision: so, if Esme wasn't slouching around Paris, there was always the trendy hilltop Chiado area or Bairro Alto close to the center of Lisbon with its tangle of streets, tight alleyways, sidewalk restaurants and miles of stairs. She had connections and a former lover there and she had more than enough Portuguese to get by. Then there was her charming ex-husband Alessandro's scenic winery in the Piedmont area of Italy. It was off the beaten path so she could hide out easily. I knew that Alessandro would do anything for her. I couldn't rule out Cinque Terre, the picturesque quintet of hillside towns clinging to the cliffs on the Ligurian coast. Esme loved Cinque Terre and had at least one ex-lover there. With all the tourists, she could pass unnoticed. And she could easily have flown into Milan from New York, or to Genoa with connections. Then she could have rented a car or taken a convenient train.

England was also a possibility, but I decided Esme would find it easier to slip from one country to another in the European Union, post Brexit. Plus, Americans stuck out in the UK as much as English speakers did in Europe.

I took a deep breath and made the choice.

"We will start in Paris."

Chapter 13

Plan for comfort on flights: stock a small bag with sanitizer, masks, wipes, snacks, chargers, headset, a warm shawl or scarf, earplugs, eye mask, music, water and something diverting to read or watch.

I wiped off my tray, arm rests and the buckle on my seat belt and sat down, sighing with relief. The good news was we'd been lucky enough to get same-day tickets, without attracting too much negative attention from security. Jack had set up some meetings with suppliers and had the email trail to prove it, although he'd probably need to cancel those meetings. I'd been careful to book a return trip, as I knew that last-minute one-way trips set off red flags. We could always change our booking depending on what happened.

I adjusted my seat, took out my phone and charger, plugged in my headset, and pulled out my puffer jacket to use as a pillow. I considered wolfing down my chocolate protein bar, although the plane was still loading. Have I mentioned I hate to travel? Jack did not have a comfort kit. He had not given a moment's thought to this trip. If he hadn't stuffed his passport and ID in his shorts' pocket, after the apartment was trashed, he wouldn't be on the plane. I just hoped he'd brought a change of clothes. He was already conked out with his head at an unnatural angle, his arm occupying our mutual armrest. Even with our business class seats, his long legs protruded into the aisle. Because he's Jack and not me, the flight staff would be understanding about his soft guzzling snores, if not outright affectionate toward him.

I felt a bit sorry for myself. It's not every week that your mother goes missing, your home gets trashed and an old friend is murdered. The whole situation made me very twitchy. My nightmares had just made it worse.

Arriving in Paris after flying overnight without sleep might jeopardize our search. I needed my wits about me. I fished out my lavender-infused eye mask, selected the sleepy music playlist, starting with *Weightless* by Marconi Union and then mixing it up with Adele and Enya. I pulled my soft wool blue-and-gold shawl up to my chin, snuggled into the puffer jacket pillow and instructed myself to sleep immediately. It seemed like weeks later when I tore off the eye mask, glared at Jack and sighed loudly. Fine.

I had hoped to discuss our strategy for finding Esme on the trip. Jack didn't really like strategies that much. He's more of a serendipitous person, likely to say, "Let's chill and see what happens." Nothing worried me more than the idea of the two of us blundering across Europe scratching our heads and pondering the next move while we paused to eat yet again. We already had more than enough unknowns.

A seven-hour flight should have left plenty of time to figure out a mutually acceptable strategy and still manage a half-decent night's sleep. But no. I decided to take over the plan. Jack would probably find ways to derail it from time to time but at least there would be a base.

The main goal was to find Esme as soon as possible. Paris was full of elegant, stylish women and Esme would fit in like one of the gorgeous residents. She was familiar with the streets and habits of the locals. As soon as we settled into our Airbnb, I would hit the shops she loved, the restaurants and the parks, although I worried she might just stay in her apartment. Even so, she'd still need to eat and Esme never cooked.

Fears and worries danced in my head. Lola's face swam in and out of my consciousness. Lola, surrounded by flames. Unknown villains causing havoc. I shivered. Jack snoozed on with a small smile on his face. I had to fight the urge to wipe it off.

• • •

The smoke is so thick and tastes awful and I'm coughing and coughing. Mummy's holding my hand too tight and it's hard to hold the wet towel over my mouth. We're running down the metal stairs. I'm afraid that hands are reaching out to grab me. I trip and bang my knees on the hard stairs but Mummy just yanks my arm hard and we keep going. I'm crying because now my arm hurts and my knee is bleeding and my eyes are stinging and we have to get out of here. Other people are pushing past us on the staircase. Some people are screaming and running. Mummy says, "Idiots. Panic is our enemy. Don't forget that. Ever."

People push through the fire doors to get outside, but we're not going outside. We're going to hide in the building because the people who set the fire will be waiting for us. Mummy says I mustn't snivel.

• • •

"We need to get out!" I must have been shouting because Mummy was shaking me.

"We need to get out!"

Jack's bright blue eyes stared down at me. He was gripping my arms and shaking me. "I had to wake you up. We're thirty thousand feet in the air. So there's no going out, Charlotte."

I blinked and glanced around at the cabin. No long metal staircase, no smoke, no sore knees. A few fellow passengers were staring at me and a flight attendant hurried along to put an end to the "going out" idea.

"Sorry. I was having a nightmare about a fire."

"Another nightmare," Jack said with his brow furrowed. "We need to talk about this."

"Now I need to sleep."

"Fair enough," he said. Shortly after, Jack was in dreamland while I remained awake for the duration of the flight.

• • •

As we shouldered our way through Charles de Gaulle Airport, I hunted for a mobile phone vending machine to buy a ready-to-use Bic mobile with a prepaid SIM card from Orange France. I'd planned for this. Jack and I could each use one for calls, texting, and listening to FM radio in Europe. Apparently, these phones could stay charged for four hours of use. Mine was orange and Jack's was lime green, a virulent shade that featured in many of his Hawaiian shirts.

Despite the fact we were arriving in fashion-conscious Paris, Jack had switched from his borrowed clothes to his usual attire of cargo shorts, Hawaiian shirt and Converse which he'd managed to bring along. For some reason he was sporting a baseball cap, marking him as an obvious tourist in Paris.

At least we managed to hop onto a shuttle ahead of schedule. The twenty-three or so miles of modern roadway from the airport to the city is very unlike Paris with its beautiful architectural tradition.

Jack frowned out the window. "I like the historic part, that doesn't change."

Travel always makes me contrary. "Me too, except for the terrorist attacks, yellow jacket protests and shutdowns. And the fire at Notre Dame. Then the pandemic. Everything changes."

Jack said mildly, "It's been Paris since the third century and it existed long before that under other names, so I'm willing to bet it will continue to survive and thrive."

"You're right. And it *is* the most romantic city in the world."

Jack leaned over and gave me a hug. "We're on the run from the cops and thugs so that's pretty romantic too. Bonnie and Clyde but without all the bodies."

I looked down at Margaret's oldest Court suit, now sweaty and rumpled, and then over to Jack's Hawaiian shirt. "Right, and without all that pesky style."

Jack laughed. "We make up for it in other ways."

"I'd ask you to name those other ways but right now I want to concentrate on my missing mother and whatever the hell trouble she's in."

"Once we find her, we'll be here in Paris. Then we can really have a romantic getaway. Win-win, as you like to say."

We'd blown a hole in our renovation budget with those business class return tickets—extra leg room needed for some people.

I didn't even have my travel wardrobe with me, the one that covers all my wardrobe needs out of one carry-on bag and allows me to travel without undue anxiety. That capsule wardrobe was a victim of the trashing and fire in our house. Now I had what was in my emergency bag: my skinny black pants, graphic T-shirt and jean jacket, the blue-and-gold patterned shawl (and occasional blanket), a pair of red sneakers, plus leather sandals and the toiletries travel kit that I kept in my bag. I couldn't forget Margaret's suit and pale blue blouse, currently not at their best. Hardly the way to blend into a Parisian crowd.

Win-win? I wasn't so sure.

• • •

We arrived in the charming Batignolles neighborhood well before our check-in time. Jack was hungry after all that sleeping. I was too after all that worrying.

We found a patisserie with bistro tables and chairs outside in the bright afternoon sun and contacted our Airbnb host, Maxime. We decided to grab a bite while waiting for Maxime, who didn't mind letting us in a few hours ahead of regular check-in time.

We selected some lovely warm *pain au chocolat* and coffee. We inhaled the fragrance of the pastries as we waited. Jack said, "You can always tell you're in Paris by the delicious scents in the air."

Once we got our order, we made ourselves comfortable and wolfed down everything. Jack followed his pastry with another one for dessert. Why not? He was awake and it gave us a chance to talk.

"Let's see if I understand this," he said between mouthfuls. "Esme's apartment is somewhere in this neighborhood?"

"Yes. We often stayed here. She loved the mix of students and families, young and old, and not a lot of tourists. A French-speaking person could go to ground here easily."

"Uh-huh. But now, from your vague comments, I figured out that she has bought an apartment but you don't know where it is. Is that right?"

"Um, yes, it's a recent purchase. She gave me the address and I should have put it in my contacts, but I didn't think I'd have an emergency need for it. We didn't have any trips planned and Esme and I talk every week and—"

"You are obsessive about recording information and storing it for easy retrieval, but not your mother's address in Paris. What would Freud say?"

I ignored that. "Esme sent me some photos of the apartment, inside and out. She was really excited about the purchase. It's not far from the Metro and near La rue des Dames and the great little food shopping areas. You know Esme loves bread and fruit and take-out meals."

"And I remember cheese too."

Not wishing to be sidetracked by a sudden trip to a cheese shop, I said, "Batignolles is not that big. I can figure out where her place is by walking the area street by street. It's a low sandstone building with fantastic grilles forming Juliet balconies on the second and third levels and a huge glossy black double door at the entrance. Very striking."

"This winging it approach is not really like you," Jack said, munching his breakfast dessert.

"What choice do I have? Now there's no way to get the address without talking to Glenda and she's lying low, probably on Esme's instructions.

We're in a compact and walkable community. Do you have a better idea?"

He shook his head. "Nope. That should work."

Jack approved and that made me nervous.

My plan was to settle into our Airbnb first and then find the apartment. "If she's in Paris, she'll make the rounds of small grocers, fruit vendors, wine boutiques, bakers and take-out meal makers, all those places, including—you'll be glad to know—cheese shops." I'd followed her into enough of them on our trips, filling cloth bags with selections of pâté, salami, ham, croissants and so much more, often for a picnic. Esme's French was fluent and that made it easier for her to get good service. She'd spent plenty of time and effort working on her accent.

"Next to visiting the Musée d'Orsay or an afternoon on a *bateau mouche* cruising the Seine, casual eating with Esme is what I enjoyed about those trips. If she's here, I'll find her. And I don't think anyone from her past would know about her habits in Paris." I let my mind drift back to memories of our visits.

"Earth to Charlotte," Jack said with a grin. "You were a thousand miles away."

I shrugged. "Just planning my strategy. I have that photo of Esme and me, the one you took on her last visit to Woodbridge. I uploaded it to my burner phone and I've already copied it onto this new one." I waggled the orange cell. In the photo, Esme and I looked relaxed and possibly even happy. It didn't quite capture Esme's pale, ethereal beauty but it was a fair image of both of us. "I'll make the rounds and find out if any of the shopkeepers or neighbors have seen her."

Jack said, "Seems like a good plan."

I felt a wave of guilt. "I know you love Paris, Jack."

"I did a lot of research here when I was working on my dissertation."

"Right, and I wish we could be here just as visitors instead of . . ."

Jack squeezed my hand. "There's always next time. We're a team. We'll get this done together."

I had a catch in my throat, but managed to say, "Yeah, we're a pretty good team."

"For sure. So, are you going to finish that *pain au chocolat*?"

• • •

Jack and I were in urgent need of showers and I tried to keep my distance from Maxime when he arrived. We got our keys, lock code and instructions for the various appliances, lights, WIFI (pronounced *weefee*) and Maxime's contact numbers in case of emergency. We could expect clean linens on the bed and fresh towels waiting, plus spares available. I knew there would be an information folder inside the unit. At least we had a place to call home for our unknown number of days in Paris. Maxime had studied at NYU and spoke excellent English. He was friendly and happy to help us. No wonder he got five stars on Airbnb. "Anything I can do, just let me know."

The apartment on the third level of the traditional sandstone building seemed just right. The fridge, microwave, and induction hot plate would do the trick for food. I appreciated the kettle (electric!), the Italian coffee maker and the small cupboard with key staples: oil, vinegar, coffee, tea, salt, pepper and spices, plus sugar cubes. I even found a small ironing board and iron tucked next to the extra towels on a shelf. These small comforts would let us focus on our task. The living/dining room had a comfortable dark leather sofa, a relaxed lounger, books in the bookcase and popular French magazines, including a stack of *Paris Match* and plenty of local maps. The teak table and chairs were pleasantly vintage yet currently back in vogue. Maxime had plenty of battery-operated candles in case we felt romantic.

Although two people couldn't fit in the kitchen or the bathroom, it felt just the right size for us. The balcony had barely enough room for a bistro table, two chairs and a jungle of vigorous green plants. The view of other charming mansard-style zinc roofs could only be in Paris. Maxime had left a bottle of red wine and two glasses on the table in the dining area. Too bad we wouldn't be spending much time there. We had a task and a target. We showered and changed and I popped our travel clothes into the washer/dryer combo in the bathroom. This time I was glad that Margaret's suit was a polyester blend.

The apartment had a masculine vibe. I had a feeling this was Maxime's home and he just rented it out from time to time. I found myself distracted by how I'd like to spruce it up if I lived here. I would have to do something about the closet situation for sure. The sole closet was stuffed with clothing and bedding belonging to our host. On the bottom shelf, he'd tucked his printer, paper and cables and a box of files, plus some nice leather shoes and a small suitcase.

I admired his taste in clothing and the taupe fedora on a hook. We had a single shelf for our belongings. Didn't matter as we had hardly any clothes and much bigger fish to fry.

I picked up one of the maps and folded it to show Batignolles.

Jack was ready to go before I was, perhaps because he didn't care what he was wearing. He also seemed to be in the middle of a conversation that I had missed. "Wouldn't lots of people recognize her? I mean readers?"

"Esme? No, she just blends in. She looks French in Paris, Portuguese in Lisbon, British in London and Italian in Milan. It's a gift."

"But she's famous."

"Her writing name is, sure. But her face is not."

"Are you kidding? Her image is on the back cover of millions of books. Millions! Translated into how many languages?"

"Forty-three."

"A well-known face."

I laughed out loud for the first time in days. "Have you ever looked at the back of those books, Jack?"

"You have them all, so yes."

"I mean closely."

"Why would I need to look closely?"

"Because Esme always looks incredibly glamorous. She has her hair and makeup professionally done. But her face will be turned slightly to the left, and she'll be wearing a scarf and sunglasses like a movie star from the fifties. Or a hat obscuring her face just enough. Plus, and this is key, Jack—"

"What?"

"She looks really tall."

"But she's not tall. Taller than you, of course, but what is she? Five-four?"

"On a good day, five-three. But she somehow always looks tall in those professional photos. Tall and mysterious and not at all like herself. So people are not going to recognize her on the street in Paris based on her book covers. I wouldn't have recognized her myself if I hadn't been present for most of the shoots."

"I guess that's a good thing."

"Now, I see why it was necessary. Esme always wanted to be a writer. She intended to be a *famous* writer. But she didn't want to be a celebrity. Being recognized by strangers or, worse, people from her past would not have been a good strategy for her."

"Makes sense. So now what?"

"Now we check out Batignolles. She likes her little routines. Despite all the money and travel, Esme tends to be simple and low-key when she's at home."

"And the ex-husbands and partners would have been the same?"

"No. Alessandro is very grounded, but mostly the rest of them were all flash and dash. Chateaux and villas and yachts. Private islands. Fast cars. But in the end, maybe that's what bored her."

"Do you really believe that?"

I stopped pacing and thought about that. "She just enjoys having men fall in love with her."

"She is beautiful," Jack said, flopping on the sofa.

"She's kind of in love with love, you know, but none of it ever endures. So far, two years is the longest any of her marriages or passionate relationships have lasted. That was Alessandro."

"Whoa. And then what's she left with?"

I shrugged. "A few more diamonds. A property or two that needs to be managed and rented out. A bit more money in the bank, not that she needs any more. But then she's restless again."

"I wonder if she was always like that?"

I sat on the sofa beside him. "It was just the two of us until her books started to sell. She was restless when I was young but I don't think she was looking for anyone. She was in love with her writing at that point. And I think she still missed my father. Not that she told me anything about him."

"Do you think he's still alive?"

I shook my head. "Esme told me he'd died in a plane crash."

"You never talked about your dad."

"I don't remember much about him. Even what Lola told us was new to me. I think Esme was protecting me from the past. When we find her I am going to make sure she tells me our story. No matter how bad it is."

Jack sat up and met my eyes. "You have a right to know, but you may not be happy with what you find out."

"Pretty sure I'll be very unhappy, Jack."

Chapter 14

Use free services like WhatsApp to stay in touch when traveling.

I noticed that Lilith had contacted "Dolly" on WhatsApp.

I was not used to WhatsApp but "Dolly" called Lilith back. Our Paris sojourn was starting with a shock.

"Where are you? The police are looking for you!" Lilith's usually calm tones were shrill.

I turned to Jack, who was eyeing the pastry display like a man who hadn't just eaten breakfast and breakfast dessert. "Jack. The police are looking for us."

Lilith said, "You know they've found two bodies in the fire."

"Pepper mentioned it, but I don't know who—"

"They are asking for you to turn yourself in. It's all over the media."

"Oh, no! Am I all over WINY?" Call it vanity but the first thing I thought of was all those terrible film clips being shown on TV again.

"Um, yes, but it's more serious than that."

"We didn't kill Lola. I don't know why—"

"Who's Lola?"

"The woman who died, an old friend. Of course we had nothing to do with the fire."

That got Jack's attention. "They think we *killed* Lola? That's just crazy."

Lilith shouted to be heard, "Two bodies were found. A man and a woman. The cops are serious about tracking you. Pepper Monahan made me show her my phone to prove we're not in touch. Good thing we made this plan."

"Of course, she can't insist on seeing your phones without a warrant but it's good that you showed her. She won't suspect us of being in touch."

"I hope not. Where are you?"

"Better you don't know. Can you keep in touch and let us know what's happening?"

"Whatever I can find out, but it doesn't look good for you."

Jack and I stared at each other after the call.

He said, "Lola did have a gun and was pretty clear that she was prepared to use it."

"Lilith said 'a man.' Maybe he was one of the people in the SUV and he tried to kill Lola. She was probably defending herself. Maybe he burned the house down and got caught in it afterward."

"Pepper will have a good idea of what happened from talking to the arson investigators."

"But we won't be talking to Pepper. In the meantime, we should get out while the shops are still open."

"Aren't you hungry?" Jack said. "All this talk is making me think of food."

I didn't argue because the quest for Esme and the quest for food would overlap perfectly.

"Just remember to say *bonjour* to everyone, Jack. Esme taught me that it's rude not to."

"*Bonjour*. Of course."

What was I worried about? People like Jack no matter what. It's his superpower. I changed to my black pants, graphic tee and jean jacket. I grabbed a pair of cotton string bags to pick up food. My new phone was in my jean jacket pocket, where I could get it easily. At least I didn't need to be in disguise and there was no disguising Jack under any circumstances.

We headed down the long dim corridor toward the stairs when the light went off. Jack crashed into me. "Shoot," I said. "I forgot that the stupid hallway lights are on timers and they turn off when the time's up. You have to be careful not to tumble down the stairs. Nobody ever tells you these things."

Jack grumbled, "There must be a better way to save electricity."

"We just need to remember to click it on when we leave the apartment. Usually there's plenty of time."

"Can you turn it on again?"

"I can't see where the switch is because it's pitch—"

Lucky for us, the lights came on as one of the residents on that floor arrived home.

"*Bonjour,*" we said, but she scurried into her apartment.

"So much for *bonjour*," Jack said.

We made it alive to the heavy wooden door and rushed out onto the street. Most of the food shops were in the surrounding blocks, along with some tempting cafés on the way.

"Focus, Jack."

Our first stop was a *boulangerie* that I remembered for its crusty baguettes and burly owner. *"Bonjour!"* We bought two croissant, two more *pains au chocolat* for breakfast the next day—although I doubted they'd last that long—and a long, fresh and crusty baguette. As Jack fished out the euros, I flashed the photo at the proprietor and asked in my rusty French if he had seen my "auntie," claiming she loved their Suisse pastries. We were trying to catch up with her and thought she might have dropped in to get some, I explained.

The baker nodded at the photo and told me he had seen her but not for at least a week.

"So she has been here," Jack said.

"But not recently. *Désolé.*"

"*Merci.* We'll keep checking."

After we left, Jack said, "*Désolé* sounds so much better than sorry, doesn't it? More sincere."

"It isn't really. Just another automatic response." But Jack had drifted across the street to snag a roasted chicken that looked and smelled heavenly. I tried the auntie ploy again. The proprietor, who seemed to be from North Africa, broke into a wide smile. My aunt had indeed been there and had purchased a relative of that same chicken. When? A dramatic shrug. Last week? "*Très belle,*" he added. "*Très élégante.*"

Oh, Esme, always a hit with the men. Very beautiful, very elegant and very missing, I thought. The vendor pointed at the bouquets of flowers, hope in his eyes.

Jack said, "Those are cheerful. Let me get them for you."

"Thanks," I whispered, "but can we wait? There are so many flower vendors and Esme used to make the rounds. If we buy them too early, we can't really shop for flowers. Does that make me a jerk?"

"Makes you a strategist."

"That's a relief. I am so worried about Esme that I can't shop for fun. I hope I can do something nice for you."

"Cheese?" Jack said, hope creeping onto his face.

"Right around this corner." Sure enough, there was a cheese bar that could make your head explode. Jack started making selections right after *bonjour.* He bought Muenster, Comté, Roquefort, Boursin and Camembert before I put the brakes on.

I muttered, "We don't need *all* the cheese in Batignolles. There are several shops and Esme likes to play the field when it comes to cheese and other matters. She's only really faithful to the *boulangerie*."

Again, I was able to confirm that Esme had been there, but not for several days.

"Let's find a salad bar," Jack said plaintively. "We need to eat soon."

The salad bar staff did not recognize Esme or just plain didn't care, also very possible, but we had what we needed. Esme hadn't been seen for a few days in Batignolles, but I wanted to check a couple more spots in case. First, I bowed to pressure to rush home and eat.

"An army marches on its stomach," Jack said. I reminded myself that Jack had saved my life more than once and that I loved him. Then, I reminded myself again. We could get back on our quest quickly and maybe we shouldn't have too many bags of food. Plus, it was getting late back home and I should have already spoken with Sid to see if he'd tracked down Glenda.

We wove in and around people on the route back to our Airbnb, savoring the aroma of fresh bread, cooked meals and alluring scent of flowers. Although a lot had happened since I'd been in Paris last, the city maintained its usual *joie de vivre*. People kept their distance more than in the past and seemed a bit warier. But Parisians had stayed calm and elegant even in the middle of war and occupation, while running resistance underneath. The twenty-first-century behavior was the same.

I entered our code on the pad on the massive wooden door to our building and minutes later I was setting out napkins and place mats on the bistro set on the tiny balcony. Jack plunked down the rustic plates. We made sandwiches with chunks of the fresh baguette, crisp lettuce, slices of white chicken and Boursin cheese with herbs. I made him promise not to eat anything straight out of the paper bags. Maxime had left two large bottles of Perrier in the fridge and that was good because the shopping had been mostly a ploy to find out about Esme and I had forgotten about drinks.

"There's that bottle of Bordeaux on the table too," Jack called out. "And two wineglasses."

Even with a delicious meal in front of me, I wasn't hungry, maybe because it was too late for lunch and too early for dinner. And I needed to keep my head clear so I suggested we leave the wine until we finished our search. I'd have to settle for the view of the vibrant streetscape and the could-only-be-Paris buildings.

I turned to Jack. "This would be perfect if only we had a few flowers. I should have taken you up on your offer."

Jack nodded, because his mouth was already full.

"If she's still in Batignolles, Esme always needs fresh bouquets wherever she is."

Jack raised his eyebrows, probably because of the word *need.*

"So I will head back out and hit all the local flower kiosks with my photo of Esme and ask. If there's no sign of her in the last few days, we can conclude that she's moved on."

"I can see why people live in this city," Jack said, before turning his attention back to what might have been the world's largest sandwich and opening his mouth wide.

"Especially around here. Life might not be as great in the northern suburbs, but it is lovely in Batignolles."

"With such amazing food," Jack said, or something like it.

I picked up my sandwich at last. "If it wasn't for all our friends and the dogs at home, I think I could live here. People already seem familiar."

I dropped the sandwich.

Jack said, "Why are you so pale?"

"There's no reason for anyone to look familiar. I have this creepy sense they might have tracked us."

"How? We left in disguise from Margaret and Frank's place. We didn't go home, not that there was much to go home for. I don't believe we could have been followed."

I jumped to my feet and started pacing. "How did they find me in the first place?"

"Sit down, Charlotte, and take a deep breath. Remember that Regis accidentally told them you live in Woodbridge."

Why did I feel like swatting him?

Jack stood up and enveloped me in a comforting hug. "Okay, we both have our own obsessions and we are just letting our imaginations run wild."

"I have a weird feeling that I saw one of the fake dog-walkers from home."

"But what would bring them here?"

"Maybe they found out where Esme likes to travel."

"Again, how?"

"What if they tricked Glenda the same way they did with Regis? That's a possibility. I'm calling Sid right now. Why did I let myself get distracted by food when it wasn't even a mealtime?"

I used my burner to call Sid. "Hold your fire, Sid. It's me. What do you mean, you've been calling me? Sorry I haven't answered. I, um, don't have access to my regular phone so I missed your messages. It's been . . . crazy here. But I need to know if you found Glenda."

"Oh my God," he blurted. "You don't know."

"What?"

"I went to her place, with the couple I'm visiting, and we couldn't find Glenda. The door was open and . . ." He struggled to speak. "The place had been trashed. The cockatiel cages were open. The birds were gone. They won't survive long."

"Oh, no!" I thought my heart would explode. "And Glenda?"

Sid's voice wobbled. "There was no sign of her. The landline phone had been ripped out of the wall. Her car, purse and wallet are gone. Her phone and computer too. And some other electronics. We spoke to the neighbors. Nobody heard anything that they'll admit to. No one can remember seeing Glenda this week."

"You called the police?"

"Of course. I explained that I'd been trying to reach her."

"And did they come and take it seriously?"

A long pause. "They did take it seriously, Charlotte. Because of the broken window and all the blood."

All the blood? My head spun. So much for Glenda playing hard to get on Esme's instructions.

Finally, I was able to croak out the words to Jack: "They got Glenda. She must have been injured because there's a broken window and a lot of blood. Her phone and computer are gone, and if they can get through her computer security, they'll have access to everything they need to know about Esme's travel and habits." I gripped his arm. "Oh, Jack, what if they've killed Glenda?"

Jack said, "There's no way to find out from Paris."

My voice rose. "Things are escalating. We have to find Esme before these people do."

"You realize that you're stomping?"

"Can't help it, Jack."

"It's not like you to disturb the other tenants. Look, I'm worried about your mom too. If we can't find Esme here, where would she go next?"

"I suppose she could have taken the Eurostar to London. She loves the train and London's huge, so she could keep a low profile. Or she could have flown to Amsterdam or Berlin. Maybe Milan. It's hard to know."

"Okay, we need to exhaust all possibilities, besides the flower kiosks."

I'd lost my interest in eating. My stomach was in a knot, and regardless of how delicious the food was, I didn't think I could choke it down.

"It's a life-or-death situation, Jack."

"When you go out, I'll stay behind you in case you're being tailed. I'll spot them and rescue you if you need it."

"I don't need rescuing. Anyway, you're obviously not from here with your Hawaiian shirt and baseball cap and shorts."

"I'll remind you we couldn't pack properly and mostly it doesn't matter because we are on a mission. But!" He jumped to his feet.

"But what?" Honestly.

"There are lots of clothes in the closet here."

"We can't raid our host's closet!"

"Well, you can't because it's full of men's clothing, but I can because—"

"That seems totally wrong."

"It may even *be* totally wrong, but as you said earlier, a matter of life and death. I'm just suggesting borrowing a few things. A pair of jeans, a white shirt and a black sport jacket. I saw a scarf too, but that might be too much for me. I think my Converse will be okay. They're actually in style here."

"I don't want to steal clothing—"

"Borrow."

"Fine. I'll message Maxime and ask."

I texted our very helpful host and explained that we had arrived without our luggage, glossing over the fact that we hadn't brought it on the trip. I chose not to mention the life-or-death situation, as I figured hosts don't care for that sort of thing. I added that Jack was about his size and we would like to buy (or even rent) a few items of his clothing as we didn't have time to shop. *I suppose this is the strangest request you have ever had! Don't feel you have to agree.*

Maxime responded immediately. *It isn't strange at all. You would be surprised what people ask for.*

We can send you a photo of what we borrow and you can let us know about charges. Merci beaucoup.

Pas de problème. Take whatever you need.

So Jack would now blend in with the street traffic, but what about me? Use what you have is one of my mottos. I stuck my nose in the closet and reached for the fedora on the hook. I whipped a white dress shirt off its hanger. A white dress shirt is part of my capsule wardrobe that I didn't have with me. An oversize boyfriend shirt is always on trend, as the fashion people like to say. Maxime was quite slender so the shirt would do. I took off Margaret's suit and made a decision. Using the kitchen shears, I cropped the navy pants to a more stylish above-ankle length. I set up the small ironing board, then basted and pressed the new hem. I had just enough thread in my emergency repair kit and enough length on the pants for a small cuff, disguising the less-than-perfect hemming job.

With the boyfriend shirt collar open and tipped a bit and the sleeves rolled up, I defined the waist with Maxime's woven leather belt, tied, not buckled. The shirt looked good with the newly cropped pants (if you didn't look too closely). I tucked my hair up under the fedora and arranged my oversized blue-and-gold scarf to look flattering. I fished out my large sunglasses. *Voilà,* as they say. Jack strolled by, transformed by Maxime's left-behind wardrobe.

"I love the new you, Jack. The closet and its contents have been plundered with permission. How do you like my look?"

"You look amazing. You could be a genuine Parisienne."

"That's what I'm going for. Local and not too noticeable. If you leave after me, I think we may be able to do our tour of the flower shops and a few other places without drawing attention."

"What about the old city? Would Esme not have gone there?"

"Of course. She would have taken the Metro several times and made the rounds of her favorites. She always goes to the Musée de l'Orangerie at least once on every visit. She loves to see Monet's water lilies. She'll just sit there and watch them. She never misses a visit to the Musée d'Orsay, and lunch by the Polar Bear."

Jack said, "Maybe that's a Canadian thing."

"And she always dropped into Shakespeare and Company, even if she didn't have a book event there. She loves to read and she had developed relationships with them. Then there was a *chocolatier* she loved and a place where they made the best macarons and madeleines."

"What about a *bateau mouche*? Would she have done a little boat trip on the Seine?"

"She's hiding out. She'll stay in this neighborhood and we need to focus on here."

Jack seemed quite dejected at missing the center of Paris. I felt bad but we really needed to focus on the task at hand. "We're not here as tourists. We need to find my mother before . . . someone else does."

"I get it. We'll come back as tourists as soon as we can."

That deserved a hug. "I'm beginning to think that Esme has already moved on. We'll just check out a few more spots before we move on too. If we can figure out where."

"Ready to try our flower sellers?" One of the many good things about Jack is that disappointment never sticks.

"Right. I'll head out then."

Jack said, "I'll observe from up here to see if anyone seems to be watching you. Then I'll shadow you from about a block away. Don't make it too hard for me."

"How would I do that?"

"By disappearing into shops."

"Don't worry."

"I see that you have taken one of those larger canvas shopping bags."

"They don't use plastic bags anymore so you need to be prepared."

"Just stay in view. Things could be dangerous."

"Oh. But . . . all right. I'll be visible. But I will duck into any boutique that Esme might have visited."

"First thing, stop at that little pizza shop at the end of the street and pretend to study the menu. Chat a bit. I don't want you loose on the street until I'm down there. We can pick up some pizza on our way back."

"We just ate!"

"We'll need something for dinner, although I know you are going to fall asleep early."

"Fine."

I headed down the stairs to the front entrance and opened the door. After the dim (Jack had called it dreary) interior, it was a thrill to see and feel the late afternoon sun. I peered around and adjusted my fedora. I turned left and tried not to look as though I was checking out the street. I kept going to the pizza shop. Why wasn't everyone in Paris eight hundred pounds? It must have been because of all the walking. Inside the pizza shop, I pretended to study the menu. Minutes later Jack came in and said *bonjour* to the proprietor. That reminded me that I had forgotten.

"*Au revoir!*" I said as I stepped out the door. "A *bientôt!*" I knew Jack had his heart set on pizza for dinner or second lunch or third breakfast or whatever.

The street was busy and people were enjoying the afternoon. I stopped to smile at a small black and tan dachshund. He reminded me of Truffle and I felt a lump in my throat. Before I could ask his owner if he was friendly, the pooch lunged for my ankles, teeth bared. He'd probably roll over for a belly rub when Jack encountered him. I reminded myself that dachshunds don't like hats and I was wearing the fedora.

Several people passed with bouquets sticking out of their shopping bags. I stopped at the next kiosk and remembered to say *bonjour*. The proprietor wore a shapeless gray sweater and a stretched-out navy beret. She hadn't read any rules for the fashionable Parisienne but her kiosk was beautiful. I smiled and chose a bouquet of tulips in a gorgeous shade of lilac. As the flowers were being wrapped and money exchanged, I managed to show the photo of Esme and me. I managed to say in French something close to: "*Merci, madame.* I am getting these for my mother."

Madame blinked at the photo. I asked if Esme had been there and bought tulips for herself. She shook her head. "*Mais non.* Not today. Last week perhaps?"

"So I am safe with the tulips for her."

"*Oui.* One can never have too many tulips. The gentleman didn't get her any though," she sniffed.

Chapter 15

Wherever you are traveling, get to know your new neighborhood. It will pay off.

I blinked. "What gentleman?"

"Just another person asking about your mother. He had a picture too."

"Of both of us?"

"Just your mother."

"Did you tell him that my mother had been here?"

She shrugged in that oversized French way that I both love and hate. "Why should I? He bought nothing."

"Do you mind telling me what he looked like?"

"Boring. Running shoes. Jeans."

"Oh."

"A baseball cap. Hardly proper on a man of that age. But, you know"—she shrugged—"Quebec."

"He spoke French?"

Madame rolled her eyes.

"Um, did he have small eyes?"

She brightened. "*Oui! Comme un cochon.*"

Okay, the arrival of a piggy-eyed person from Quebec was bad news for us. It was a link that sent shivers down my spine.

"*Merci*," I said. The flower vendor seemed like the type of person who would expect to be thanked more than once. "Please don't mention that I asked about my mother if anyone else inquires. She needs to avoid some unpleasant people."

She nodded gravely as if this was something she understood all too well.

I meandered along, with my wonderful tulips, pausing to gaze in boutique windows. Jack hadn't wanted me to disappear, but what harm could it do to duck into this one? I turned around, pretending to watch a few parading pigeons. I could see Jack ambling along the street looking like any carefree Parisian *flaneur*. This was another one of his undiscovered gifts, master of disguise. It made me realize in that moment how lucky I was. Jack had never been a "bad boy," although I'd been susceptible to that type myself back in the day. That should be no big surprise based on Esme's choices, like more brains than looks, more money than brains and none of the above. There were a couple of bad boys in the mix and I suspected my father was one of them. Although I was very fond of one of my stepfathers and didn't mind the other two, Esme never met anyone who made her happy. Never anyone like Jack though. Sean Doyle may have made her happy but he sure hadn't kept her safe. But who did she need to be kept safe from?

I settled on a bench and pretended to be admiring the street scene. I tried to equal Jack's relaxed posture and lifted my face to the sun. I wasn't sure if a Parisian woman would do something like that. They were famously protective of their skin. I shielded my eyes with my arm, admiring the sight and scent of a flowering cherry tree. I saw no one in the strolling crowd who connected with any of my memories. Jack was now squatting to pet the little black and tan dachshund on the dog's return trip. Apparently the pooch had been living in anticipation of this moment. Although Jack engaged with dog and owner, I knew he was keeping an eye on me and the surroundings. I rose, stretched slightly and passed in front of him and entered one of Esme's favorite boutiques. The clothing was elegant and flowy, much of it white. Esme would have looked great in anything there. I am more earthbound and practical. Still, I needed more than Margaret's mutilated suit pants and Maxime's pilfered shirt, hat and belt.

On the other hand, I couldn't pick anything white that would need frequent cleaning, or worse, ironing. Nothing delicate. Nothing noticeable. Would anything in this beautiful shop fit the bill? I was able to find a beautifully cut silk blouse in navy and a pair of high-waisted, slim-cut, dark-wash jeans and a cashmere pullover in yellow. The sleeves of the blouse and the hem of the jeans could be rolled until I could get them altered. I worried about the cashmere sweater, but hadn't Jack said it was only money and you can't take it with you?

Jack was lounging by a statue eating ice cream when I emerged. Ice cream is my favorite thing and he knows it, so I assumed I was being punished for "disappearing," although it had been clear where I was going.

Jack obviously didn't have a care in the world. A few passing women gave him subtle but assessing glances. I made a point of not being jealous.

I crossed the square again, nodding to the pigeons, stopped at another flower vendor to ask about Esme. No luck. I was disappointed but bought a small green trailing plant to leave for Maxime. After a few pigeons and pooches, I stepped into another boutique, pausing to adjust my fedora in the mirror by the door. Outside, Jack was paying attention without appearing to. Good.

I quickly purchased a navy and white *mariniere*. Those cotton sailor sweaters are stylish and timeless. I found a faux silk scarf in celadon, blue and yellow that would come in very handy. Scarves can go missing easily so, unlike Esme, I didn't spring for real silk.

Now I had a mix-and-match wardrobe that would take me to London, Madrid, Lisbon or wherever without looking too suspiciously scruffy.

As I exited, dark banks of nimbus clouds swept in to cover the sun. April showers were on their way. It would be a good time to get a leather jacket or a trench coat, but the change in weather meant I'd better scurry to talk to flower vendors. I felt briefly happy about the purchases in my canvas bag, until I reminded myself why we were in Paris without proper clothes. Now I needed an umbrella. Umbrella vendors spring up like magic as soon as there's a whisper of rain in Paris so it was easy to score an inexpensive one.

Jack had moved on from socializing with passing dogs and was now admiring a sleek-looking bicycle parked outside a small fruit shop. I was pretty sure I'd be hearing about it over our next meal.

I hurried to the next flower vendor, a very good-looking man in his twenties, just Esme's type for a fling. I pointed at a bouquet of fragrant freesia. The young man looked to be Algerian and spoke in the beautiful fluid French that you hear in the city. "*Bonjour!*" I said. "They smell so lovely." I showed him the photo of Esme and me. "*Si belle,*" he inhaled.

Fine, so she was beautiful. "She was here?" I said in my best French.

"*Oui, oui.*"

"When did you see her last?"

What a magnificent shrug! But he ruined the mood by switching to reasonably fluent English. "Six days ago. I am pretty sure."

Still, it was a relief not to have to carefully consider every word that left my mouth. "I urgently need to find her. I think she may have left Paris."

"Why don't you send her a message?"

Right. "It's a long story but she wanted to be alone so she left her devices."

"Then why do you not let her relax and be alone?"

"Because there's a dangerous situation and she needs to be aware."

Alarm flashed through his dark eyes. "Dangerous?"

I raised my chin. "Quite dangerous."

I could have sworn he was worried. But then, my mother can have that effect on strange men. "Are the police involved?"

"Yes, in America, but not here. I don't believe the police can help. My mother needs to know what is going on and then she can decide what she wants to do. Did you say she was here in Batignolles a few days ago?"

"Yes. She was planning to leave."

"She spoke to you about leaving Paris?"

"Not in those words but . . ."

My heart was thundering. "Did she say where she was going?"

He shook his handsome head. "No, but I figured it out."

Can no one ever give a straight answer?

"And where was that?"

"Well, we were talking about pastries."

Of course you were.

"She loves pastries."

"She definitely does."

"And she said she was looking forward to her favorite *pastel de nata*."

Pastel de nata is a Portuguese egg-tart pastry dusted with cinnamon.

"Did she? So that might mean—"

"Portugal, naturally."

You can get a good *pastel de nata* all over Europe these days. I knew that, but Esme adores her treats and prefers them authentic, a madeleine or macaron in Paris, a *pastel de nata* in Lisbon, a gelato in Italy, a scone in England.

I bought a lovely bunch of lavender from him. I needed to make sure that anyone watching thought it was an ordinary flower-based conversation. And lavender is a wonderful soothing fragrance. It could come with us in our hand luggage.

"I hope she will be safe," he said, taking my euros.

"So do I. Other people are looking for her and you must not tell anyone about Portugal. They may be watching us even now."

He said, "So we should act naturally, is that what you are saying?"

"Yes." I pointed at some dried roses and he made a big deal about shaking his head.

"They have already asked," he said.

I gulped. "What did you say?"

"I told him nothing."

"What? Him? Who?"

Another shrug. "An American man."

"Can you describe him?" I pointed at some daffodils.

He pulled out a bunch of daffs for me to examine. "There was nothing special about him. He was about my height. A bit heavier. Maybe fifty years old. He wore a baseball cap. What's that you Americans say? 'Not a good look for him'?"

"Piggy little eyes?"

He shrugged again. "Sunglasses."

"And could the man have been French-Canadian too?"

"I don't know. He spoke English with an American accent. I don't really know the difference between a Canadian and a U.S. accent in English."

On the upside, I now had a description of the man searching for Esme. On the downside, he had found this neighborhood and probably had spotted us.

• • •

All that remained was to find Esme's apartment and see if that yielded any new information. I turned onto a side street, glancing around in case anyone was behind me. No one, not even Jack. I was a bit rattled as I searched for the elegant façade on Esme's pied-à-terre. Five doors down on the left side I recognized a building with well-tended pansies in large pots at the door—I'd found it. Now what? We needed to find out what her neighbor knew about Esme's whereabouts, we needed to keep our thuggish follower from finding her, and we needed to get the hell out of Dodge. But, I was alone. Pushing down panic, I called Jack. "Where are you?"

"I lost you."

"How could you lose me?"

"I picked up a few things for dessert as part of my cover and when I turned around again, there you were, gone."

"I'll meet you back in front of the pizza place. Wait for me there."

I gritted my teeth and, as I hurried to meet Jack, struggled to remember the name of the woman who kept an eye on Esme's apartment. Once we reconnected we headed back to Esme's apartment. "We need to stick together now. I just need to remember the name of her helpful neighbor. We passed a hand-lettered sign offering *Poulet Chasseur* take-out and Jack said, "Do you feel like chicken for dinner because—"

I did a double take. "It's Madame Chasseur!"

After a long pause, Jack said, "What?"

"Esme's neighbor. That's who takes care of Esme's apartment when she's away. Madame Chasseur."

"Okay. So we'll either find Esme hiding under her bed or we'll be on our way to our next destination," Jack said without missing a beat. "We'll come back when this is over. We'll walk in every park, float on every boat and get our pictures taken with every statue."

I didn't ask what if this whole adventure ended badly and I never saw Esme again. I didn't ask what if something happened to one of us. Some questions are better left unasked.

As we walked my admiration for Baron Haussman and the design of Paris grew. The man had a sense of organization. Similar building materials and a limited number of styles left me feeling soothed. Paris was a huge, busy city and yet, aside from the crowds in the tourist areas, there was a serenity about it. I found it amazing that one person could have such an impact. I made the mistake of mentioning this to Jack. He was not a fan.

"He caused the destruction of much of historic Paris. People were outraged. And—"

I put up my hand. "Well, this is historic Paris now. Let's agree to disagree. And there's the street." We'd reached the familiar corner. "Now to get in."

"Can't you go into the foyer and just press the buzzer for this Madame Chasseur's apartment?" Jack said as we reached our destination.

"That would be too easy. Esme's big on security. She told me you need a code to get through the main door. Anyone who needed to see her or Madame Chasseur would have phoned and made an appointment. They'd get buzzed in. And of course, we don't have the code, and, before you say anything, yes, it is because I didn't write it down when Esme told me."

"We'll just have to ask the next person who comes along."

I held out no hope for that tactic, but Jack said "*Bonsoir*" to a man carrying a computer bag and wearing a stylish leather jacket. He explained that we had a family problem and urgently needed to speak to Madame Chasseur but didn't have her phone number. Could he help? "Charlotte Adams needs to speak to her."

The man nodded curtly and we paced outside the glossy black door feeling foolish for a very long time.

• • •

Just as I was about to give up and form a new plan (possibly breaking in through a window), a woman I assumed was Madame Chasseur appeared in the door and looked down her long nose at us. I introduced myself and Jack. She beckoned us in. Her hair was silver and cut in a chic bob, and I watched her tall, slender figure as she preceded us to the elevator. Her slim charcoal pants and loose-fitting caramel-colored sweater looked like they'd been designed for her. Her discreet pieces of jewelry—small gold earring and a chain with a tassel—fit in with this elegant foyer with the gold-framed mirror and striking modern art.

"Madame Adams told me to expect you. I brought the key to her unit. Are you planning to stay here?" she said as we exited the elevator.

"Would you be kind enough to join us for a few minutes?" I asked as she opened the first door on the left.

"But of course." Her smile didn't reach her eyes—in fact, it barely reached her lips.

There's something eerie about an apartment that has been vacant for even a few days. A large vase of wilted freesia sat on the table, the usually pleasant scent cloying. Esme had left in a hurry if she didn't take a minute to empty that. Madame Chasseur frowned at the dead flowers. I picked up the vase and carried it to the kitchen. The unit was open and airy with white walls, tall windows and quality pale furniture—two Eames chairs, a long white leather sofa and a huge raw-edge coffee table covered with stacks of art books.

On the opposite wall, a mid-century brass and wood bar cart, well-stocked. Esme had told me there were two comfortable bedrooms and she'd complained about her pokey little office. Of course, mostly if she had to work, she chose the dining room table.

I returned and smiled at Madame Chasseur. I wondered what her first name was or if she had one. "As we mentioned, we've gotten our travel arrangements confused. I hope you can help."

"*Naturellement.*" She inclined her head ever so slightly and tried smiling again. It was as though she was new to the concept and wasn't sure she'd be sticking with it.

I gestured for her to sit and she did with more dignity than most people can produce at a funeral. Jack sank happily into one of the Eames chairs.

"Can I offer you something? Cognac?" I said.

My mother had mentioned that she and Madame Chasseur shared conversation and cognac when Esme was in the Batignolles apartment.

"*S'il vous plaît,*" she said.

Esme liked good cognac served in crystal snifters and there was a beautiful bottle of Camus Borderies X.O., three-quarters full on the bar cart.

I poured generous portions into three crystal snifters. Perhaps cognac would clear my head or calm me down. Mainly, it was to loosen up Madame Chausseur.

I distributed the drinks and sat on the other end of the sofa. I raised my glass. "To old friends."

She nodded.

I said, "So you were expecting me?"

"Oh, yes, Madame Adams said you might be along with your friend." She nodded knowingly at Jack. He raised his snifter with a grin.

"We really need to catch up with her, so any help would be appreciated."

"She is expecting you to follow her."

I took a deep breath. "Follow her where?"

"She said to tell you to meet her in your favorite place in England." Madame did not hold any British location in high esteem if her expression was anything to go by. Probably that view had been enhanced by Brexit.

"My favorite place?"

Madame Chasseur gave a classic Gallic shrug indicating she couldn't imagine having a favorite place in that unfriendly land. "I assume that is London. Do you have her address there?"

I have always liked the United Kingdom. My favorite place would be Mevagissey, a scenic village on the rocky coast of Cornwall, much like the location of the television show *Doc Martin*. I was pretty sure Madame would rank Cornwall much lower than London.

"Thank you so much. We'll have no problem finding her, now that I know what country she's in. When did she leave?"

"I have been very busy and I didn't really notice her departure."

"By the way, did anyone else ask about Esme?"

Her surprise seemed genuine. "Who would be asking?"

"No one important, but if anyone does, you must not tell them she's in England."

Her eyes widened and her hands went to her throat. If she'd had pearls, she would have clutched them. "But—"

"Perhaps say you think she's in Amsterdam. She's crazy about tulips."

"*Oui.* Amsterdam." Another serious nod.

"I just want to check around for a couple of minutes before we leave. I know Jack is interested in talking about art with you."

This was news to Jack but he rose to the occasion. "Art? For sure. Do you have a favorite gallery in Paris to recommend, Madame?"

I scuttled into Esme's bedroom and tapped at the back of closets and checked the underside of drawers. The same with the small office. I am familiar with where she usually hides things.

Madame stood up when I returned. Jack said, "Got some hot tips on galleries. Did you know that Monet's Water Lilies are shown in two oval rooms at l'Orangerie?"

Jack and I were both well aware of that. "Fantastic. We must check it out before we leave for London." I washed up the glasses and put them away, thanked Madame and said goodbye.

Back on the street, we checked both directions and spotted none of our would-be stalkers.

"London and then Cornwall?" Jack said.

"No way."

"But Madame said—"

"Exactly what Esme wanted her to say. She figured I'd end up here although she'd be very miffed to know how long it took me to remember where the place was. She's sending me on a wild-goose chase. It's a long train or car trip to Cornwall from London. At least five or six hours each direction, but it would get me out of the way for two days. I'm not falling for it. But Madame didn't need to know that."

"Okay, so that explains her weird expressions. She's not used to being deceptive."

"Not sure she knows she's being deceptive. Esme wouldn't include her in that. But here's the news: Esme always keeps an emergency bag hidden behind a panel in her bedroom. Always. I found the hidden panel, but there was nothing left behind it."

Jack turned toward me, eyebrows rising fast.

I said, "That means she needed to use other ID, other credit cards, a burner phone, all the stuff I showed you."

"So she's on the run."

"Definitely. And she doesn't want my help or interference."

"Now what?"

"We stick with the plan. Based on the information from the flower vendor, I'd say Lisbon's our best bet. Let's head home and make that happen."

I saw no one even vaguely familiar on the way. For some reason that wasn't soothing. It's better if you can see the enemy. I could hear Jack whistling behind me so I knew we were together. I was grateful.

We stumbled up the dim stairs and along the gloomy corridor, and although the automatic lights went out just as we made it to the apartment, I said, "We're going to book a flight, pack and get to the airport without being seen. They've been asking about Esme and they may know we're here."

"Not very likely," Jack said, eyeing his shopping bags. "And by the way, my stomach says it is dinnertime. Or at least time for appetizers."

"I'm packing. You're booking the flight. We'll talk about dinner when that's taken care of."

• • •

By a minor miracle, Jack managed to book our trip for that night at ten forty-five. It involved three separate flights and would get us into Lisbon in the morning. I zipped the carry-on bag as soon as he shouted out success.

He couldn't resist saying, "If we're going to be traveling, we should have a really good meal. It's our last night in Paris and we'd be crazy not to treat each other well. So, before you put up a fight, it's not too early for dinner, we have plenty of time to get to the airport."

I didn't bother to argue. Even though I knew there would be no shortage of wonderful meals in Lisbon, tonight's dinner would make him happy.

We settled on a tiny dark bistro off the beaten track. The advantage was that it served early dinners and many restaurants wouldn't start until later. Plus, the scent of fresh bread drew us in. We made ourselves comfortable at a discreet corner table that gave us a good view of anyone passing in front and ordered from the chalkboard *menu du jour.* I ordered the sole *bonne femme* and Jack chose the *boeuf bourguignon,* traditional French dishes, rich and delicious.

Flickering candles cast shadows on the red and white tablecloth and on Jack's face. There were only two dozen tables in the little bistro and because it was earlyish, there were only a handful of other diners. A pair of men who might have been professors at the music school waved their hands as they spoke passionately in French. A middle-aged couple commiserated about their day. Two young women with spiky blue and green hair lingered over appetizers. No sign of the shadowy villains who had been tracking us and Esme. I could relax with a glass of good wine for a short time and tomorrow we'd begin a new adventure. Jack had a seafood bisque to start, but I merely nibbled on a slice of freshly cut warm bread. I wished I could slather it with butter. French butter is an experience in itself. But I'd learned on an earlier trip that in France one does not butter one's bread at dinner.

Even when our main courses arrived preceded by their delicious aromas, my heart wasn't in our meal. For one thing, it was ridiculously early for a romantic dinner. For another, the past twenty-six hours had about a month's worth of drama, action and travel. Still, I appreciated Jack's support in this crazy chase. When he decided to have crème caramel for dessert, I went with chocolate ice cream and it helped a bit. We just had to get to Lisbon without disaster.

As we were getting ready to leave, I heard a WhatsApp call coming in. I reached for the phone, wondering who could be contacting us. It was after midnight back in Woodbridge. My heart fluttered as I read.

Chapter 16

It's always wise to have some blister stick with you on a trip to save your feet.

Charlotte: This is Alison Erikson. I am a friend of Vanessa Vallerin's at McGill library and have been looking into your query about a missing mother and child in or near Montreal in 1995. The following information may be relevant to your search, although the story is broader than a mother and child. This is my very rough translation of an article in French by Jean-Claude Dion, a well-respected crime journalist who covered the Hummingbird Gang, a group of dashing bank robbers in the mid-nineteen-nineties. Dion went on to write a book about their escapades and the sad ends of their lives. The book was published in English and French, but unfortunately not in electronic format. Our English copy has gone missing, but I have summarized the key points. I will try to locate a copy and scan it. I hope that helps. Let me know. There may be more to come. I believe Jean-Claude is working on a new book about the gang. Ali.

The Hummingbird Gang was a group of young men of mixed French and Irish parentage who had been in and out of foster homes and juvenile detention since their early teens. Sean "Shonnie" Doyle, Léo "le Loup" Lemire, Danny "Danno" Hanrahan and John "Boy" Nadeau, all from broken and abusive homes, bonded and worked together to protect each other from bullies and thugs when behind bars. Originally from the rough-and-tumble Pointe-Saint-Charles area of Montreal, they extended their reach into Notre-Dame-de-Grâce and points west, where they acquired new contacts and gorgeous girlfriends. They picked up useful skills while incarcerated and emerged determined not to get caught again. Apparently, none of the four considered going straight as an option. The gang members were good-looking, intelligent and daring. They stayed out of direct competition with the bigger, more established Montreal posses such as the dominant West End Gang and the vicious O'Byrne Crew, and they were not prone to violence. They weren't known for repeating the tactics of a robbery either. Sean "Shonnie" Doyle, the planner, was said to enjoy putting together an elaborate scheme for each heist. Doyle, who was a talented amateur artist, liked putting his creative stamp on a robbery.

Before long, they had developed some effective methods of targeting downtown bank branches at the best times. Police believed that the gang had inside information about bank operations. Léo Lemire's wife, Lucie Vachon, at one time worked in a branch of the Bank of Montreal and by all accounts made many friends there. Later police learned that Shonnie Doyle's young wife, Evelyn Acheson, a former student at Concordia University, was the daughter of Graham Acheson, the manager of a BMO branch. Unnamed sources say that the Acheson family disowned Evelyn when she became pregnant by her gangster boyfriend. She stayed with Doyle, who had acquired a sort of rock star image in the Montreal media to the point where some said that tellers were reluctant to trigger the alarm system. As the alarm systems were always triggered, that would appear to be an urban legend.

Evelyn Acheson had a summer job in a bank branch when she met Lucie, who in turn introduced her to Léo Lemire's friend, Sean. Sparks flew. Both women knew the routines and knew how the alarms worked. Nadeau and Hanrahan would arrange a major distraction near the bank. Fire hydrants were opened to the delight of children. Fires suddenly erupted in multiple dumpsters and, in one case, a load of live chickens was released, creating a lot of excitement as people tried to catch the wayward chickens, perhaps for dinner!

To stymie the police and facilitate the gang's getaway during one robbery, Nadeau and Hanrahan stole four vehicles from long-term parking. They also took over a semitrailer. They swapped plates on the vehicles and sprang for parking in the streets adjacent to the target bank. Once the others were in the bank, they staged a crash between two of the cars, blocking access to the block for other vehicles. Nadeau legged it to the other end and waited in the semi while Hanrahan guarded the door. At the signal, Nadeau blocked access to the street with the semi and disappeared. Cash in hand, the other three raced down the block, crawled under the truck and vanished into a waiting vehicle driven by Nadeau. By the time police reached the area, the Hummingbirds had flown. The gang and their women were living the high life. Everyone bought fast cars, and Shonnie Doyle was rumoured to have taken flying lessons and purchased a Cessna 172, although there is no evidence that he had a pilot's license. Under her own name, Evelyn Acheson paid cash for a penthouse in Cote Saint-Luc. Life was good for these little birds.

The final job had a new twist. A rumour had surfaced that just before he was indicted on murder charges the notorious West End gangster Bobby "Bullets" O'Byrne had deposited a serious stash of cash in several safety deposit boxes in a BMO branch on rue St. Henri and he was said to have big plans for it. At one time both Lucie Vachon and Evelyn Acheson had been employees of the branch. Hanrahan was heard to say that Shonnie Doyle was wanting to get out of the game and settle down with Evelyn and their young daughter, Seanna. Léo Lemire was also feeling a bit old for the life. Hanrahan and Nadeau felt they had many more heists in them, but "they was a team." The Hummingbirds set out to locate those safety deposit boxes before someone else got the same idea. Sean Doyle and Danny Hanrahan both had francophone mothers, and while they were fluent in English, French had been their first language and they had attended French schools. The bank branch was next to the office of a notary public. Adjacent to that was a small restaurant space for rent. Shonnie and Danny established themselves as the Dufour brothers, a pair of French-speaking restaurateurs who wanted to open a high-end steak and seafood restaurant, called Dufour. During the economic slowdown of the time, it was a buyer's market. They asked to secure the space for a three-week period while they nailed down the approvals and licenses, using cash as an enticement to the owner. That cash was eventually traced to an earlier heist. The owner had no clue that his potential purchasers were the very newsworthy Sean Doyle and Danny Hanrahan. Hook, line and sinker, as they say. With the site secured, the team set about to make their plan work. Both the bank and the notary closed at four p.m. on Fridays, a charmingly old-fashioned approach that worked well for the Hummingbirds. They set to work in the basement, with concrete cutting equipment, opening the basement wall of the notary's office. One of the team was always on watch outside in case anyone came into the office. Unconfirmed chatter says that Evelyn and Lucie took turns posing as pedestrians but keeping guard. Everyone in the gang was rumoured to have the latest in mobile phones, although those would be laughably chunky by today's standard. From the notary's office, the team moved on to the bank and its much more challenging wall. Léo Lemire had worked in the mines in northern Quebec and learned his way around a fuse. Hanrahan and Nadeau were welders and at ease with acetylene torches. Rumour has it that the crew got the plans for the block from a corrupt city employee but this has never been proven. While the Hummingbirds easily worked unobserved to open up the two interior basement walls, the vault would be another thing altogether. Dynamite would be needed, but the explosion would be heard. The solution was another diversion. At the moment of the breech of the vault, Hanrahan and Nadeau were busy setting off fireworks in the surrounding blocks. They stayed in touch by walkie-talkie and the fireworks went off on time, raising a racket and creating much excitement in the neighborhood. They then melted into the night and back to the rear door of the Dufour restaurant, where they were needed to open and clear the safety deposit boxes. While the streets flooded with people enjoying the fireworks, some, perhaps of a more nervous disposition, called police. No one seemed to notice the extra boom, let alone the drilling of the safety deposit boxes. The security guards had been previously tricked into leaving by a replacement team, almost certainly the Houdini-like Nadeau and Hanrahan. By Monday morning, when the bank staff arrived, all four Hummingbirds had taken flight. Things were looking good until someone in Bobby Bullets' crew put two and two together and came looking for the Hummingbirds. Apparently they had flown the coop with Bobby Bullets' cash—millions awaiting the right laundering facility—gold bars, jewelry and incriminating evidence against people in business and government. The underworld gossip laid it at the feet of the Hummingbirds. Before the week was out, Hanrahan and Nadeau were shot execution-style behind a warehouse on the South Shore. A police officer deep undercover in Bobby Bullets' crew later produced a recording of Bobby admitting he'd ordered the murders and celebrating the executions. Bullets expressed disappointment that Hanrahan and Nadeau did not reveal the location of Shonnie Doyle and Léo Lemire before they died, most likely because they didn't know. O'Byrne was sentenced to twenty-five years with no

> parole, for these and other crimes. The day after the murders of Hanrahan and Nadeau, Léo and Lucie Lemire disappeared. Lemire's remote northern cabin was found burnt to the ground. Their bodies are rumored to be buried in a forest in the Laurentians. There was an arson attack on Evelyn Acheson's penthouse and Sean Doyle, Evelyn, and their young daughter went into hiding. Less than two weeks later, the family of three was presumed dead after Sean's small Cessna went down over Lac des Larmes, one of the deepest lakes in the Laurentians, on April 7, 1995. Fragments of the plane and belongings, including a locked suitcase with nearly two hundred thousand dollars in cash, were found scattered along the shore. The fuselage of the plane and bodies of the Doyle family have never been found. Despite ongoing investigations, no one has yet been implicated in the deaths of Sean Doyle and his family or in the arson attack on the penthouse.
>
> *Here is a scan of a photo of the Hummingbird Gang with Evelyn Acheson and Lucie Vachon.*
>
> *I will try to put you in touch with Jean-Claude Dion but he has been injured in a mugging and is in hospital. It may take a few days before he is able to talk to you.*

I stared wordlessly at the photo of eight people and tried to keep my head from exploding. Four cocky young men entwined with four glamorous women. Esme was front and center, gazing at a man who looked a lot like the legendary and doomed actor James Dean. Next to her was Lola, snuggled up to a dark-haired and swarthy fellow. I took a deep breath and handed the phone to Jack. I stared around the bistro while he read.

"Well, that's sure something," Jack said when he finished. "*Lac des larmes*. That means lake of tears."

I nodded numbly. My name was Seanna. I knew that on some level, of course, although I hadn't heard the name for more than twenty-five years. It was just one more surreal and disturbing element in my real history, but it left me feeling weak in the knees.

"I think that this information explains the kind of things that have been happening to you before and during this trip."

"Yes. We don't know how Esme and I managed to stay alive, but the photo tells me who Lola is. And the article tells me why Esme is on the run."

"Right. I'm glad you stayed alive."

I shivered. "So far."

"Right. And it looks like our troublemakers are connected to this O'Byrne."

"They want to spook me into panicking and leading them to Esme."

I responded with thanks to Ali and asked her to send any more parts to the story she could uncover. I added my hope that Jean-Claude Dion was recovering and that I could speak to him soon.

Jack was busy searching for something on his phone. "Let's see what we can find out about Bobby Bullets."

"No matter what you find, we need a new plan." I was having trouble processing all this new information about my past and my parents. I couldn't stop shivering.

Jack raised his phone and waggled it under my nose. He put his fingers to his lips. I read what he'd located in a Montreal paper, dated a month ago.

> *Robert "Bobby Bullets" O'Byrne, 74, was released today from his maximum-security cell in Port-Cartier Institution on compassionate grounds because of his diagnosis of terminal cancer. O'Byrne had served twenty-four years of his twenty-five-year sentence for killing Daniel (Danno) Hanrahan and John (John Boy) Nadeau, members of the glamorous '90s Hummingbird Gang. Several witnesses to the murders also disappeared in suspicious circumstances.*

Jack scrolled down to a photo below: a seemingly frail white-haired man was being helped to a vehicle by a group of people. Bobby Bullets might have been gaunt and stooped, yet he still had a few chins. I'd imagined his eyes would be small and mean and they were. Jack pointed at the other faces.

Two women and two men, all in their late forties, early fifties, apparently the children of Bobby Bullets. The women had classy blonde hair with well-executed highlights, the kind that cost several hundred dollars at upscale salons. The hairdos and well-cut clothes couldn't minimize the heavy jawline, extra chins, tiny eyes and the awkward posture of our female dog walker. I also recognized the person who had taken my course at the library. Both women were dressed in heavy but pricey-looking winter clothing: black coats trimmed with fox fur, high-heeled leather boots. They were the same duo who had tried to trick Regis into letting them in to see my mother.

The men wore expensive overcoats. I was betting the coats and the scarves fashionably looped around their necks would be cashmere. We recognized the face of our male dog walker. The ponytail was gone, if it had ever been real. The fourth O'Byrne, also a burly man in a dark coat, kept his face averted from the cameras. All four radiated menace, even the faceless one.

So now we knew.

To add to my worries, another WhatsApp message came in from Ali. She was very active for a librarian in the middle of the night.

> *Just learned that Jean-Claude was not mugged. He was savagely beaten in his home and only survived because his grocery delivery driver interrupted the attack. He is in an induced coma. I'm not sure when he would be able to talk (or if) but will keep you posted. Be careful! Ali.*

• • •

The walk back to our apartment was creepier than any stroll through a graveyard. We were in a safe neighborhood of a city with plenty of people strolling the narrow streets on this spring evening but I could almost taste the threatening vibe. The hair on the back of my neck was standing up. Annoyingly, Jack didn't seem to smell danger. He still had a happy glow from his successful research. As we rounded a corner, without warning he hustled me into a dark bistro and piano bar, featuring low lights and a jazz piano. We found an even darker corner, where Jack could keep an eye on the street and I could slouch against the red leather of the banquette.

Jack leaned forward and whispered, "I saw a hulking guy that might be one of them. You can't miss that lumbering walk and the—"

"Piggy eyes."

"Exactly."

Jack slid out of his seat and whispered to the bartender. He gestured at the menu and talked up a storm. Surely he couldn't have been thinking about more food. I saw some money change hands. Seconds later, the bartender waved us into the kitchen, apparently to see how something was done. Then boom, we were racing out through the back exit into a small courtyard mostly home to garbage containers. Our bartender knocked at a closed metal rear entrance to the building on the street in back. When the door opened, more money changed hands. We scuttled through a loud and frenetic restaurant kitchen smelling of seafood and *frites* and into a crowded, noisy *brasserie* where people were enjoying intense conversations over wine or beer. Quite a few euros poorer, we took a roundabout route to our Airbnb. I kept an eye out ahead and Jack made sure we weren't followed. If our pursuers had been watching, our escape would have slowed them down.

The benefits of our excellent dinner had evaporated.

• • •

Back in the apartment, Jack said, "You should wear those hummingbird earrings you've been hanging on to. Be a shame to lose them after carrying the guilt all these years. When you find Esme, you can have it out with her. She dragged a small child on a dangerous and bewildering journey and never let her speak about it. She's got some explaining to do." Jack's eyes flashed. He is gentle and easygoing, but he has his limits.

I said, "Speaking of birds, we're sitting ducks here. We need to figure a way to get to the airport without being seen."

I calculated how much we should pay Maxime for his clothing. I'd leave the fedora as any watchers would recognize it by now.

We used the printer to print the photos of the O'Byrne family and then scanned them and sent the image to Ramona via Lilith's pal Zak, along with the suggestion that Ramona find an anonymous way to let Pepper know they were linked to the dog walkers. The fingerprints seemed like the right link.

I hunched in a corner and texted Maxime: *Am trying to avoid a persistent former boyfriend. He is stalking me even though Jack is here. Is there a rear exit to this building? Also may need to "borrow" extra things, including your carry-on case.*

Again, will reimburse you. Plus, we need a cab to the airport. We're cutting it close.

That was putting it mildly. I am always early at the airport, but tonight it looked like we'd barely make it in time for boarding.

Maxime responded almost instantly. *Take what you need. Yes, there is an exit through the laundry area. I will be right over to guide you out. You will never find it by yourself.*

I answered. *Perfect. Merci.*

While we waited, I changed into my black pants and tee, added my jean jacket and speedily repacked using Maxime's suitcase. Jack was busy doing something with blankets and every candle in the apartment and a bottle of wine with two glasses. Had he lost his mind?

As I finished, leaving my suitcase open on the bed, I went to check. Jack gave me a flamboyant embrace in front of the window. With the lights on in the room we would have been visible to anyone watching from across the street. It was all I could do to resist looking.

Jack turned on all the battery-powered candles. Stepping out of the line of sight of the window, he set up one of the rolled blankets in a chair. As I watched openmouthed he crouched down and set up the other one on the opposite side of the little table. One leaned forward.

Maxime texted that he was outside the door. I grabbed my suitcase and cross-body bag and Jack picked up his pack. As Jack flicked off the lights, whoever was watching would imagine a romantic scene, or so we hoped.

Jack explained to Maxime, "We just need the distraction of the candles until we're out of here."

Maxime said, "The worst that can happen is the batteries die."

We left the lights off and crept down the stairs to the main floor and turned toward the back of the ancient building. It was spine-chilling even with Jack and Maxime. Maxime unlocked a metal door that connected to a building on the next street. "You see this a lot here, if you know where to look," he said. We found ourselves in another apartment building and followed Maxime to the front door, where he had a cab waiting for us. Getting a cab to the airport wasn't necessarily easy in Paris, so Maxime again deserved his five stars.

• • •

We barely caught our breath at Orly airport before our flight was ready to board. There would be no more watching for menacing figures behind every pillar. As we got our documents in order for the flight, my phone kept dinging with notifications. Ali Erikson, our new source of articles in local papers relating to the Hummingbirds and the disappearance of the Doyle family, wasn't getting any sleep tonight. Now we had more scanned articles that might keep us up all night too.

I forwarded the new scans to Jack.

As soon as our flight was in the air and we could turn on our devices, we started to read

The Montreal Daily News
April 3, 1995

> *The Sûreté du Québec revealed today that items found in the area of a crash near the icy shores of Lac des Larmes, a remote body of water north of Montreal, are believed to be the property of Sean "Shonnie" Doyle's wife and child. Neighbours have identified the Barbie case as similar to the one little Seanna Doyle owned. The Doyle family is believed to have perished when their small Cessna crashed near the shore of the lake. Doyle was the alleged mastermind of the Hummingbird Gang, whose most recent heist was looting of safety deposit vault at the Bank of Montreal on St. Henri. Although debris was scattered on shore and in the shallow edge of the lake, no bodies have been recovered to date and recovery operations will be difficult with the winter weather and the depth of Lac des Larmes. Investigators have revealed that a suitcase submerged near the shore contained nearly two hundred thousand dollars in cash and a nine-millimetre handgun. They have also confirmed rumours that one wing that was recovered from the doomed plane had been pierced by several bullets from a high-powered rifle or rifles. Personal effects strewn in the area included the sad sight of a child's striped toy rabbit. A silk jewellery bag with a diamond necklace was found hanging from a tree branch.*

Police suspect that Doyle had used a phony name to rent a winterized cabin near the site of the crash and intended to hide out after the arson attack on his wife's penthouse and the execution-style murder of John "Boy" Nadeau and Danny "Danno" Hanrahan, two other members of the Hummingbirds. Léo Lemire, the third member, and his wife are missing after their remote chalet was destroyed by fire.

Police divers are continuing to search for bodies in the lake. Lac des Larmes is one of the deepest bodies of water in the province.

When I finished reading. Jack and I stared at each other.

"A very sad ending," I said.

He nodded. "Except . . ."

"That Esme and I are not dead?"

"Exactly. Not only are you not dead but you were already in Woodbridge, where you started Kindergarten on April first."

"Your birthday!"

"I'll never forget. You were so small and perfect and I thought you were like a birthday present to me."

I blinked.

Jack continued. "That's a very real memory and so I am not likely to be mistaken."

"So this flight, loaded with items that made it look like Esme and I were on board, was a decoy."

"I think the whole thing was a setup."

"But the money and the diamond necklace . . ."

Jack shrugged. "Wouldn't that be a small price to pay for having Bobby "Bullets" O'Byrne and the cops think you and your family are at the bottom of Lac des Larmes?"

I inhaled and processed that thought. "I have to agree. So my father set it up. And then someone fired high-powered bullets at the plane to shoot it down?"

"What if he parachuted out and had an accomplice to fire at the plane just after he jumped? Your dad would have needed nerves of steel," Jack said.

"Look at how he made his living. He wasn't afraid of taking dangerous chances. I think it would be exactly the type of stunt Sean Doyle would love."

Montreal Daily News
April 12, 1995

> *The large sum of money found in a half-submerged suitcase at the edge of Lac des Larmes has been confirmed as part of the loot from the second-to-last Hummingbird Gang heist, according to La Sûreté du Québec. A nine-millimetre semiautomatic with the serial numbers removed was also located. Although some of their possessions have been located, including a child's clothing and toys, in addition to jewellery and the cash, the bodies of Sean "Shonnie" Doyle, his wife, Evelyn Acheson, and their five-year-old daughter have not been found despite a major search by SQ divers. While rumours that this was a mob hit are circulating, at the time of his death the twenty-eight-year-old Doyle was dodging a warrant for his arrest by Montreal police. With his reputation for reckless daring, police speculate that Doyle was making a run for it with his family before the police and the mob closed in on him. Police are also searching for the bodies of Léo Lemire and his wife, believed to have died when arsonists torched their remote chalet.*

"That's the accomplice," I said. "Léo Lemire."

"Of course, and we know that his wife, Lucie, was the woman you knew as Lola and she was already in Woodbridge too and not at all dead. They all planned to vanish. Once they were in a different country with new identities, they could get on with their lives."

"Disappearing with however much loot they had left over from the heist."

"With safe-deposit boxes, there will be no way to know how much was actually taken."

"I don't know what happened to Léo in the end. I never saw him or anyone like him at Lola's. I am guessing he was the man the neighbors said had died a while back."

Chapter 17

Always pack shoes that can handle whatever you encounter: cobblestones, steep stairs, long distances.

"City of spies," Jack said happily the next morning as we sat in the back of the cab heading into the center of Lisbon.

"That is the history of Lisbon, especially in the Second World War."

The cabdriver didn't react to this, not even a glance at us in the rearview mirror.

Jack said, "Behind every door there was double-dealing going on. It's sort of thrilling just thinking about it. Double agents, even triple agents."

I didn't even want to think about what a triple agent might be. "That was what Esme loved about the city, aside from the fact that it 'absolutely drips history and intrigue.' Her words."

"I wonder if there were quadruple agents?" Jack said.

"Maybe. It there were any of those anywhere, I suppose this would be a good place for them. It makes my skin crawl to imagine what it would have been like during the war."

"And before and afterward, in many parts of Europe. I wish I'd studied a bit more about that period and about Portugal. Too bad I got seduced by philosophy. Although many of the philosophers I studied had their ideas stolen and twisted in ways that led to wars."

"Esme claimed she always got the best ideas for plot twists on visits to Lisbon. And she said it was good exercise too. You can eat all the *pastel de nata* you wanted and never gain an ounce because you've climbed so many stairs just getting through the day."

The driver shot us a grin. "*Pastel de nata!* Very good," he said, giving us the thumbs-up. I would have preferred he kept his hands on the wheel, but you can't have everything.

With the help of a map, we managed to get set down in the older part of town. Our plan, which we didn't reveal in the hearing of the cabdriver, because you really do never know, was to find Carlos Pereira, Esme's former lover. We had not discussed that in the cab. Now here we were at a crossroad that led to a swirling network of ancient streets. Every path seemed to stagger up a ridiculously steep hill. I suppose it was lucky that there were so many stairs leading this way and that way up that same hill. Somewhere in that tangle of streets lined with centuries-old buildings, I hoped to find Carlos. I tried not to be distracted by the beautiful purple-blue blooms on the jacaranda trees that were starting to strut their stuff in the squares and parks. We were not tourists. We were on a life-and-death mission. First step: find Carlos, one of Esme's more congenial exes.

When I'd seen Carlos last, he had been maintaining a guest house and several Airbnbs. I knew from Esme that he'd also invested in renovating derelict properties with a plan to expand into online good-quality, short-term furnished apartment rentals. Esme had stayed in one on her last visit to Lisbon, but I couldn't remember where it was, a worrisome pattern for me. All I had was a memory of Carlos from seven or eight years earlier. He was handsome and laughing, holding court in his guest house breakfast room while a flock of British widows fluttered admiringly at surrounding tables. If I could find him, that would be the best connection to Esme. But where was he? I figured somewhere in Bairro Alto, one of the charming and historic parts on the hills of the city. I knew that the façades on these ancient buildings hid surprises and not always good ones.

I was glad I'd worn my sneakers. The traditional Portuguese pavement was made of small pieces of limestone and its relative, black basalt. Although they and their mosaic designs were gorgeous, I'd heard more than enough about them from Carlos on my last visit. They had quite a history and displayed amazing artistry, especially the ones in the Praça do Comércio, the grand square facing the harbor. I'd found the tiles treacherous when wet so I was grateful that it wasn't raining.

As we scanned the buildings, I was beginning to think that there were more restaurants here than in Paris. We turned off onto the jumble of side streets, only to find even more eateries tucked into alleyways, with chairs, tables and mostly red umbrellas already outside, although it was much too early for lunch.

"Are you hungry?" Jack asked hopefully.

"Let's find Carlos first. I think he was around here somewhere."

"Maybe we can get a bit of pizza and do a plan," Jack suggested. I figured his mind was more on pizza than plan, but I understood. I wasn't ready to stop just yet, having flown across Europe in a very indirect way to get here.

"His guest house had a blue door and I know it was around here somewhere. The name of the street was Duque or something like it."

"I think we just passed that, by that really nice-looking bakery," Jack said.

We turned and walked back up and along what seemed like dozens of streets, and sure enough, there was Duque. It seemed too easy and yet familiar.

I stumbled ahead, knowing that Jack was staring with longing at pastries in a bakery window. But at the end of the street, no blue door, no sign indicating *Guest House*. I turned and slumped back. "Nothing here."

Jack was chirpy. "But what about the other side?" Sure enough the street continued with a little jog on the opposite side of the cross street.

"You're tired," Jack said. "Have one of these sandwiches and you'll get your pep back. A few minutes isn't going to make a difference."

It was barely past breakfast time, but then again we hadn't had breakfast, a tough situation for Jack. We plunked ourselves at a small bistro table and chairs outside the hole-in-the-wall bakery, savored the aromas and studied what was on offer. Jack said, "I'm having a *bifana*, whatever that is."

"It's another Portuguese specialty. Strips of seasoned pork with spices and garlic on one of those beautiful crusty bread rolls. Yummy."

"Do you think one would be enough or should I get two? Those stairs really burn up the fuel."

"One would be plenty for you and I probably won't be able to finish mine so you can have that too. But if you're still hungry afterward, get another *bifana*."

"Good idea. I'll order it now."

I decided that I'd probably think more clearly with some food.

Jack arrived with our *bifanas* and squirted bright mustard on his, as the locals do.

"None for me," I said. But it was too late. And when in Rome, as they say. Jack had also brought beer, which the locals traditionally enjoy with these sandwiches. I stuck with bottled water. One of us had to be on our toes for when we met Carlos, or for whatever plan we adopted if we couldn't locate him. I always felt better when there were plans. I may have already mentioned that.

The sandwich was delicious, but I could only manage half. My stomach was knotted from the travel, the threat to Esme and worry about ending up with mustard stains on my jean jacket.

Jack cut into my thoughts. "Is it safe to contact this guy? How do you know that Carlos isn't connected with any of these people?"

That I was confident about. "Carlos has nothing to do with anyone in Canada or the U.S. Esme met him here, right in Lisbon. I was with her on that trip. I was a surly teenager, so I think she probably deserves some retrospective sympathy."

"Okay, if you're sure. You going to finish that sandwich?"

I pushed the remains of my *bifana* toward him. "We met him down on the waterfront. We were at an outdoor restaurant under red umbrellas on a beautiful sunny day with just the perfect breeze, and that same breeze picked up Esme's straw hat and blew it across the tables. Carlos rescued it. When he brought it to our table you could see the sparks flying between them. Of course, as a teenager, I was mortified. He found out where we were staying and courted Esme, over my objections. He was so handsome and urbane and nothing like any of the men that Esme had been seeing. His hobby was studying the espionage industry—his words—before and during World War Two. That's how I learned quite a bit about that era."

Jack was hooked by this kind of talk, as I knew he would be. He would like Carlos if we ever found him. They could discuss spies and pavement surfaces. "Carlos didn't have anything to do with the book world either. He could speak English fluently and read it, of course, because he was in business, but he didn't read novels in any language. He'd never heard of Esme before they met. She liked that. She could let her guard down with him. He was into music and had done a lot of producing and promoting. Esme had no interest in the music business, so they were even."

"The relationship didn't last?"

"Well, she didn't marry him."

"Did he ask her?"

"I think he did. Now I realize that her reluctance would relate to my father as well and all the turmoil that must have . . ." It suddenly occurred to me that Sean Doyle might be alive and that could account for Esme's inability to have a lasting relationship.

"So she said no?" Jack was intrigued by the story but more interested in the pastries in the window of the shop.

"Esme didn't always confide in me about her love life. I was glad of that at the time. Now I wish I knew more."

"We're confident about Carlos?"

"Yes. I trust him. And no one has any way of knowing we are here."

"Never mind. I'll still be keeping an eye out and watching behind us."

"I'm fine with that. History tells us that in this place, nothing is what it seems."

It didn't take long before we were ready to move on.

Sure enough, turning right instead of left onto a narrow, twisty street made all the difference. Halfway up, I spotted a *Guest House* sign, in English yet. The door was blue as I had remembered it. It was also locked. We looked around for a bell and finally just banged on it.

Nothing.

"I think Carlos makes all his arrangements online or by phone. He wouldn't be expecting any walk-in business."

"Let me google the guest house and see if there's contact information," Jack said.

Why hadn't I thought about that? Because I was tired and rattled, that's why.

Sure enough, while I leaned against the wall and watched people trudge up the many steps, Jack located a contact phone number. Before I could finish inputting it, he had called. Someone answered. "Ask for Carlos himself," I said.

I reached for the phone while we waited for Carlos to come on.

It was a thrill to hear his warm tones. It seemed like such a long time since we'd heard a friendly voice on this trip.

"It's Charlotte Adams, Carlos. I'm right outside. I need to speak to you."

The door clicked and Jack pushed it open. We headed up a well-worn narrow staircase. No two steps appeared to be tilting in the same direction. Traditional Portuguese blue and white tiles decorated the walls. On the second floor was a sign that said *Serviço*. Carlos's office was to the right, and to the left the cheerful breakfast room and lounge that I remembered. A slender middle-aged woman with wavy grayish blonde hair emerged from some mysterious back room and said, "Hello, Charlotte. I am Beatriz, the assistant of Carlos."

"Of course, I remember you, Beatriz."

"I remember you too, of course. Carlos asked if you would wait for him here for a minute." She spoke English quite well with a charming accent.

Many people in the tourism business in Lisbon can switch easily among four or five languages. "Please, sit and be comfortable." Beatriz's wide smile was probably her best feature. I remember that she put people at ease as soon as she flashed those pearly whites. Odd that she wasn't quite meeting my eyes this time.

We sat at a blue table with a small vase with fresh white carnations on an embroidered place mat. Beatriz said, "Would you like coffee?"

"Yes," I breathed. "Please."

Jack just nodded and went back to looking around, studying the interior of this ancient building.

"I bet parts of this building are three hundred years old," he said. "Maybe more."

Beatriz arrived quickly with the fragrant coffee, cream and sugar, two cups and a plate with large wedges of cake. She poured us each a cup of coffee and smiled. "I made a fresh pot. I will be in the office dealing with reservations, but please just knock if you need anything else. Carlos is on the phone. He reminded me that you love yogurt cake, so here are a few pieces. This one has Carlos's own homemade plum preserves as the filling."

Jack's eyes lit up. He'd probably never heard of yogurt cake before that minute but he was prepared for love at first bite.

"You look great, Beatriz."

She flashed the smile. "I have a young daughter now. It is a happy time."

I sipped my coffee. Fabulous. As anxious as I was to speak to Carlos, I wanted to savor every sip. I nibbled on a piece of the yogurt cake. If it hadn't been for the worry about Esme this would have been heaven.

Jack said, "Great cake. I wonder if it also comes in chocolate."

I was on my second cup of coffee and Jack was finishing his second wedge of yogurt cake when Carlos bounded through the door. "Charlotte!" His energy filled the room.

Carlos was still trim and handsome and, like Beatriz, he had aged a bit. His hair was now shot with silver on the sides. It looked good on him, the kind of hair a smart man would pay for. He was very European in his T-shirt, fitted leather bomber jacket and slim pants. He was a small man but we felt the warmth of his big personality. "Charlotte, this is wonderful. I had no idea you were coming. What can I do for you? If I had known, I could have had–"

I couldn't help smiling back at him. I think it was the flashing dark eyes and the coiled energy radiating from him. Five minutes with Carlos and you'd feel like you could move a mountain.

I said, "It's kind of short notice, an impulse on my part. Don't worry about us. I am trying to catch up with my mother and we seem to have gotten out of sync."

Carlos slid into a chair and twinkled at me. "She's a bit of a . . . what do you say . . . a whirlwind?"

"She sure is, though you are no one to talk."

Carlos chuckled and then nodded pleasantly at Jack. I said, "Excuse me, Carlos, this is, um, my friend Jack Reilly. He is helping me try to catch up with Esme before our European trip ends."

I trusted Carlos, but I wasn't taking a chance of giving away too much, especially in the city of spies.

"I wish I could help you, Charlotte. I had heard whispers that Esme has been in Lisbon, but, sadly, I haven't seen her for a few years now. I think she has been disappointed in me."

I could have told him that sooner or later Esme was disappointed in every man.

"Sorry to hear that. I was hoping you could give us a bit of help."

"She didn't get in touch on this trip. I suspect she's been back several times over the years since. She always loved Lisbon, but . . ." He shrugged. He was disappointed perhaps, but far from heartbroken. A man like Carlos would always have a lineup of women to console him. He and Esme were two of a kind really.

Beatriz arrived back with the rest of the yogurt cake as we had polished off the first batch. Jack beamed at her. She smiled tightly at him. Her eyes remained guarded though, something I didn't remember about Beatriz. Our bizarre trip was making me see strangeness and danger everywhere.

I said, "So Carlos, I was hoping you might remember some of her contacts in Portugal. I was only with her in Lisbon for a couple of short trips over the years and we didn't really meet many people except for you and Beatriz, but I know she has other friends."

I didn't really know that, but I was hoping.

Beatriz focused on straightening up the table and refilling the coffeepot. She seemed ill at ease, although I remembered her as relaxed and friendly.

She wasn't meeting my gaze. As I've gotten older, I have realized that people's moods and reactions most often come from whatever is going on in their own lives and aren't a reflection of their feelings about me. Even so, this made me curious.

Carlos shook his handsome head. "No one comes to mind. When we were together, it was just the two of us, if you know what I mean, except for the times when you came along."

"Mmm."

"But where are you staying? I will get in touch the minute anything comes to mind."

"Oh, well, we just arrived in Lisbon. We haven't found a place yet. It's all kind of seat of our pants until we catch up with Esme, and we'll decide what's what then."

Carlos laughed. "I like that expression. Seat of our pants! Do you need a place to stay in the meantime until you find Esme and decide? I can certainly put you up as long as you need. We're full here but, in Casa Pereira, there's room."

"That's a very kind offer, but I don't want to take advantage. I'm not even sure how long we'll be in Lisbon."

Jack shot me a glance of the "say yes to this great deal" variety.

Carlos grinned. "You wouldn't be taking advantage. For one thing, business has been slow and for another, I just had an English couple cancel at the last minute. They forfeited their fee and it's too late to rent out their space. It would be my honor and pleasure to put you up on their dime, as Esme likes to say. I love your American expressions."

Jack said, "Thanks. We need to crash a bit."

Casa Pereira was up about six more flights of outside stairs and around a half dozen corners and along one very claustrophobic alleyway. It was near the top of Bairro Alto and I figured Jack would have already burned off that cake. The building lay behind what looked like a pale green historical façade. A façade was what it turned out to be. Once you were through the massive wooden front door with its surprisingly modern security locks, everything was new, spotless and minimalist. Once again in Lisbon, things weren't what you thought. I figured Jack preferred the older buildings, but I was ready for a clean room, lavender-scented bath products, luxurious bedding and a fridge full of delicious cheese and fruit. I plunked on the bed for a minute to sort out my thoughts about next steps. When my eyes finally opened the sun was setting. Outside our window the Lisbon night was coming to life.

"I wasted the day!" I wailed.

Jack turned from the window and said, "There are at least four restaurants within one block."

"How can you think about food at a time like this?"

"You mean dinnertime?"

"Oh. Didn't we just eat those *bifanas* and all that yogurt cake?"

"That was hours ago before we walked up a million stairs and along who knows how many alleys and before you slept all day. I'm ravenous."

"There are snacks in the fridge. Ham, cheese, rolls. Fruit."

"Um."

"Really? You ate everything?"

"All this dashing around Europe brings out the hungry beast in me. We'd better hurry."

I knew there was no rush as the restaurants would start serving late. But I remembered Esme always used to say, 'Eat when you can. You never know what's coming.' She learned that from experience.

"Sure, Jack, but I can't believe you let me sleep all that time. I have things to do."

"It's been how long since you actually slept? You needed it. And now we're in this beautiful city with all this atmosphere. It seems that your mother is not here. And probably hasn't been, so we may as well enjoy a dinner and wine while we figure out our next steps in the great Esme hunt."

I couldn't come up with a good argument against enjoying dinner. We had hit a wall on our search for Esme. We needed to think and to talk and to plan our way forward.

While Jack paced hungrily, I freshened up. I put on my new blue silk shirt and the dark-wash jeans and slipped into my one pair of heels. Why not? We wouldn't be walking more than a few yards and it was nice to feel normal even if nothing was really normal. I twisted the celadon, blue and yellow silk scarf into a loop and put on the hummingbird earrings. I shoved our now revolting travel clothes into the washing machine and ran it so as not to waste any more time. No procrastinating. Who knew what the future held for our laundry?

Jack was right. There were four restaurants within steps of our door. Plus, around the first corner, tables lined the narrow road. Twinkle lights glittered on wires strung overhead for the diners. The night was surprisingly warm, even for late April, and haunting music ramped up the ambiance. I teetered on the rough surface so we settled into the first restaurant for dinner. Jack was excited about the seafood grill while I played it safe with *frango*, aka chicken. Jack made short work of the crusty Portuguese bread and salty butter on our table. He moved onto the small bowls of juicy olives. Our waiter spoke English. He'd learned it in Toronto, he informed us when asked. We heard him switch seamlessly to French, Italian and German depending on who was seated at what table.

I was almost relaxed when I saw a familiar face passing. Beatriz. She seemed lost in thought, her shoulders hunched, head down. Worried? I waved, but she didn't glance our way. "I'll be back," I told Jack. "I just need to ask Beatriz something."

When I caught up, she jumped.

"So sorry. We saw you passing and . . . I didn't mean to scare you."

"No, no. It's nothing."

I took a chance. "Something's obviously wrong. Can I help?"

She leaned against a wall and shivered. "Maybe I can help you. But you must promise not to tell Carlos."

I felt a tingle of alarm. "Not to tell Carlos what?"

"Promise first."

"Carlos has been so good to us and–"

She shrugged.

"Fine. I won't tell him whatever it is."

She glanced over her shoulder. "Esme is here, or she was. I saw her three days ago."

"But Carlos said he hadn't seen her."

"He didn't know she was in Lisbon. She was shocked to see me and she asked me not to tell anyone. I felt wrong about keeping it from him."

"I know what that's like."

"But I promised her. She looked . . ."

"What?"

Beatriz bit her lip. "She was afraid of something. Or someone."

"Not Carlos."

"Never Carlos! Esme said, 'I don't want him to get involved in this.'"

"Involved in what?"

"She did not say. But I think something very serious. Carlos would do anything for Esme."

"So she's afraid that whoever she's worried about could hurt Carlos too."

"And Carlos would jump right in with no concern for himself."

"Okay, but I need to know where you saw Esme, Beatriz."

"I must call home to say I'll be late and then I will show you. I didn't notice the street address but I will recognize it."

I was familiar with that approach.

"I'll get Jack to pay for what we've already eaten and we'll go."

"Jack can wait here. We won't be long."

Beatriz made a quick call to reassure her daughter and we paused at the restaurant. Beatriz spoke rapidly to our waiter in Portuguese and he nodded. She turned back to me and took my arm. "They will leave Jack in peace, and if you are not back soon, they will make up a box for you."

We hustled along another narrow street lined with outdoor cafés and colorful umbrellas. Music filled the air. The inevitable stairs lay ahead and I was regretting wearing my heels.

I was nearly breathless keeping up. Of course, Beatriz lived her life amid these winding streets, cobbled surfaces and steep stairs. Plus, she was already late and doing me a favor. I could hardly ask her to slow down. I promised myself a few extra pastries to make up for it.

After a half dozen sets of stairs followed by three or four rapid zigzags, we stopped abruptly at the base of a curved street. I almost plowed into Beatriz. Most houses were decorated with the traditional blue tiles, and what wasn't tiled was a lovely soft umber shade. Lush plants in large pots stood guard by the entrances. I noticed gates on the doors. "Is it here?" I asked.

"I don't want anyone watching to know which house it is. You understand."

It took everything in my power to remain calm. "But you saw Esme come here?"

"She looked quite different. Her hair was dark and curled. But there is something about the way she holds herself, you know. Anyway, I was surprised, because Esme usually stays in one of Carlos's properties, but that was not my affair. Carlos would think it was his business though. Perhaps there is another man?"

"Did you speak to her?"

"She jumped when I called her name. She pretended to point out directions as if I was a stranger. She was afraid of someone, but she didn't want me to know."

That rang true.

Esme would never want anyone to know she was afraid.

"She *is* in danger and I really need to know where she went."

"She went through the third door down. The one with the best plants and the little balconies above. The name on the door is Salazar."

"Salazar," I repeated. That was a historic name in Portugal but also not uncommon.

"I will leave you here and go home the other way. Pretend I am instructing you and giving directions." Beatriz's dark eyes glittered in the dim light and I felt the hair rise on my arms. "In case."

"Sure." Beatriz did a very dramatic job of showing an alternative route back to the restaurant with elaborate hand gestures. I nodded equally dramatically. But I wondered if I could trust her. She had led me to a seemingly deserted street. Had it just been a fluke that she passed by when we were eating? Or was this a setup? As Beatriz vanished around the corner, I reminded myself of my promise not to take stupid chances. I texted Jack the address and told him that Esme had been seen there. I squared my shoulders and prepared to confront Esme's latest lover, apparently called Salazar, like the late dictator. I was glad that the traditional iron lights attached to some of the buildings illuminated the deserted roadway. On this street they all seemed to have the symbol of Lisbon, a sailing ship with two ravens.

• • •

The deep teal-blue door with the grille over it was so beautiful that I almost forgot my worrying quest. I could drool over charming Lisbon once we'd found Esme.

No one answered the little bell. I stood anxiously switching from foot to foot. Restlessness and the start of blisters. With nothing to lose, I banged on the door. I waited. I banged again, imagining L. Salazar: Large black mustache? Flashing eyes? Esme always had a thing for flashing eyes. She wasn't big on mustaches though, so I wasn't sure where that thought had come from. After the third time banging, I thought I heard footsteps. I drew myself up to my full height.

The teal door creaked open slowly, revealing a willowy woman with a silver streak on each side of the dark hair that reached her collarbone. Her green eyes glittered. She reminded me of a panther, smooth, lithe and dangerous. She was closing in on fifty, but if she lived to one hundred she would probably still have that wild feline beauty. Esme would have enjoyed meeting her. This woman would have turned up in a book at some point, disguised just enough that she wouldn't recognize herself, seeming more like a leopard perhaps or even a tiger.

"Boa noite, senhora." It never hurts to say good evening. "I'd like to speak to Senhor Salazar please."

The willowy woman laughed out loud. "Would you?" Her silver filigree hoops gleamed in the glow from the streetlight. Her black dress was obviously silk.

I faltered a bit. She was very cool. She spoke English perfectly. His sister perhaps? "Yes."

"There is no senior Salazar here."

"Oh. But–"

She raised a dark curved eyebrow and waited.

"I am looking for this woman and I know she has been here."

A flicker of interest crossed her face as I pulled out my phone and showed the photo of Esme and me. Her eyes locked on to the image and then searched my face.

Was I going to have to push my way through this door? Luckily, it didn't come to that. She glanced up and down the street, twice, even checking the surrounding balconies. But unlike the rest of lively Lisbon, there was nothing happening on this street. "You'd better come in." She stood back and I eased into a cool white foyer with a spectacular black and white tiled floor and an elaborate plaster ceiling. The heavy door creaked and closed behind me.

"This way." I did my best not to gawk as I followed her into a large living room. In this historic house, I'd been expecting dark rooms, heavy wooden furniture with dusty brocade upholstery, items that had been with the

Salazar family for a century or more. Instead, the walls were ten-feet high and those at each end painted bright white. The trim on the long narrow windows was also painted white. Impressive green plants showed well against the walls. Two pearl-gray leather sofas faced each other on opposite sides of a massive wrought iron and glass coffee table. Oversized books were stacked four high in various piles on it and a huge modern crystal ashtray sat on one stack. I tried not to check the titles.

One wall was sandblasted brick, the opposite covered by a custom bookcase. Unframed canvasses hung on the brick wall. Some hung from wire holders and I caught sight of vivid red and gold splashes, full of emotion and meaning, although I had no idea what that meaning might be. In contrast to the modern furniture, an ornate antique desk had pride of place on the brick wall along with the paintings. The tall thin windows looked out on an interior courtyard, invisible to the street. If I hadn't been scared to death, I would have wanted to move in.

She gestured to the sofa. "Sit down."

I sat.

"Would you like a glass of port?"

Not likely.

I shook my head. "I just need information. I won't take much of your time. Mr. Salazar is . . . ?"

She sighed. "I suppose I am Mr. Salazar. You may call me Leonor."

"Oh." Where had I gotten the idea that L. Salazar was a man? Probably because of Esme's tendencies. "I apologize. My mother was seen to visit this house and I need to find her."

"Your mother?"

"Yes. Esme Adams. I am with her in the photo. I should warn you that people know I am here."

She threw back her head and laughed. "Well, Charlotte, I'll try to keep you safe in that case."

"How do you know my name?"

"Like you, I have my sources. Esme is not here."

"But I know she *was*."

"You have been misinformed."

Had Beatriz misled me? Unlikely. Leonor knew my name. I turned away and stared at the bookcase trying to get my emotions under control. There were books in Portuguese, Spanish, French and English. Most of them looked very serious and heavy-duty. At the end of a low shelf, a few familiar-looking spines. To my surprise, Esme Adams works had a place of pride on these shelves. Every one of her books was lined up proudly. Including the latest one, *What Lies Beneath the Dark Hills.* The one that was about to be released. A few weeks earlier, Esme had sent me an image of the cover and had asked what I thought of the bright blue. She hadn't been happy. But then she was never satisfied with her covers. She must have received her author copies before she left. She would have brought a few as gifts for friends in Europe. She liked to give signed first editions of the hardcover. The books would be much harder to get here in Europe, not her main English market.

I stood up and pulled out the copy. "Yes. This is her latest book."

Her mouth tightened. "That means nothing. I was able to order a copy. I have been waiting for it."

"Nope. It's not actually available yet." I flipped it open and checked the title page. Sure enough. "To Leonor, with admiration." I raised my right eyebrow. "So don't you think it's time to tell me the truth?"

She stared at me flintily. I stared back, trying to match her flintiness.

Finally I tried again. "The truth?"

"Fine. Esme needs to be unimpeded. No one should be on her trail. Especially you."

"What do you mean, especially me?"

She gave me a smile that was equal parts pity and condescension. "You will put yourself at risk and you will also expose Esme to danger. Is that what you want?"

I sputtered, "Of course it isn't. But—"

"So, be a tourist here. Enjoy Lisbon." She glanced at my feet. "Maybe not in those shoes."

"You need to tell me where Esme is."

"Let me be clear. You must stop this quest. You will do more harm than good."

"My mother is on her own and people are pursuing her. What do you know about them?"

She shrugged. "I don't know anything about them. She didn't say a word on who she was avoiding."

"Avoiding! This is way beyond avoiding. These people are dangerous."

"That may be, but I have no idea who they are." Her dark eyes glittered. She was a woman who enjoyed a challenge. Her foot tapped ever so slightly, so I figured she wanted this to be over.

I said, "Have you considered that you might also be in danger?"

"Don't be ridiculous."

"I found you. And if I did then they might find you too. Her other friend who was so good at keeping secrets was murdered and her house burned. Did she tell you that?"

She turned her head away. "Nobody knew she'd come." I wondered if she was planning to bean me with the crystal ashtray.

I shook my head. "Wrong."

We both jumped at a hammering at the door. Had Leonor called for reinforcements? A glance at her white face told me she hadn't. The banging continued. It sounded like the very solid door could be battered open. She reached into the desk drawer and pulled out a gun. It was slim and elegant-looking, but all the same, alarmingly lethal. Leonor moved toward the front door and a security camera and peered at it. I did too and gasped.

I said, "It's okay, he's with me."

My jaw dropped as she unlocked the door, opened it and raised the weapon.

I flung myself at her, pushing hard and yelling, "Look out! She's got a gun."

A shot rang in my ears. Jack tumbled through the door and landed with a splat on the beautiful tiles.

Chapter 18

You can never do too much research for a trip.

"Have you lost your mind?" Leonor said, sticking her elegant head out the door to look around and then pulling it in again and engaging the lock. The gun dangled from her hand. "Look what you've done to my ceiling."

A bit of antique plaster fluttered down from the ornate ceiling.

"What were you thinking?"

"You were going to shoot Jack."

Jack picked himself up and glared at the gun. He hates being shot at.

"Is this Jack? Why would I shoot him?"

"Why did you pull out the gun?"

"And as you said, there are some dangerous people, possibly following Esme and you. I didn't want one of them to push his way through."

"But I told you."

Leonor glanced up at the ceiling and frowned. "I suppose that can be fixed."

Jack brushed bits of plaster from his Hawaiian shirt and stared sadly at the containers with our boxed-up dinner. "I missed some relevant background information."

"Jack, this is Leonor Salazar. She knows Esme, and although she claimed that Esme had not been here on this visit, this turned out to be incorrect."

Jack nodded, as if he might have been expecting that. "It's very nice to meet you, Senhora Salazar."

She nodded graciously. "I am attempting to discourage Charlotte from pursuing Esme and putting her in danger."

"I gather you don't know Charlotte very well," Jack said. "You might as well tell her what she wants to know."

Leonor pointed the way back to the salon. "Can you excuse me a minute please? I need to phone my neighbor and tell her not to worry about any noise she may have heard. Make yourselves comfortable." I would have bolted, but she entered the salon and slipped the weapon back into the drawer of the elaborate desk. I guess she wasn't worried about us shooting her.

Following a quick phone conversation, she returned. "Let me offer you a glass of wine and a bite of cheese. I feel that we got off on the wrong foot."

That was putting it mildly.

"I have some nice bread and olives."

I was about to decline, but Jack said brightly, "That sounds excellent."

Maybe this could work for me. "Why don't you give Leonor a hand in the kitchen, Jack."

They blinked in unison.

"Jack has a thing for olives and cheese. He'd really love to see what you would have in your authentic Portuguese kitchen."

Jack said, "You have different kinds of olives? Awesome."

Leonor seemed to stifle a sigh. "Come along then," she said, beginning her panther prowl out of the room. "Have a seat, Charlotte. We'll be right back."

Jack was saying, "How many kinds of cheese would you have on hand as a rule?"

I shot right out of my chair. On the third shelf from the bottom of the bookcase, I'd spotted a clump of books, pamphlets and maps. That clump had bothered me throughout my chat with Leonor before Jack arrived. After snatching Esme's book off the shelf at the opposite end, I hadn't found a way to check out this discordant element in the otherwise immaculately organized bookshelves. The messy area contained a few guidebooks, some maps and scraps of paper with scribbles. They looked like they'd been hastily stuffed onto the shelf. I pulled them out one by one and took shots of each item with my phone. I stuffed it all back and barely made it to my chair in time. Leonor led the parade into the room. She leaned over the dramatic coffee table and set down a large ornate silver tray, three crystal glasses, an open bottle of *vinho tinto* and a bowl of big, juicy olives. Jack was carrying a wooden board with some soft cheese along with a knife and a small basket of crusty bread. He was already lost to me.

"Let me pour," I said. "Barging in like this, I should really do something. I think Jack is also quite taken with your library."

"I am," Jack said. "It's heavy on philosophy and history."

"Yes. My two great loves." She smiled as if she meant it.

I was never going to get him out of here at this rate. I poured the wine and distributed the glasses randomly. If there was something dangerous in the bottle, we were all going to sip it. If there was something in one of the glasses, any one of the three of us could end up with it. Leonor paid no attention.

"And two of mine," Jack said. He grinned at me. Not too subtly.

She sank into a leather chair and smiled her panther smile. I tried to relax. Who had she really called? Were we about to be surrounded by thugs? I decided that if she tried anything, I would reach for the desk drawer and snatch up the gun.

Jack announced, "Did you know there are seven varieties of olives in Portugal?"

"I didn't," I said tightly.

"Leonor seems to have plenty of each."

"Mmm." Have I mentioned that I do not care for olives?

"These little dark ones are *galega*. They're kind of sweet and fruity. I plan to try them all."

"Good for you, Jack."

"You'll love the cheese." He seemed to have picked up on my mood. "Try the Azeitão. It is deliciously creamy. Spread a bit on a piece of bread and tell me what you think."

Leonor studied us as if Jack and I could be just as tasty as any olives or cheese. "I am enjoying Jack's enthusiasm. I think I am missing that sort of thing in my life. You are turning our strange little meeting into a party."

Strange little meeting? Did she mean her refusing to help me find my mother? Or did she mean pulling out that gun?

I said, "We really should be heading off soon. Jack will polish off that whole tray otherwise and we have our dinner waiting for us." I didn't mention that the dinner was in boxes inside of the bags on the floor and was probably not going to be at its best by the time we staggered up the hills and stairs to our apartment.

Jack raised his wineglass and said, "*Saúde.*"

Leonor said, "*Saúde*" too. I muttered something like it and tried not to roll my eyes. I wanted to get back to check out the information I had taken pictures of.

Luckily, it doesn't take Jack long to hoover up a tray of food. I was starving too and managed to eat two pieces of very good Portuguese bread spread with the creamy Azeitão. It was to die for, although I hoped not literally.

Jack said, "Leonor is a history professor."

She said with a deep nod, "I am retired now, of course."

"How did you meet Esme?" I asked.

The green eyes glittered. "A few years ago, she approached me when she was doing research for one of her novels. It had to do with spies in Lisbon during World War Two. A fascinating topic. She wove it into *A Gift for the Hidden* with great skill and talent. I think Esme has a gift for the hidden. And you know how she loves a twist at the end."

Indeed she did. *A Gift for the Hidden* was the title of one of Esme's best-selling books.

Jack stopped his amiable chatter and said, "Her gift for the hidden has become really dangerous."

I added, "It might be the gift that gets her killed, so please tell us what you know."

She shook her elegant head.

I said, "We need to protect her."

"Have you stopped to consider that she doesn't want you to?"

"It doesn't matter what she wants. Dangerous people are pursuing her and they're getting closer. She can't be left on her own."

"You are wrong about that," Leonor said.

"I don't think so," Jack said, scooping up a couple of olives in case we wore out our welcome.

"Here is why you are wrong." She leaned forward.

Jack and I leaned forward too.

"You are worried that the people pursuing Esme will harm her. But the problem is that you have it backward."

"What?" we said in unison.

"Perhaps Esme is the one in pursuit of someone. Perhaps they should be worried. I don't for a minute think that poor little Esme is without allies. She is very capable of finding her prey and then . . ." She shrugged in a perfect expression of feline languor. But I could sense tension behind the pretence.

Leonor was worried too.

"Well," I said, gathering my bag. "You have been very kind and helpful. We've had quite a hectic twenty-four hours and we have to be getting back."

"Can you give me your address? I'll let you know if there is anything useful to tell."

"Absolutely. I'll text it to you."

In your dreams I will, I thought. I had no intention of letting her know how to find us.

Jack looked longingly at the rest of the cheese, but I stood up. He must have figured that I meant business because he unbent out of the chair.

After a flurry of phony goodbyes, Jack picked up our dinner containers and we found ourselves on the deserted street again. I turned in the opposite direction from our accommodations high in Bairro Alto.

He said, "Are we throwing someone off our trail?"

"Exactly. I think if we duck in and out of these alleys and little streets we can still find our way home."

Jack's eyes lit up. He loved that idea. He walked confidently and I limped after him around and around and up and up and up. Just when I thought I'd have to go barefoot on the streets of Lisbon, I spotted our building.

"I didn't recognize the approach. You did well," I said with relief.

Jack said, "I thought it was better to come up from the back, just in case someone was keeping an eye out for us near the restaurant. Did you think we could trust Leonor?"

I shivered. "I wish I did."

• • •

Back in the apartment, Jack reheated our cold food while I soaked my feet in the tub with the Epsom salts and concentrated on the photos I'd taken of the materials on Leonor's bookshelf.

Jack called out, "Dinner will be ready soon. And after we eat, let's plan what we'll do in Lisbon tomorrow." I smiled. Jack knows that making a plan usually cheers me up.

"Bad news on that front," I said, drying my tender feet, rubbing on soothing cream and hobbling to the table. "You need to see what I found on Leonor's bookshelf."

"Can it wait until we eat?"

I decided it could. Jack was showing a lot of domestic talent on this trip. He had set the table and even added napkins. He'd poured us each a glass of *vinho tinto* and lit some candles. This time we could enjoy them and not just use them as a decoy. Even reheated, our dinner looked surprisingly appetizing.

"Everything looks great, Jack, but I'm not really hungry after our stressful night."

Jack eyed my plate with interest, but he did the right thing. "Didn't Esme once tell you to eat when you got the chance because you never knew when you'd get another opportunity?"

"She also told me never to invest too much emotional capital in a man, but I pick and choose from her advice."

"Huh."

Before Jack could say "You finished with that *frango*?" I ate enough to keep myself going.

Somehow Jack had snagged some flan or what I would have thought of as crème caramel. I wasn't sure how it managed to get from the restaurant without turning into scrambled eggs in its little plastic containers, after being dropped on the floor at Leonor's and its long slow trip uphill to our table. It still looked perfect.

"If I can't have ice cream with chocolate chunks in it, then this is definitely the solution."

Jack paused, his spoon halfway to his mouth. "Why can't you have ice cream?"

"Because we don't have any."

"We can always get some. There's a Santini not too far from here. Everyone says their ice cream is the best. Let's go."

"First, let me finish swallowing our first dessert before you add another, and second, I'm not walking anywhere." I could almost hear my feet saying *Move us and lose us.*

"You don't have to come. Relax. Check in with the gang at home or close your eyes. I'll be back soon."

I hobbled to the door behind him. "There's lots of flan left. You bought more than enough. Why are you doing this?"

Jack turned and said, "Because your feet hurt and you love ice cream. And I love you."

It's not like the two of us to be mushy so we left it at that.

I said, "We have to take the first plane out. I've figured out where Esme went when she left Lisbon."

"Where are we going?" Jack said as he opened the door and we both screamed.

Carlos joined the choir. He yelped and stared around wildly.

"You startled us, Carlos."

"I startled *you*? Why are we screaming?"

"Never mind. What can we do for you?"

"I wanted to see if you were all right."

"My feet are killing me but aside from that, I'm fine."

Carlos blinked. Jack hesitated. I could tell that he'd decided not to leave me with Carlos while he hunted down the nearest Santini.

Carlos said, "Don't let me keep you, Jack."

"I was just checking that the lock was working," Jack responded.

I hobbled back to the small sofa and sank into it with a sigh. "Would you like a bit of flan and a glass of wine?"

"Wouldn't say no to either. Join me?"

"I still have one of each going."

"You stay there," Jack said to me, then, "*Vinho tinto*, Carlos?"

"Excellent."

Carlos accepted his glass of red wine graciously and settled back in his chair, every inch the suave man around Lisbon. "I saw you in the Alfama earlier, Charlotte. I tried to catch up but I couldn't find you anywhere."

"It's such a maze there. I think I was moving like a drunken fly, a bit panicky."

He smiled seductively. "But you found Leonor Salazar's place with no problem?"

I would have denied it but Carlos's eyes glittered knowingly.

"Yes."

Carlos took a sip. "Very nice, if I do say so myself."

I took a sip of mine and tried to match his relaxed body language.

"You cannot trust Leonor Salazar. She is . . . not what she seems."

"She seems like a retired professor of history," Jack said.

Carlos laughed. "Yes, she is that, but much more. You should be careful."

"I'm not sure what you mean."

Carlos shrugged in that way European men do. "She could have given you wrong information."

"She didn't give us any information."

"Not a scrap," Jack said, "although she did have some very good olives and cheese."

"And fantastic bread," I added. "Wine too, of course. Not as good as this, mind you."

Carlos spread his arms without spilling a drop. "You are here in Portugal. It's the least you can expect. But along with snacks, she must have told you something."

"Like what?" Jack said.

While Carlos turned toward Jack, I scanned his form-fitting leather jacket for any lump or bump that might indicate a weapon.

"I imagine like where Esme is." Carlos flashed his charming smile again.

"We asked. Several times and various ways, but she denied that she had seen Esme and made it clear she had no idea."

"And you believed her?"

"Why wouldn't we?" Jack said.

I broke first, "So how did you know that we had been there?"

There were only a few possibilities: Either Carlos had followed me and Beatriz. Or—and I hated this idea—Beatriz had told him, after first warning me not to tell him I was visiting Leonor. A shiver ran down my spine. Could Carlos have seen Beatriz and forced her to tell him where I was going?

Carlos said, with a smug smile, "I know a lot of people all over Lisbon, but especially in Bairro Alta, Chiado, and the Alfama. I just made inquiries. When I was near Leonor's, one of her neighbors told me they heard a gunshot."

"A gunshot?" Jack could play the game as well as anyone.

"Yes, just as a man matching your description collapsed into the house."

Jack said. "That might have been a vehicle backfiring. Or firecrackers perhaps. It startled me so much that I fell in when Senhora Salazar opened the door."

"My mistake."

"An understandable one, Carlos," I said. "But I don't think you get a lot of gunfire here. Am I wrong?"

"We suffer badly from pickpockets, not gun crime. But I need to make sure you are not in danger or planning anything . . ." He glanced around, apparently trying to chose between *foolish* and *unwise*.

I said, "Tell me about Leonor Salazar."

He sighed. "She looks like a cultured and sophisticated professor, doesn't she?"

Jack and I nodded.

Carlos said, "Of course. But dig into her family and you will see she is no aristocrat."

"Interesting," I said. "To tell the truth, I didn't care for Leonor Salazar. A bit too superior for my liking."

"That is it," Carlos said, "and inappropriate if you consider her background."

"Don't tease me, Carlos!"

His grin lit up his face. "I do like to tease you but the truth is not so amusing. The Salazar father and uncles were involved in the criminal business of providing false documents for people who wished to, say, disappear."

Jack said, "Disappear for their own safety?"

"More often to avoid arrest or prison."

"That is interesting," I said.

Jack butted in, "But Leonor is not her father nor her uncles."

"What do they say in your culture? The apple doesn't fall far from the tree?"

"Fine for apples," Jack said, warming to the idea of a bit of debate, "but I can't say I'm prepared to believe she is a criminal."

Carlos admired his manicure briefly and then turned to Jack. "It is common knowledge that she keeps her hand in with the family traditions. Perhaps this was why Esme wanted to see her."

"But we don't know that Esme saw her." I hoped my nose didn't suddenly begin to grow.

"These neighborhoods are like small towns really. Not much happens without someone noticing."

Jack raised his eyebrows. "Did someone see Esme visit her?"

"There is always talk in Lisbon," Carlos said with a shrug.

I said, "We need certainty. Leonor said she hadn't seen Esme and we had no reason to doubt her."

Carlos flashed his winning smile. "And you didn't think Esme might have needed documents so that she could, what do you say, fly under the radar?"

Jack managed to look shocked. Perhaps he'd missed a career on the stage. "Are you suggesting that Esme would buy false documents? She's hardly a criminal."

"But perhaps she wishes to disappear for her own reasons."

I was quiet during all this. I hoped my mother wasn't a criminal, but I now knew she'd been involved with a gang. She went into hiding rather than go to the police about whatever was going on. And in fact, we both lived under other people's names. So it wouldn't have surprised me at all if Esme wanted new and different documents. I had no intention of telling any of this to Carlos.

"Well, that's an interesting theory, Carlos," I said, "but it's not much use to us. We have figured out that Esme wants to be by herself and we have decided that we have to accept that and head home."

"Head home? But you just got to Lisbon! Aren't you going to stay and see the sights?"

"We've both seen them before, Carlos. We've left a big renovation project behind and Jack's business needs his attention right now. And this thing with Esme has taken the fun out of our trip anyway. We'll come back when we're feeling more relaxed."

"And less broke," Jack said.

"In fact, we were just about to get ice cream from Santini's and then book our flights home."

Jack nodded, although this was news to him.

"Please allow me to take you to the airport." Carlos loves that sort of thing. "It would be my pleasure."

"Thank you. We'll let you know when we've got a booking and see if the time works for you."

"You have my number?"

"Of course. I put it in my phone when we were at the guest house.

Carlos got to his feet, smiling sadly. "I must go. Never a quiet evening in the hospitality business. I hope you'll get a chance to enjoy some Fado before you fly away. You could still go tonight."

I didn't think I could really cope with the traditional mournful musical genre that has its roots here. I knew better than to say that to Carlos. I'd been to more than enough Fado houses with him and Esme back in the day.

I gave him a hug. "We'll try."

"The next time let me know before you come, Charlotte. And you too, Jack. I will line up some unique experiences for you. And an even better place to stay."

"Can't wait, Carlos," I lied.

"And please come for breakfast at the guest house tomorrow. Beatriz and I will make up something special for our last meal together."

Why did that sound so ominous?

"Thanks so much, Carlos. We'd love that, wouldn't we, Jack."

Jack produced a wide grin as the talk was of food.

Once Carlos headed out, Jack watched from the window. "I saw him turn the corner. Do you feel safe if I get the ice cream now?"

"Yup. I'll be busy booking."

"It'll be good to get home."

For sure, it would have been wonderful to get back to our dogs, our friends and our ruined home, but I couldn't tell Jack where we were actually going. Carlos owned this unit and he had keys to it. I wanted to trust Carlos, but I couldn't take a chance. For all I knew, he could have planted an audio bug or worse, a camera, in the unit.

"Make sure there's chocolate in that ice cream!"

Chapter 19

Always do your homework: check out your airport and the terminal you'll be departing from. You don't want any last-minute hitches.

Carlos opened his arms to welcome us to breakfast. You would have thought it was a wedding feast. He looked his suave self, this time in a gray fitted leather jacket and jeans. He pointed to a table in the window. Fresh carnations decorated the table, pink this time. Carnations are an important flower in Portugal, getting plenty of respect. A platter of cheeses and ham waited for us, with slices of fresh pears along the edge. Carlos poured freshly squeezed orange juice for us. It did smell fantastic. If only I wasn't quite so nervous.

"Beatriz is ready to prepare the eggs and sausage if you wish them."

Behind Carlos, Beatriz seemed pale and furtive. Was she worried about what I might have told Carlos? I smiled at her and gave her a little wave.

"Can you do scrambled, please?" I asked.

Jack said, "Mmm, with toast. And sausage. This is great."

Carlos arrived back with another blue-flowered cake stand, this one holding several pieces of yogurt cake. Jack's eyes lit up.

Beatriz skirted the table when she deposited our plates, carefully not making eye contact. Dark circles under her eyes suggested she hadn't slept at all.

Carlos chattered away throughout. "I have a meeting after this but I have arranged a driver for you."

"No need to do that, Carlos. We–"

He held up a hand. "I insist."

That created a small problem but I accepted with thanks. Just one more challenge.

Beatriz carefully wrapped up large pieces of yogurt cake, mostly for Jack. I couldn't imagine ever eating again. Carlos said, "We got you some treats. Heard you liked them." I reached for a *pastel de nata* with a smile on my face.

Shortly after, we were bundled into a large dark car driven by Joao. Carlos had already headed out but Beatriz was in charge of getting us into the car without forgetting anything. I had to bite my tongue. Jack and I were seasoned travelers, even if I didn't care for it and he had never made a list in his life.

Beatriz leaned in as she helped put our cases in the trunk. "I am sorry," she whispered. She pulled back before I could ask her what she was sorry about.

"Don't worry," I said.

I wondered if she had told Carlos about my visit to Leonor Salazar's home. And if so, why. Was there something else I should have known about that visit? But it had all ended well, so I hoped I had nothing to worry about.

The driver dropped us at Terminal 1 and made sure we got inside. I gave him a nice tip. He protested politely but finally accepted it. As soon as he was out of sight, we hustled ourselves to the shuttle to Terminal 2 and the flight we were *really* taking.

• • •

We were in plenty of time for our flight, leaning back in the blue molded chairs in Terminal 2 in Portela Airport. I was rigid with tension and Jack was digesting the latest news.

"So we're not going home?"

"Eventually, but not yet. I found some maps and documents at Leonor's, as I said before. She'd hidden them in the bookcase. It was very out of keeping with her immaculate shelves."

"But you said they indicated Esme was heading to the USA."

"That was for Carlos's benefit, which is actually for our benefit because I don't know if we can trust him, or anyone else for that matter."

"Who else can't we trust? You definitely didn't trust Leonor Salazar."

"Correct. But also, and I couldn't tell you this because I thought the apartment might be bugged. Remember I wrote that on the note I slipped you before you left?"

"I might not have actually read it."

"You were distracted by the ice cream, I realize. I knew I could fill you in once we were through security here."

"Right. And that's why Carlos told his driver to drop us at Terminal One?"

"Exactly. But I'd done my homework and I knew we could get to

Terminal Two with the bus. All the cheap airlines depart from here. The overseas flights would all be from Terminal One."

"You hugged Carlos like he was your oldest friend."

"You are my oldest friend. I hugged Carlos like he was a man who didn't need to have his suspicions aroused."

"Okay."

"There's a good reason we are in Terminal Two waiting for a Ryanair flight. But I didn't get a chance to tell you. I believe Esme was going to head for Piedmont."

"So Carlos will let down his guard because he thinks we've given up and gone home? And because we're not sure if Carlos is a good guy or a bad guy?" Jack said.

"I've always liked him, but right now, I only trust you."

"It's a lot of responsibility," Jack said with a grin. "I'll try to live up to it."

"I'll hold you to that. Check out my phone: I took photos of everything on that shelf when you were off on your olive safari with Leonor. I found information about trains and car rentals in Northern Italy and there's stuff about Cinque Terre."

"Cinque Terre? But those towns are in Liguria."

"Clever boy."

"I've never been. Always spent my time in the classical cities like Florence, Rome and Venice. And Verona, of course. Turin is in Piedmont and I've always wanted to go there."

"But we're not touring. We're trying to track down Esme."

"So scratch Turin?"

"Unfortunately. As I think I mentioned, Esme's ex-husband Alessandro has a winery in Piedmont. But Esme had a 'friend' in Cinque Terre too."

"And you believe we'll find her?"

"The documents at Leonor's point the way, although Esme's capable of laying more than one false trail. However, she had no way to know I'd end up there. I suspect Esme did use Leonor to get new ID for her trip. For sure, she'll be traveling as someone else."

"Do you believe Carlos about Leonor's family 'business'?"

"I did recall a couple of trips ago Esme consulting with someone in Lisbon about false documents and slipping across borders undetected, ostensibly research for her book."

"You didn't let on to Carlos. But didn't he really care for her?"

"Oh, sure. And she threw him over. He might feel just the tiniest bit of resentment and someone could have gotten to him. All to say, just in case, we're giving him the slip."

"Okay. I'll follow your lead."

"I've booked us on the noon flight to Linate in Milan. I couldn't get any flights that worked from Genoa. But that's fine. I've arranged to rent a car."

"You're going to drive in Italy? When you haven't slept in a week?"

"I've slept."

"Not enough. You have huge circles under your eyes and you're very—"

"I do not have circles under my eyes! And I am not very—"

"Grouchy."

"I'm perfectly capable of navigating the roads in Italy and, unlike you, I know the way, but I'll get both of our names put on the rental."

"Good."

"Regardless of cost," I snapped. True, I was sleepy, although I wasn't pleading guilty to grouchy. Jack loved to drive, so I'd booked us a Fiat 595 Abarth with GPS and back-up camera. The rental agent swore that it was roomy enough for any tall man and more fun than any of the other choices, which were all unavailable anyway because of something I didn't really understand. I was about to pass on this information, but by then Jack had lost interest and was busy strategizing about future food opportunities.

I picked up a good bottle of port and some beautiful locally made candles for Alessandro since we were going to be descending on him without warning.

On the flight, I read and reread the documents from Montreal, including this last one.

Montreal Daily News
April 15, 1995

> *Rumours continue swirling in the Quebec underworld that the Hummingbird Gang made a big mistake with their daring robbery of safety deposit boxes from the Bank of Montreal on rue St. Henri. Anonymous sources say that multiple safety deposit boxes belonging to an unnamed gangland figure were*

> *taken in the heist. The boxes contained large sums of money, jewellery and incriminating documents. Two of the Hummingbirds have been found shot execution-style. Léo Lemire and his wife are believed to have been murdered in their remote chalet and their bodies hidden in the woods. Sean "Shonnie" Doyle is presumed dead, along with his family, after his four-seater Cessna was apparently shot down on the edge of Lac des Larmes.*

"Unnamed gangland figure," I said. "Bobby 'Bullets' O'Byrne."

"Recently released from prison, by strange coincidence."

"Yes. Just when all this started up and Esme went missing and our home was trashed and Lola murdered. Let's hope they don't figure out we're heading for Italy."

For the rest of the flight I worried about Glenda. There was no news on her and I hoped the O'Byrnes hadn't done their worst. I fretted about Lola's death too. Who else had died in her home? Was it one of the O'Byrnes? Or someone close to Lola?

While I worried, Jack had been dozing. Suddenly his eyes popped open. "I wonder what started all this?"

"What do you mean?"

"These villains must have believed that Esme, you and Lola were all dead until just this year. And then somehow they learned you were alive in Woodbridge."

"And through me, they found Lola." I couldn't shrug off the guilty weight of Lola.

"Not your fault, Charlotte."

"And I am beginning to wonder if my father is also alive and they have figured that out. It would explain a lot."

"I'd put money on it."

That gave me plenty to think about on our otherwise uneventful flight to Milan.

• • •

Jack and I both loved arriving in Italy, once we got through the airport and the car rental bureaucracy and out onto the Autostrada. I commented that while the autostrada was like any interstate in the U.S., we could look forward to some great vistas ahead of us, on the A4. Before I could expand on this, I drifted off and Jack was left alone with the GPS and his thoughts of Italian food.

I jerked awake as we drove up to the impressive iron gate at the front of the even more impressive hilltop villa. How disappointing! I was sorry I'd put the address into the GPS and had missed the scenic drive and the chance to do a commentary for Jack. Still, for the first time in days, I felt a flutter of happiness. With the exception of our own home in Woodbridge, until it was trashed, I'd been happier visiting Villa Dolce than anywhere else on earth.

"Glad you're awake," Jack said.

"I don't think I actually slept."

"Someone was snoring. I can't unhear that."

"There's an intercom. Just press the button. I'll speak to Alessandro."

A familiar voice crackled over the intercom. A pair of dogs began to bark loudly.

I shouted to be heard over the crackle and the dogs. "Alessandro, it's Charlotte. Charlotte Adams, I am here with my fiancé. We were in the area and took a chance at finding you home. I'd like you to meet Jack."

A brief silence and then, "Of course, I am at home. Where else would I be? I am happy to meet your fiancé and even happier to hear your voice. Please come in."

The massive iron gates swung open gracefully and we rolled in and around to the back of the villa and the pea gravel parking area.

I said, "He wasn't flustered. That probably means that Esme hasn't been here."

Alessandro emerged from the house smiling, arms wide. Two Labrador retrievers arrived with him, bouncing and barking.

Alessandro was even taller than Jack. Esme used to joke that he had the legacy of his barbarian ancestors. Now he was a bit stooped and his fair hair was sprinkled with silver. I noticed he walked stiffly, using a cane. His handsome face seemed drawn and gaunt, but his warm blue eyes still gleamed charismatically. He enveloped me in a hug. All I felt was guilt for never being able to convince Esme that, of all the choices, this was the man she should stay with. "Pick your own partners, Charlotte," she'd said. And then she was gone, leaving another devastated man in her wake.

Alessandro had been my favorite of Esme's husbands and partners, consumed with his love of his vineyards and winery, a generous man whose home was always full of wonderful food and warm conversation, a man who kept in touch with dozens of cousins all over the globe, and one stepdaughter. Me. Villa Dolce had been a haven for me as a teenager.

I luxuriated in that hug before I introduced them. "Jack, this is my stepfather, Alessandro Zuccari." I didn't say former stepfather. The two men seemed to size each other up, then shook hands firmly. I hoped no bones were crunched. Alessandro said, "Didn't you have a close friend named Jack Reilly when you were growing up in Woodbridge? I am sure you mentioned him on your visits."

"That's our boy," I said, "friend and fiancé, two for the price of one."

Alessandro chuckled. "That worked out well then. I hope you will be able to stay for a few days."

I hesitated, not sure when we'd need to gallop off. "We didn't give you any notice. We don't have much of a game plan but we can find a place. A little visit this afternoon would be nice though."

"Are you trying to insult me? It has been too long and I demand a proper visit. For at least a week."

I had to grin. "You win. Today and tonight, anyway. We may have to hit the road quickly without much notice. Jack has a cycle business and he has been setting up meetings with suppliers for us, European products. We have a lot of balls in the air. Thank you so much."

Jack managed not to look too surprised at his business plans. I was sure he could come up with names of potential suppliers if backed into a corner.

"I have many contacts in that industry. I will be very happy to talk about who you've been meeting. Would you please show Jack the guest house, Charlotte? Ornella will bring you lunch on the terrace when you are ready."

I smiled but not as much as Jack did.

Alessandro said, "Unless you want to have a little rest first?" Did I really look that bad?

"Something to eat sounds really great. We could rest afterward," Jack said quickly. Nothing shy about him. I remembered that Ornella, the melancholy housekeeper, was a brilliant cook.

The guest house was up a curvy set of stone steps halfway to the top of another hill. Would Alessandro have trouble with those steps now? I wondered why he needed a cane, but I knew he was a proud man and I'd be careful how I inquired.

Jack was knocked out by the view from our balcony. "It's like something out of a golden fairy tale." He stared out at the vista. "Look how those houses are perched on the tops of the rolling hills. Incredible."

"I love it too. That's how the villa and the guest house look from the other side of the valley. This is one of my favorite places in the world."

I managed to have a shower and change into my skinny black pants, my *mariniere* top and my sandals. I pulled my hair into a ponytail and added gold hoop earrings. Jack found a fresh pair of cargo shorts and a Hawaiian shirt with purple volcanoes. We were as presentable as we could manage when we appeared on the terrace.

An informal feast had been set out on the table. A large wooden serving board was heaped with local cheeses and paper-thin slices of prosciutto, Genoa salami, crusty rustic bread, plus slices of pears and fresh figs and something called *mostarda*. Naturally there was wine and three glasses. Ornella bustled out with more on a second board. She was a tall, still-slender woman somewhere between sixty and seventy, her blonde hair streaked with gray. I seemed to remember that she was a cousin of Alessandro's. They'd both been fortunate to score good genes from those Northern barbarians.

Ornella eyed Jack with interest. He was a man who looked like he appreciated food, even if he could do with a bit of fattening up.

"You must try our new barolo," Alessandro said pouring with pride. "We called it Esme and we won the Medaglia D'Argente this year. I thought you'd like to sample that."

Ornella slipped the new board near Jack, who lit up appreciatively.

I said, "A silver medal? Wow. I'm saying yes to that." Of course, Esme would never be happy with less than gold, but never mind.

I slipped back into the kitchen after Ornella. I wanted to ask her about Alessandro's health and I hoped my rusty Italian would do.

"Alessandro è malato?"

At the best of times, Ornella has that aura of sadness. It intensified before my eyes. Her eyes filled and she placed her hand over her heart. *"Cardiaco."*

I gasped. A heart attack? She shrugged and said, *"Sta meglio adesso."*

Even though Ornella assured me that he was better now, I kept a worried eye on him as we chatted and shared the meal. No wonder Ornella looked even gloomier than usual.

When we finished our lunch, it turned out that Ornella had some *crema caramellata* waiting for us. Jack would never say no, but I was already wondering if the delicious bread, the carefully chosen cold cuts and condiments and now dessert would knock me right out given my ongoing sleep deficit. I didn't want to flake in the chair and snore again. Or worse, drool. I felt my eyelids growing heavy.

Jack gave my knee a nudge. "Get a look at that swimming pool."

I jerked awake.

Alessandro said, "It's still cool, but I hope it will be warm enough to swim one day when you are here."

He was sticking to his weeklong visit idea. I needed to correct that. "Oh, well, I—"

"That would be awesome." Jack could have been a close relative to the two bouncy retrievers.

Alessandro pointed to the vineyard rising on the hill behind us. "Would you like to check out the plants? It's quite pleasant to stroll between the rows of vines. Charlotte has done it many times, but I think you will enjoy it."

Alessandro and I needed to talk and alone would be better. Jack took the hint.

"So," he said as Jack headed off, followed by the dogs, who had taken a shine to him. "What really brings you here, Charlotte?"

He'd seen right through me. "I am searching for Esme."

"Esme? Why don't you just call her?"

"She's not taking my calls. She's on the run from some very dangerous people and I need—"

He raised his hand to stop me. "Dangerous people? What dangerous people?"

I decided that caution was overrated. "Gangsters. Or the grown children of gangsters."

Alessandro blinked. "Gangsters? You mean *mafiosi*?"

"No, just plain old Canadian thugs."

"Canadian!"

"Long story. The point is that they are after her and they are after me and they have killed some people."

"But—"

"Are you sure you haven't been in touch?"

"I haven't been in contact with Esme for years, her choice, not mine. I am happy that you call when you can."

"I should be better."

"You are good, Charlotte, and I appreciate it."

"I always wished she had stayed with you," I said, fighting the sting of tears.

He shrugged. "She was not a woman to keep still."

"I know that."

"So these thugs are dangerous and apparently Canadian." He chuckled and I assumed that was about the Canadian part.

"Do you know where she is?"

He shook his head. I believed him. He'd never been good at bending the truth.

"She was planning to come to Italy, I learned that much in Lisbon."

"She would have been welcome."

Alessandro filled up my wineglass before I could say no. "She's running from trouble," I said.

"She'd be much more likely to run straight toward trouble." He grinned. "Am I wrong about that?"

"You are not." Leonor Salazar had said pretty much the same thing. "But I believe they will kill her if they catch her."

"Is it not more like her to—how do you say that?—turn the tables on them?"

He had a point. "In this case, she'd be crazy to try to outwit them. They are extremely vicious and we don't know how many of them there are."

Alessandro patted my hand. "So what will you do next?"

"Not sure. I hoped she'd be here."

"Remember, *bella*, Esme is very intelligent, very strategic and very courageous. She's not a panicky vulnerable woman."

I felt a whoosh of relief.

"In spite of your difficulties, I hope you will take time to plan your next step. Stay as long as you need."

Why not? The Villa Dolce was wonderful. And I wasn't sure what to do next. I could bounce ideas off Alessandro. "Of course."

Throughout our talk, I could see Jack ambling through the vineyard, accompanied by the bouncing dogs, enjoying being able to stretch his legs and checking out the vines. I missed my own dogs. I would have done anything to stroke Truffle's silky fur and Sweet Marie's velvety coat.

Jack arrived back and rather than interrupt had struck up a conversation with Ornella. They were both distractingly animated. Jack's Italian might not have been perfect but it was more than good enough for a lively conversation. Strangely, Ornella appeared to be confiding in him.

Finally Alessandro announced that he had some work that couldn't be avoided. "Why don't you have a nap, Charlotte? You seem exhausted. Give yourself a break. Ornella will make us a beautiful dinner in the Piedmontese style and you can have an early night. Tomorrow you will be able to focus better."

"I can't really relax until—"

"You will find Esme. But you will be more effective if your brain is rested."

Alessandro was so charming, it was easy to forget he'd been a high-powered businessman before retiring to his vineyard paradise. "You're right. I'll take your advice. But first let me help clear the table."

Alessandro didn't argue and we quickly got that job done.

I glanced out the window and noticed that Jack had discovered a blue and silver bicycle and was examining it with great interest. "Is that yours?" I asked. I had no memory of Alessandro cycling anywhere, and Esme would never have considered it.

"Ah, my Cinelli. I keep it for visitors, although we don't have many."

"Jack would rather go for a spin than take a nap."

Alessandro chuckled. "He's welcome to it. I hope he's good with hills."

• • •

I had no intention of resting. Here in this serene environment, in the soft golden light of the guest house, I needed to plan my next steps. I was stuck. I had not a clue where else Esme could be. I'd hoped she would have come here. But of course, that wouldn't have been such a good idea. There had never been any public announcement when Esme married Alessandro, but it hadn't been a secret. Those thugs who were pursuing us had found me, had tracked Sid in New York and located Esme's condo. Apparently, they had followed us to Paris. Although they didn't seem to have figured out Lisbon, they could find Alessandro.

How could I feel safe here? And where was Esme? Alessandro was probably right. A rest would help me but I was too worried to doze. I needed to do something. Too many names whirled in my brain, too many unknown villains lurked on the edges of consciousness, and too many possible locations beckoned Esme to her death.

But I had a great idea. For once in my life, I decided to use Nick. I knew that if I contacted him, he would *never* tell Pepper, because she was jealous of any contact between me and her dim-witted husband with the wandering eye. If Pepper found out I'd contacted Nick, she would then discover I was in Italy and she would make Nick's life hell and mine, too, eventually. But I wouldn't be in this location for more than overnight, so there wasn't much chance she'd track me down or engage the local police. And Nick would get over it. He was always in trouble for one thing or another.

I sent Nick a message from "Charlie" on WhatsApp. He responded almost instantly, indicating Pepper was nowhere around. I greased the wheels by commenting on his policing skills and asked my question.

"Yeah. They've identified the bodies from that arson, Charlie."

I took a breath. "And who were they?"

"The woman who lived there was ID'd by the neighbor. She died of smoke inhalation and wasn't burnt to a crisp."

I shivered at Nick's description. I had hoped that Lola had gotten away.

Nick said happily, "And a guy name of John Doe. They don't know who he is yet."

"Right," I said, waiting to insert some information.

"But get this, Charlie. There was security camera footage of a guy buying a container of gas at a nearby station. They found fingerprints on an empty gas can outside the house. And guess what?"

"They match the fingerprints in the stolen rental car."

I felt the air ooze out of Nick's balloon. "Give a guy a break, Charlie. How did you know that?"

"Sorry, Nick, but it had to be the same people and they were the ones who trashed my home too."

"Well, he sure took a chance, leaving his prints. But a weird thing: those prints are not on file. And something else. No vehicle was found near the arson site so they think the dead guy must have had an accomplice." I thought back to the three beefy faces in the Ford SUV.

"He had accomplices, all right, Nick."

"You're getting ahead of me, Charlie."

"I think those criminals are from Montreal. And I told Pepper that one of our fake dog-walkers left prints on the side of the house. I don't think she took it too seriously."

"She did, Charlie!"

"I doubt she checked those prints with Canadian authorities, Nick."

There was a long, worrying pause during which I decided that Pepper must have come within hearing. Finally, Nick said, "Do you mean *I* could suggest that?"

"Excellent idea. That could be a hunch that comes to you in casual conversation about the case. *So, Pepper, did you guys check those prints with any other countries? Canada? Mexico?*"

"Whoa. I can do that. You want a report, Charlie?"

"Nope. Just take credit for the idea and good luck. That guy burned to death but he was trying to kill someone else."

"What?" Nick was tickled to add, "Guy was shot first. Nine-millimeter bullet was recovered. Right in the face."

"That's bizarre." I hoped that Lola hadn't gone out without a fight.

"Yeah, no kidding."

"Maybe it was one of his accomplices. Maybe the guy was unstable."

"Musta been."

"I'll check in again to see if you learn anything more."

"We'll stay close, Charlie. Oops. Gotta go."

• • •

Every room in the guest house had a desk, a chair and a magnificent view. Naturally, there was paper and a selection of pens from Vinicola Dolce, next to a tray with one-euro coins and small bills for the convenience of Alessandro's visitors. There was a coffee machine too, and mugs as well as tiny espresso cups, because Alessandro knew the habits of his American visitors, such as me. I made myself a double espresso, tossed it back in very non-Italian fashion and settled in to make progress even though my head was empty of anything but worry.

My attempt at purposeful activity led to flaking out on the duvet cover. Twenty minutes later, the caffeine jolted my system as planned, one eye opened and then the other. I sat up, my head full of Esme headed straight for trouble.

Questions. Yes. I knew that journalists often use five *Ws* and *H* to make sense of a story for readers. I had nothing to lose. I started with *Who*. There were so many people involved in this whole scenario, that I had trouble keeping them all straight. I started with everyone who had any contact with Esme or me or any relationship to what was going on. I separated names by location, hoping that by looking at the lists, a light would go on over my head.

It did not.

Woodbridge

Me
Jack
Sally
Margaret and Frank
Pepper and Nick
Ramona
Vanessa
Jack's part-timers
Lilith
Rose
Lola
Woman at my workshop (one of Bobby Bullets' people)
Faux dog-walkers (part of Bobby Bullets' family)

Montreal

Esme Adams/Evelyn Acheson
Lucie Lemire, Lola Lachance (deceased)

Léo Lemire (deceased)
Sean Doyle (possibly alive?)
Evelyn's parents (most likely dead?)
Danny Hanrahan (deceased)
John "Boy" Nadeau (deceased)
Ali Erickson
Jean-Claude Dion (injured, possibly dying)
Bobby "Bullets" O'Byrne (dying)
4 family members—two known women, one probably dead, and one man we don't know anything about.

New York

Sid Greenberg
Glenda Walker (missing, possibly dead)
Regis, the concierge
Would-be robbers at Esme's place (two of Bobby Bullets' daughters)

Paris

Maxime (Airbnb host)
Madame Chasseur
Flower vendors
People in boutiques and food vendors
Bartenders and waitstaff
Bobby Bullets' man and woman spotted. Was the man the fourth sibling?

Lisbon

Carlos
Leonor Salazar
Beatriz
Driver, Joao

Italy

Alessandro
Ornella
Ex-lover in Cinque Terre?
No sign of Bobby Bullets gang! So far, so good.

Maybe a light didn't go on over my head, but somehow the list helped me to think. I knew that already from the work I'd done on decision-making, an important part of organizing anything, especially if you've had some sleep. Tables and lists can lead to clarity. And that was what I needed.

Using the key question, *Where*, the Bobby Bullets gang had been active: Montreal, Woodbridge, New York City, and Paris. But not in Lisbon or Italy yet. Had we given them the slip?

That brought me to *How?* How did the gang discover our whereabouts in Woodbridge? I knew the gang found out about me from Regis's slip, but *how* could they have known that Esme was connected to the Hummingbirds in the mid-nineties?

None of my friends or colleagues had any clue about that. Sid, Glenda, and Regis would have no idea about Esme's history with the Hummingbird Gang and wouldn't have believed it if they'd heard it. Then there were Esme's neighborhood contacts in Paris and Madame Chasseur. What were the chances Esme would have let them know her murky past? Zero, I decided. The food and flower vendors were unlikely to have been involved.

Maxime was an Airbnb operator I had chosen almost at random, and I'd used my fake ID so he wasn't a suspect. Ali, the intrepid librarian, had been brought in by Ramona and Vanessa after Esme had vanished, our house had been trashed and Lola had been killed. Ali was unlikely to have been involved. Also she had no idea where we were at any time.

There were only two people who could have explained how the Bobby Bullets gang found us.

Lola was the first one. Had she been forced to tell the gang what she knew before that? But the arsonist had died too. Still, I doubted that Lola was in the loop about Esme's travels. I suspected the long-ago split between them had actually been a rift.

I decided to look at things in different ways to see if things got clearer.

The Dead

Sean Doyle (not so sure now)
Léo Lemire
Lola
John "Boy" Nadeau
Danny Hanrahan
The attacker (one of the O'Byrne boys) in Lola's burnt-out home
Evelyn's parents?

Missing

Esme
Glenda

Injured

Jean-Claude Dion
Sid (slightly)

I stared at Jean-Claude Dion's name. He was a formidable researcher. Ali thought he had been working on a new book about the Hummingbirds when he was attacked. I had assumed that he'd been targeted because he wrote about Bobby "Bullets" O'Byrne in the past, but why attack him now? Unless he'd learned something about Esme and by extension, me, in the course of his research. What if the O'Byrnes got wind of that something? The attack on Jean-Claude had been not long before the faux dog-walkers showed up in Woodbridge. Had he spilled the beans during the attack? I sat back and thought hard. Jean-Claude was a journalist and apparently a very good one, so perhaps he'd been able to uncover Esme's path somehow. Had she contacted him in Montreal?

I listed four action items:

1) Follow up on Evelyn's parents
2) Follow up on Esme's trip to Montreal

3) Find out if there had been contact with Jean-Claude Dion
4) Ask Ali to somehow alert the Montreal police that the O'Byrne family may have been behind the attack on Jean-Claude.

• • •

I was obsessing over these actions when I heard a commotion from outside. I rushed to the balcony and stared down on the terrace below. A pickup truck was parked at a crazy angle and the driver was gesticulating wildly toward the house. Of course, we were in Italy so he might have just been saying good afternoon, but I thought there was more to it. My heart raced when I spotted a crumpled blue and silver bike in the back of the pickup.

Alessandro emerged from the house and limped quickly toward the truck. He pulled out his phone while Ornella hurried to the truck, flapping her hands in distress. They both peered into the truck bed and then into the passenger side. Ornella dashed back into the house. I stumbled recklessly down the stone steps. Alessandro stopped me and said, "We think he's okay. A doctor is coming."

I peered into the truck. Jack was leaning back in the passenger seat, eyes closed. Blood trickled from a cut on his forehead. "Jack?"

His eyes opened slowly and he stared at me, dazed.

Ornella elbowed me out of the way with a bowl of water and some cloths. Jack closed his eyes again. Alessandro said something to Ornella. She wasn't having any of it. The truck driver got in the middle of it too. For a minute it looked like a three-person riot. I had just enough Italian to figure that Ornella wanted to clean the wound and Alessandro insisted on waiting for medical help. I let them fight it out. I leaned close and said: "Jack. Open your eyes. You have to stay awake because you hit your head."

"You should see the other guy," he mumbled.

"What guy?"

"Bo Jangles people."

"What?"

"The ones you are so worried about."

I jerked back. "The Bobby Bullets gang attacked you? In Piedmont?"

Jack put his hand on his head. "I stopped to admire the incredible vista. This big sedan passed me heading toward Villa Dolce. They must have recognized me because they made a U-ey and gunned it. Then I was sailing through the air."

Alessandro said, "Lucky for you there was a pile of hay to land on. Severino found you unconscious. He doesn't have a *telefonino*, but he recognized my Cinelli and he brought you here to get help. He thought you might have been a bicycle thief." Alessandro chuckled at that.

I felt a rush of outrage at the idea of Jack stealing anything, but Jack managed a weak grin. "That Cinelli is worth stealing."

"But not worth being killed for," I sputtered.

"Still alive," Jack said.

Alessandro butted in. "However, you have injuries that need to be checked out. I called my good friend, *la dottoressa*. Ah, here she is."

A white Mercedes sedan squealed into the parking area and a short, very curvy woman with a mass of salt-and-pepper curls jumped out and took charge. Even Ornella held back.

Jack had to answer some questions before he could be moved into the villa to be checked out by *la dottoressa*. Once we were inside, she waved us away. No problem with her English. Alessandro and his friend went off to lift the crumpled Cinelli from the back of the truck.

After that, Alessandro pulled me into the kitchen while Ornella rocketed around assembling food and drink.

"Did your friend see what happened?" I asked.

Alessandro shook his head. "Severino didn't see the accident, but a black Volvo sedan passed him on the bend just before and then again coming back. We will need to talk to the police."

"Would Severino recognize the driver of the vehicle?"

Alessandro shrugged.

"I have some photos to show him."

The doctor put an end to our conversation. "We need a scan of Jack's head to make sure there's no bleeding. I am glad he was wearing your helmet, *caro*. It probably saved his life. You can kiss the helmet and your bicycle *arrivederci*."

Alessandro said, "As long as he's all right."

"Let's find out," she said.

"We will replace the bicycle," I said.

Alessandro shook his head. "No. It's just an old thing I had lying around."

"It's probably worth ten thousand dollars. We'll replace it."

"Pick your battles, *bella*."

Jack went to the hospital with the doctor. Alessandro and I rode together. I took a minute to thank Severino before we left. He was happy to look at the photos I had of the O'Byrnes in Montreal. He squinted at them and nodded slowly. He said, "*Anche una donna nella machina.*"

Also a woman in the car! Bad news. Severino didn't get a good look at the woman, but we knew that the O'Byrnes were here.

• • •

On the way to the hospital, Alessandro turned to me. "Charlotte, is this attack on Jack connected to Esme's situation?"

I met his eyes and nodded.

"Hmm. I had hoped you were mistaken or merely exaggerating."

"She's done her best to keep us all out of it. But now they have tracked us down."

His forehead furrowed. Alessandro had loved Esme and me too. He still did. He deserved to know the whole story.

I took a deep breath before spilling the beans. "Esme was married to a young bank robber who was part of a daring theft of safe-deposit boxes in a supposedly secure vault. They were known as the Hummingbird Gang because they seemed to just fly away quickly. So the Hummingbirds took millions from that vault and much of it was never reported. As far as I can tell, one or more of the safe-deposit boxes belonged to Bobby O'Byrne, who headed the gang I mentioned. They called him Bobby Bullets, for obvious reasons. Murder and arson were his specialty. Bobby Bullets went after the Hummingbirds and their families."

"Where are these . . . Hummingbirds now?"

I found myself choking up and Alessandro took his eyes off the road for longer than he should have.

"Charlotte?" He swerved to avoid an oncoming truck. The driver shook his fist at us.

I swallowed. "The Hummingbirds are dead. Esme and I have been hiding out for twenty-six years. Two of the Hummingbird Gang were shot in what they call execution-style. The third was apparently killed in a fire, a theme with these thugs. My father's small plane crashed at a remote lake north of Montreal. Some of our possessions were found floating near the shore. It appeared that the plane was shot down. I believe that Esme heard the news about the crash and we took off in disguise." I modified the timeline slightly and felt kind of sleazy about that and left out the distinct possibility of Sean Doyle being alive.

A look of pain crossed Alessandro's weathered face. "She never trusted me enough to tell me this."

"Join the club. I am only just finding out this bizarre story."

He sighed. Esme had that effect.

"But that's not all. Last month Bobby Bullets got out of jail, supposedly because he is terminally ill. Now all hell is breaking loose."

Alessandro was silent for a long moment. Finally he said, "That explains a lot."

"Mmm. Currently it explains why Esme is hiding out. She doesn't want to be killed."

Alessandro said, "But, *bella*, it is a long distance to get revenge on someone's wife and a very long time to hold that kind of grudge. Surely this is old news?"

"A Montreal reporter who wrote a book about the Hummingbirds and was working on an updated version has been attacked and left for dead in Montreal. Someone doesn't think it's old news."

"Do they think she has something from the safe-deposit boxes?"

"I think they must. They found us in Woodbridge. I believe they killed Esme's former friend, Lola, in a house fire. I think Lola was the widow of one of the Hummingbird gang members. They trashed my home looking for something. They broke into Esme's agent's office and now her assistant Glenda has disappeared . . ." I choked up. ". . . and may be dead. They tried to get into Esme's condo in New York. They have pursued us to Paris. I thought we would be safe here."

"So, *bella*, whatever they are looking for, it would have to be something important. A large amount of money. Perhaps gold. Or jewelry."

"Two hundred thousand dollars tied to the last robbery and some expensive jewelry was recovered after the crash of my father's plane."

"Could Esme have had a large amount of money hidden anywhere?"

"I don't see how. We fled from what I now know was Montreal with small cases. There couldn't have been a large amount of money."

"She could have hidden some on her body. She had one of her characters do that in *Nothing Is What It Seems*."

I thought back to my mother looking fat on the bus so many years ago. Part of the game, she had called it. "She could have hidden some under her clothing and I wouldn't have known. I realize now that she looked pregnant when we were on the run, although she wasn't. Whatever she had hidden probably kept us going, but it was hardly millions."

"Perhaps it is not money they're after, *bella*."

"I don't know what else they could want. Money or revenge."

"Maybe there were documents that could damage this Bullets person."

"What could damage a dying man who has served twenty-four years for multiple murders? Well, whatever it is, these people are serious."

Alessandro turned to me. "I'm worried, Charlotte. Who else knows about all this?"

"Nobody. Jack and I have learned some of the history but only Esme knows why the O'Byrnes are pursuing her. I can't see any way to find out."

Chapter 20

Make sure you take out extra insurance if you travel outside the country.

The hospital had that eerie quiet that signals horrible unseen outcomes. We sat in silence while we waited for Jack's scan and for *la dottoressa* to appear through a set of double doors. Alessandro said, "Tell me what I can do."

"There is a way you can help."

"Anything."

"I need to make some phone calls to find out what is happening with Esme's assistant, Glenda. She's missing and I am worried that these people might have harmed her to get information about Esme." I found myself choking up, yet again. Glenda was always a lifesaver.

Alessandro frowned. "But why don't you just make the calls."

"Well, there's more to it than I told you originally."

Alessandro's eyebrows nearly hit the ceiling.

"The police are a problem."

The eyebrows stayed high.

"My former friend is a police detective and she told us not to leave town because of the fatal fire that killed Esme's friend Lola and an unknown man who I believe to be part of the O'Byrne Crew. Jack and I were seen nearby. I believe we are being set up by the Bobby Bullets family."

"A suspicious fire?"

"Yes. Lola was Esme's good friend in Montreal and the girlfriend of one of the other Hummingbirds. He also died in a fire, started by members of the Bobby Bullets gang. She moved to Woodbridge before us. We were friendly with Lola when we first arrived."

"There is a lot to absorb, Charlotte."

"Tell me about it."

"Why did you leave if the police told you not to?"

"We needed to find Esme before the thugs did. I decided to hell with the consequences."

"That's my girl. So now I know why you need to make phone calls."

"I don't want to use my phone or Jack's in case the police are tracing calls to our friends or Esme's agent. I am desperate for an update on Glenda, too. Maybe I'm paranoid but so many crazy things have happened, it might be good if the calls can't be traced to you either."

"Understood. I can help with that."

I paused long enough to consider if there was any possibility that Alessandro could be implicated. I have learned the hard way that people can be very surprising, but the evidence over the years told me I could trust him as much as anyone.

Alessandro nodded. "I remember Glenda and Sid, of course. And they are the two people most likely to have information about Esme's plans and contacts. I will try, *bella*. I have also tried to contact them more than once over the years when Esme was 'playing hard to get,' as they say. I can just call them pretending to need to reach her. You won't be involved."

My shoulders slumped with relief. Alessandro reached over and patted my arm. "Once we're home we'll get something to eat and we'll take care of this."

The doors opened and Jack loped out, grinning sheepishly. *La dottoressa* gave us the thumbs-up sign.

"Sorry to give you a scare, Charlotte." Jack leaned in for a hug.

I choked back tears of relief and held on tight.

"Alessandro, I will replace your bike. I feel bad about that," Jack said.

"No. It had been hanging around collecting spiderwebs for years. The place will be a bit neater from now on."

Before we could get into a dustup over that, *la dottoressa* said, "Your Jack is lucky he avoided serious brain injury, but I advise caution and rest for the next few days at least. This is important."

"And good food, I suppose," Alessandro said.

She laughed. "Definitely good food is part of recovery. Lucky for you, Jack, you are in Italy and even luckier, you are at Villa Dolce."

• • •

The sun had gone down, leaving a chill in the air. In this hilly area the usual high at the end of April would be around sixty-two degrees, but that dropped to the low forties in the evening. There would be no casual outdoor meal, but the prospect of eating around the rustic round table in the warm kitchen was very appealing.

Ornella's hands were a blur as she made dinner, pausing every now and then to fuss over Jack.

Although the villa had seemingly endless rooms, we were clustered near the source of all good things. I was surprised that the stone floor was heated, although I shouldn't have been: the kitchen featured European appliances—six-burner gas grill, built-in high-end coffee maker, and two dishwashers—so a heated floor made sense.

Alessandro served everyone some excellent barolo and Ornella had set out crusty bread, soft goat cheese, a chunk of Gran Padano cheese and thin-sliced Genoa salami. Jack announced he was starving, a good sign according to *la dottoressa*, who had apparently joined us.

Alessandro and I slipped away to one of his several offices to make the calls. I was too tense to relax and eat. He had no trouble finding Sid's private number.

"Signor Sid," he boomed when the phone was answered. "Alessandro Zuccari."

"Eating lunch? I am so sorry. But I need to reach Esme. You must remember me from when I was married to her for too short a time. I am sorry to disturb you but I have a pressing business issue. Esme and I jointly own shares in a small company and I have an opportunity to sell them at a good profit, but I cannot reach her to get approval. I require her signature. I wonder if you can help me?"

I could hear Sid raging in the background.

"Really? No idea. Oh, well, could you please get a message to her?"

Alessandro flinched and held the phone away. Loud squawks filled the air.

"Oh. My. And you were injured by whoever is looking for her?"

Squawk. Squawk.

"That is serious. Do the police have any idea—"

Squawk!!!

"And you think this has to do with Esme? Is she in danger too?"

Jabbering.

"That is very troubling. Perhaps I will try Glenda just in case. Please try to stay safe and get in touch if you hear anything from her."

More squawking.

"No one knows where Glenda is? Have you called her?"

Again, Alessandro found it necessary to move the receiver further away.

"Are the police investigating?" A long pause. "And they have found nothing?"

I turned the phone partially toward me and heard Sid's voice break. "A lot of blood, but still no sign of Glenda. But yesterday they found her car about two hundred miles away near a remote hiking trail. There was blood in the trunk."

Alessandro whispered to me, "Her computer and other valuables are missing. But her credit cards haven't been used, apparently. It's been all over the news."

"We have heard nothing of it over here, I am afraid. I am sorry to hear this, Sid. I will try to get in touch with Charlotte. I didn't want to worry her but now I suppose I must."

Sid's voice wavered. "Charlotte's gone too. The Woodbridge police seem to think she might be involved, but that is ridiculous. I think she's hiding because she's in danger. I've been told if she gets in touch and I don't let them know, I could face obstruction charges. So you understand that I can't help you with your business matter."

"Ah, that business matter doesn't seem so important next to this emergency, Sid. I hope you are safe now."

"I'm staying with friends away from the city. Don't think I'm going to tell you where."

After Alessandro realized that Sid had hung up, we stared at each other.

My knees felt weak. "Poor Glenda. She has always been so loyal to Esme and she's so feisty. I think she would have resisted giving them information, and they . . ." I couldn't bring myself to say "killed her."

"A bad situation," Alessandro said with a grim set to his jaw. "We must keep you and Jack safe. I will give you another *telefonino* if you need to contact anyone without being traced."

By the time we returned, the others had worked their way through the antipasti, Ornella had cleared the table and I had another burner phone. Jack attempted to help with cleanup but was put in his place by Ornella and *la dottoressa*. I thought the curvy little doctor seemed very comfortable in Alessandro's home. Her large dark eyes flashed and her hands seemed to have a life of their own. Her salt-and-pepper curls bounced as she talked.

Jack said, "*La dottoressa* was just telling me all about the war and the freedom fighters in this area. Very interesting history. Dramatic life-and-death situations."

"Yes, my grandmother was nearly killed by the Germans."

Ornella pointed to herself and said something. Ornella would have been born well after the end of World War Two. Alessandro broke in and said, "Ornella wants you to know that her grandfather also was a *partigiano* and her grandmother helped to feed and hide the resistance fighters."

Ornella won that round, hands down, and *la dottoressa* took it with good grace.

Ornella celebrated her "win" by dishing up fragrant clear chicken soup with *stelline*, tiny pasta stars and very good fresh Parmigiano Reggiano. I'd spent enough time in Italy to know you shouldn't fill up on the antipasti, the soup or anything else that looked like dinner but was actually just a teaser. A savory spinach and ricotta agnolotti followed. I loved these savory little pillows, a bit like a round ravioli, but again, I didn't fall into the trap. Jack is a bottomless pit so it didn't matter that he had seconds. Finally, with a flourish, Ornella presented the platter of chicken with mushrooms and cheese. It was all so delicious that it nearly drove my worries from my head. Alessandro continued to top up our wineglasses, including Jack's when the doctor wasn't looking. Really, who could resist?

In the end, we overcame Ornella's protests about not needing help and we cleared our plates and loaded the dishwasher. Everyone continued to talk at once and I found that very reassuring. Jack was asking to see photos and everyone promised to show him their valiant family members.

The meal ended with a warm homemade chocolate pudding with caramel sauce, toasted hazelnuts and whipped cream. Everyone reminded us the hazelnuts from Piedmont are the best in the world and in fact Piedmont was the home of Ferrero Rocher chocolates. Jack said, "Why would anyone ever leave this place?"

That got a laugh.

Despite the fantastic distraction, I couldn't stop worrying about poor Glenda. She didn't have a fraction of the survival skills of Esme. Aside from the occasional husband and myself, Glenda was the person Esme was closest too. Her two friends, Lola and Glenda, seemed to have died trying to protect her. That would be hard for Esme to deal with if and when this nightmare ended.

I found myself pacing and Alessandro offered me a reassuring hug. Not for the first time, I asked myself why Esme couldn't have simply stayed married to this wonderful man.

"I know you are worried about everything."

"I am afraid for Esme and Glenda and all of us. Look what happened to Jack today here where we felt safe."

He nodded sadly.

"It all goes back to the gang Esme was involved with, the Hummingbirds. I wish I knew what actually happened and what they took from Bobby Bullets," I said.

Alessandro chuckled. "Hummingbirds. We call them *colibri.* They are tiny and beautiful but warlike little creatures. Very fast."

"Yes. That was the point of the name. They were super fast and they seemed to be able to fly away. But in the end, they weren't fast enough and they didn't fly far enough. People are still dying because of what they did. I don't know how to find Esme and I have no idea if it's too late to save Glenda. I feel so useless."

"What is it you say? Welcome to the club? Have a bit of Barolo Chinato. It's our after-dinner *digestivo*. We make it with our own barolo. Ornella steeps it with mint, cinnamon and vanilla, her secret recipe. After that you can have a good night's sleep. Jack needs to recover too. In the meantime, don't worry about what you can't do anything about."

Later, full of food, wine, and stories of ridiculously brave locals, Jack and I thanked Ornella, *la dottoressa* and Alessandro and teetered up the stone stairs to the guest house.

"Funny," Jack said when we successfully reached the top of the stairs. "I mean funny strange or funny sad perhaps. Ornella told me that Alessandro is still in love with Esme."

"Yet she treated him so badly."

"He's kept her things, clothes, books and all that, for more than ten years. He can't bear to get rid of them."

"I guess people can't help their feelings. I hope he finds someone else. I am thinking *la dotteressa* might be a good candidate."

But Jack was already out like a light, leaving me fretting about whether his pupils were dilating.

• • •

Of course, Jack slept happily all night. I tossed and turned, my thoughts whirling.

I finally dozed off and woke with a start at four. The Bobby Bullets gang were shooting up a scenic seaside restaurant in Cinque Terre and Esme and a faceless man were running for their lives. Bullets whizzed by my ears and O'Byrne faces grinned evilly. I sat up gasping, "Hummingbirds!" Alessandro had called them *colibri. Colibri!* My heart thundered and the name rang in my head. Signor Colibri. That's what Esme had called the man who had come between her and Alessandro, long before I'd heard of either the Hummingbird Gang or the word *colibri.* Whoever Signor Colibri was, he was somehow connected with Esme's old life in Montreal.

I sat like a lump in the very luxurious guest bed, fingering the Egyptian cotton sheets and staring out the window into the darkness. I had no idea what to do, no clue where to go, no way to know what was coming next. What I had was an overwhelming sense of peril. There'd been danger in Lola's pretty garden, danger in Glenda's quirky Brooklyn apartment, danger here on the scenic road not a mile from Villa Dolce. Jack snored on, happily unaware. Of course, we weren't safe here. We weren't even safe in our own home in Woodbridge. I turned what I knew over and over in my head. Was Esme running to someone? Was that someone Signor Colibri?

I thought I knew about every one of Esme's relationships. Sometimes more than was comfortable. And yet, this one was murky. What if the relationship with Signor Colibri had endured? Or reignited? Something had been up these last few months. I wasn't the only one who'd noticed. The last time I'd spoken to Glenda she'd been frustrated with Esme. "What's going on, Charlotte? Esme's so freakin' elusive. Does she have a new toy boy in her life?" Before I could answer, Glenda had snapped, "Maybe it's menopause." And hung up without saying goodbye.

A lover, I'd assumed, but not an important one or I would have heard about him, and even been introduced. So he was somehow unsuitable. Too young? Too notorious? Too married? Unlikely. Esme had no use for men who were married to other people. She preferred middle-aged men because "they were beginning to understand their proper place in the universe." For sure, there'd be something wrong with him.

Figuring I'd never close an eye again, I dragged myself out of bed and made a bracing mug of extra-strong coffee. I carried the mug to the balcony. I curled up on the chair and wrapped myself in one of the heavy wool blankets that had been thoughtfully provided in baskets next to the door. In what should have been the false dawn, the glorious green and gold hills and valleys were shrouded in thick drifting fog. That was similar to the state of my mind: facts, figures, suspicions and assumptions merged in an impenetrable haze. Images swirled in my brain: our trashed home, the blackened remains of Lola's house, unseen pursuers in the back streets of Paris, worries in old Lisbon and now, this: the Bobby Bullets gang knew we were here. They had tried to get rid of Jack. Why? To make me panic? Or did they think that Jack had seen them and would warn me? Were they lurking in the darkness waiting to finish us off? Had I brought this threat to the idyllic Villa Dolce and Alessandro, Ornella, *la dottoressa* and Jack? How could I sort out the whole murderous situation? In retrospect, overflowing closets, chaotic kitchens and turbulent bedrooms seemed like happy dreams.

I sipped my second mug of coffee and watched the fog slowly wisp away, revealing the golden glow of dawn to come. Something similar happened in my own foggy brain. I felt patches of clarity. It was time to plan my next steps.

Everything that had happened to any of us began in Montreal decades earlier with a band of good-looking and reckless thieves. Esme had been enthralled by Sean Doyle. Sean Doyle was believed to be lying in a lonely grave at the bottom of Lac des Larmes, but that could be another false story. Now Esme's long-ago romantic visit to her so-called acquaintance Signor Colibri was beginning to make sense.

As the last of the fog vanished, revealing the lush curved and terraced vineyards surrounding us, my brain fog continued to lift too. I knew I had to find Signor Colibri and my crazy-making mother. I understood that she had kept me in the dark to protect me from danger and from finding out the truth of my own past.

I closed my eyes and tried to remember the brief glimpse I'd had of "Signor Colibri" in Cinque Terre. I compared that snatch of memory to the photo of the Hummingbird Gang.

I was fast becoming convinced that Sean Doyle was Signor Colibri. If they'd discovered he wasn't dead, he would have become a target for the vengeful O'Byrnes. Esme was up to her pretty neck in Sean Doyle's life after death.

Now it occurred to me that I had been along for that trip to Cinque Terre to give my father a chance to see me without me having a clue about what was going on. It had been yet another setup.

Whatever was going on with Esme and Sean Doyle and the O'Byrnes, I couldn't see it ending well.

I whirled as Jack stumbled onto the balcony, stretching. He seemed as good as new if you didn't count the many scratches and bruises on his legs and arms. and the bandage on his head. Today would probably have been the right day to switch from cargo shorts and short-sleeved Hawaiian shirts, but . . .

He folded his lankiness into the second chair and smiled at me. "How long have you been out here, Charlotte?"

"Hours."

"Nightmares again?"

I nodded.

Jack leaned in to comfort me. It felt good to be enfolded in his arms, but I pulled back. "The good news is that the nightmare provided a clue."

"Excellent."

"Maybe. So here's the thing, Jack. I'm pretty sure Sean Doyle is not dead on the bottom of Lac des Larmes."

"Whoa."

"And my father could be living the good life not far from here, I'm guessing Cinque Terre."

"And how do you feel about that?"

I wondered if Jack's joint loves of history, philosophy and cycling had squashed a potential career as a therapist. But that would be a discussion for another day.

"Confused, conflicted and worried. Angry and frustrated too. I believe Esme reconnected with Sean Doyle some years back, how I don't know, but when it happened, boom! That would explain ending her marriage to Alessandro. And he deserved better."

Jack nodded. "First love is a powerful bond. I know that. Did Esme know Sean was alive all along?"

I thought hard. "She wouldn't have married again if she thought her husband was still alive. But on the other hand, this *is* Esme we're talking about."

"What makes you think he's here in Italy?"

"When she was still married to Alessandro, she had an encounter. I hadn't thought much about that until my dream last night. It was more flashes of memory than a dream until . . ."

"So what happened?"

"I had just finished my first year of college and Esme had insisted that I come to Italy to celebrate. No problem. Alessandro always spoiled me when I showed up. After the birthday celebrations, Esme and I took the train to Cinque Terre, starting in Corniglia, my favorite of the five gorgeous towns. We had lunch at a beautiful al fresco restaurant overlooking the Ligurian Sea. It was fantastic, lots of white umbrellas and tablecloths, a breathtaking view of the water and a backdrop of vineyards. The food was amazing. I can still taste the fresh bread. Anyway, I was sent off to poke around in the boutiques before her "friend" arrived. I wandered around, in and out of the little shops, exploring the crooked streets and wondering what it would be like to live in a fairy-tale place like that. Minus the tourists, of course."

"So far the dream seems pretty good."

"I was a teenager so I got bored before long and headed back. They were holding hands and staring into each other's eyes when I spotted them. She must have heard me gasp and she reacted with horror. He just melted away as soon as I got a look at him. I was furious because I cared for Alessandro, but Esme said that Signor Colibri was a very special person from her past and I shouldn't worry about it. That is the memory part, but in the dream, I came back and was about to meet him. Suddenly I realized that faceless people were lurking behind the umbrellas and all the serving staff had turned into members of the Bobby Bullets gang. Esme said, 'I'd like you to meet Signor Colibri,' and that's when the gunfire started and it turned into a nightmare. Now I am convinced that my subconscious was trying to tell me that she is running to Sean Doyle. Bobby Bullets must have found out that Sean is still alive."

"But how could he find out? He's sick. He got a compassionate medical release because he doesn't have long to live."

"What if he was faking?" I held up my hand before Jack could object. "Doctors can be bribed or threatened. Maybe Bobby Bullets doesn't plan on dying just yet and he wants to recover whatever was in that safe-deposit box. And to have revenge. But how would he have learned that Sean Doyle was still alive? And not just Sean, but Esme and me. Lola too."

Jack said, "Must be connected to Jean-Claude Dion. Ali said he was working on a new book before he was attacked. What if he had a conversation that got people talking in the underworld community and the O'Byrne Crew got wind of it? Didn't you say that Esme went to Montreal?"

I nodded. "She didn't tell me and therefore she must have had something to hide."

"Could it be a death in the family? A funeral? The Bullets gang might have kept tabs on Esme's family."

I stared at him. "That makes sense. I should have thought of that. So perhaps a parent . . ."

"Or a brother or sister?"

"Esme said she was an only child. I believe that is true."

Jack nodded. "So we know that her family had turned their backs on her and you."

"Right. And we also read that Sean, Esme and I were dead. Still, I don't believe Esme was ever in touch with family again."

Jack cleared his throat before speaking. "When a parent dies, it's like nothing else you've experienced."

I leaned in and gave him a hug. He had lost his beloved parents in a car crash. "You're probably right. I bet she felt safe showing up, twenty-five years older and wearing one of those writerly getups that obscure her face."

"And Jean-Claude would have been there because—"

"—he never stopped digging. Jean-Claude must have recognized her. Her attitude makes people take notice," I said.

"If the Bullets gang heard something, that would have led them to Esme and you."

I said, "To Esme. They found out where she lived in New York and Regis slipped up and they learned where I lived and came after me. I am guessing that they really wanted Sean Doyle and they were trying to drive Esme to him."

"Now we're guessing and we need some facts."

• • •

I found myself holding my breath as we waited for Ali to connect us with

Jean-Claude Dion on WhatsApp. This man was the key to everything. But he was also in bad shape.

Ali came on the line. "Sorry, he's having quite a bit of trouble today but he does want to talk. He's quite lucid but still very weak."

I exhaled and waited. Finally Jean-Claude spoke in a quavering voice. "Charlotte Adams." He did manage to infuse enthusiasm into my name. "I may have brought you a lot of trouble. I did not mean to." His voice faded and all I heard was wheezing. Ali broke in. "Give us a minute. He's . . . this is hard on him."

After a full two minutes, she said, "Okay. Go for it."

"Jean-Claude, I need to know what the Hummingbirds may have taken from Bobby Bullets."

"Well, there is a lot of speculation in the underworld that the safety deposit box contained blackmail information targeting senior municipal officials and politicians. Bobby Bullets used damaging information to solidify his hold on crime in the city. It was a long time ago, and although most of the players are dead or retired, there are two big-name firms and some long-serving municipal officials who could be damaged by these revelations. The O'Byrnes wouldn't want to let go of that leverage. But really no one knows and Bobby Bullets isn't saying. I think perhaps whatever they found went down with Sean Doyle and the little Cessna on Lac des Larmes."

"But how did—" I stopped as a hacking cough took over the line.

Ali returned. "He's in crisis! I will try to reach you later with whatever news."

"Wait—"

But she was gone.

"Now what?" Jack got up and headed for the coffee maker. "We need to get a lead on this Signor Colibri, but he could be anywhere in Italy."

"Cinque Terre would be a good start. There's already a connection there."

Jack said, "It's a sad situation. Esme's still in love with Sean Doyle and Alessandro's still in love with her. Remember, Ornella told me that he's kept the clothing she left behind."

"That can't be emotionally healthy."

Jack shrugged. "I'm just saying that he kept those things."

"Not in his room, I hope."

"She said that it's all in the storeroom."

I tried not to feel annoyed that Jack could hold a smooth conversation with Ornella while I had forgotten so much of the language. I could hardly put together a sentence.

Jack gave me one of his more reassuring hugs. "You know that we're in this together, right?"

I nodded, my chin wobbling. "Okay. Let's think. Esme had fled from the city and from Canada to save her life and mine. What could have compelled her to return? Was it to find some of the hidden loot from the robbery? Possible but doubtful. What else? Her husband was gone, her friends were dead or gone or both. Her family had disowned her. There was nothing to return for, until . . . "

Jack nodded. "I suppose we could check the obituaries."

Of course. While I had the chance to use Alessandro's computer, I googled Acheson obituaries in Montreal and hit the jackpot.

> *Elizabeth Acheson, 78, of Notre-Dame-de-Grace, passed away peacefully in her sleep on February 21. She was predeceased by her husband, Graham, her daughter, Evelyn, and her granddaughter, Seanna. She is survived by her friends at the Riverview Retirement Residence. Service will be held at St. Lucia's Catholic Church in Montreal West on Feb 26 at 1 pm.*

I shivered as I read my grandmother's obituary. A grandmother I'd never had a chance to know. What kind of relationship had I been deprived of? Figuring that she had disowned her only child and left her to find her own way, I thought I hadn't missed much. On the other hand, over twenty-six years, people can change. Both Evelyn and Seanna were mentioned. Did that mean her mother had feelings or regrets? Did Elizabeth Acheson go to her grave not knowing her daughter and granddaughter had survived? So many questions and no way to get answers. I had one answer though. The funeral was indeed at the same time Esme had visited Montreal.

Bingo, as they say.

Chapter 21

On every trip try to be a bit adventurous. Find something fun that challenges you or is out of your comfort zone.

Stopping a determined group of murderers seemed like a challenge, if not a fun one. Jack could not be part of that in his condition. Last year, he'd taken a bullet trying to save me. Yesterday, he'd been hit and left for dead. I hoped neither one of us was going to be in the position of having to save the other one's life again.

We made our way down the stone stairs to the terrace. I kept an eye on him in case he was unsteady. He seemed to be doing the same with me. We were lucky we didn't both plunge onto the stone terrace below.

Through the open door we could see Ornella slapping plates of food on the huge rustic round table. She must have spotted us.

"*La colazione!*" Ornella trilled. Today's breakfast would be bread, butter and jam, and frittata. Coffee was ready. Even though I'd had my daily dose already, I knew I would love it.

"*Brava!*" Jack said. Of course, he was now the new favorite.

It would all be delicious, especially Ornella's homemade rustic bread, the wonderful Italian butter and her special jam, a mix of whatever local fruit was available. Too bad my stomach was in knots.

Alessandro hailed us from across the terrace and limped toward the kitchen door. "I hope you slept well."

"Charlotte was up all night," Jack said.

"Not all night," I protested.

Alessandro chuckled. "I saw you sitting on the balcony in the dark."

"I had a lot to think about." I took a deep breath and filled him in on what we now knew about my parents and the O'Byrnes. "I believe that Esme is with my father, now known as Signor Colibri. They are both being hunted and I think they are in Cinque Terre."

Alessandro took a while to absorb this strange news.

"That is a very bizarre theory," he said finally.

"Trust me."

"And don't forget the dream," Jack interjected, although that didn't enhance my credibility.

"Have you seen this man?" Alessandro said mildly.

"Our librarian friend in Montreal sent an old photo of him. We can use the aging software to get an idea of what he looks like now."

Alessandro scoffed at the idea. "Aging software? I can't believe that would work."

"How about an experiment? We can put in a photo of you at twenty or thirty and see how close it comes."

"You mean I no longer look thirty? You know how to hurt me, *bella*."

"Can we try it in your office?"

"Only after we've enjoyed our breakfast. Oh, *frittata, pane, burro e marmellata*. Must be special guests, Ornella."

Alessandro served us the coffee from the million-dollar machine. It all felt lovely. Too bad I needed to trick everyone and disappear soon.

• • •

After breakfast, we hovered around Alessandro's computer. Even a romantic venture like a winery was still a business requiring computers, filing cabinets, supply cupboards, printers, scanners, desks and chairs. Also, another high-end coffee machine, this one a Gaggia, and even a glass jar full of Ornella's chocolate hazelnut biscotti, which I love, because they also have a hint of espresso. Alessandro downloaded the "aging" app and, still unconvinced, uploaded a photo of himself as a young man, on a hike in the nearby mountains. He zoomed in on his own face. We watched the app do its magic. Alessandro was satisfyingly surprised by the results. I was happy because the aged photo was close enough to current reality.

"I look like I'm a hundred years old," he grumbled.

I patted his shoulder. "Time has been kind to you. You look better than the aged photo, but we can tell it's you."

He shook his silver head. "Vanity does not become an old man, *bella*."

"You're hardly old, but you can see how effective this is. Now we need an update on the mysterious Sean Doyle."

We uploaded the photo of the Hummingbirds that Ali had sent with the background information. We cropped it to focus on Sean Doyle and once again watched the process. The smooth-faced young robber, Shonnie, thickened up and wrinkled a bit as we aged him ten, twenty and twenty-five years. His jawline was a bit looser, eyebrows furrier, and deep lines settled around his mouth. We had an idea now what my father looked like.

"Can you print me a few copies, please, Alessandro?"

"Anything you want, *bella*." The wireless printer whirred.

"Have you seen him anywhere?" I asked.

Alessandro shook his head. So did Jack. But I gasped. The second-to-last photo was definitely the man who'd met my mother in Cinque Terre, just before she abruptly ended her marriage to Alessandro. I didn't say that, but now I knew my next steps.

Could I locate Esme and Signor Colibri in Cinque Terre before it was too late?

I beckoned Alessandro aside. "I am worried about Jack overdoing it. I wonder if you could keep him occupied. He loves to drive so he could take the Abarth we rented. It would, um, ease my mind."

Alessandro ran with that idea. As Jack ambled into the room, Alessandro greeted him. "Jack, today I am visiting the *cooperativo*. Would you like to see how we work together on the wine? The process is really interesting."

Jack shot me a look of total suspicion.

I chirped, "I've seen it all before, but if Alessandro has time to show you, I have some laundry to gather up and stuff to put in order. And you know, Jack, after your injury, it will be good to try driving. You'll have a local expert on the roads with you."

Jack said, "Alessandro must be busy."

"Well, I must visit the *cooperativo* anyway for business and I would like to see how the Abarth handles on these roads. Do you mind, Jack?"

I said, "While you're out I'll check in with Sid to see if he's heard anything. I am really worried about Glenda. I'll try to reach Ali again to see if Jean-Claude is doing better." I tried smiling innocently, which made Jack raise an eyebrow.

Alessandro was keen to fill Jack's head with obscure facts about the wine-making process. I waved as they left and I headed up the stairs to the guest house and on to the large storage room on the attic level, up a wobbly ladder. My ankles took a couple of gouges from boxes, trunks, covered racks of clothing and old exercise gear.

I whipped the sheet from a rack and found dozens of dresses and several coats that I remembered Esme wearing years back. Up close I spotted a half dozen floral hatboxes. I wasn't searching for hats. I wanted wigs. Esme loved to change her appearance. I'd always found that strange, although now I had a better idea of how she got that habit. I uncovered a large paisley box full of wigs, most obviously never worn. Frankly, it was a bit creepy. I picked out a curly blonde one, from before beach waves were in vogue, but curls are always good. Then a deep copper number with a long loose braid. Wigs had worked for the Bobby Bullets brigade and they could work for me. If I layered on some clothes I could change my size as I changed my disguise, on an as-needed basis. In the hatbox was a largish tweed poor boy cap. It had set Esme back a couple of hundred dollars. I thought it would look great with the copper braid.

Esme was taller and a bit heavier, but her clothes would work for me. So far the day was on the cool side, despite the sun. I selected a caramel-colored leather trench coat, the type that never goes out of style. It almost reached my ankles, but that was trendy too. I scooped up a cropped jean jacket, forever in style. A beautiful soft leather black tote bag hung from a hanger on the rack. It would be perfect for holding a couple of changes of disguise and enough food to keep me going. Best of all was a pair of platform boots. They'd added about four inches to Esme's height. I could definitely use the boost. They were too big but I could always stuff a sock into the end of each. I tried to chose between them and a pair of wedge sneakers that I remembered envying years earlier

I dug out a couple of casual tops, one red and two in usefully boring neutrals, a beige and a navy, and a brilliant flowered large square scarf. There was an excellent floppy woven travel hat in one of the flowered hatboxes. Esme even had a baseball cap from one of her conferences. My bases were covered. I folded everything tightly and wedged my treasures into the tote bag.

Back in our room, I gathered up my passport and credit cards, Bic and burner phones, and the printed photos of Sean Doyle with twenty-five years added, sunglasses, pen and notebook, and my practical running shoes, which I might be needing. In my waist money-holder I tucked all the coins and larger bills from the tray, plus my lipstick and eyeliner for good luck. I was still my mother's daughter.

I headed out to the kitchen to find food for the trip. The vending machines in the train stations sold dry sandwiches that reminded me of cardboard. Old cardboard, the type that should be decluttered.

Ornella was buzzing around making fresh pasta when I stuck my head in. I managed to convey that I was still hungry. Ornella didn't question this unlikely scenario. She hurried to assemble some focaccia, cheese and prosciutto, plus a copious supply of Ferrero Rocher and some bottled juice and water for a "little snack."

It was enough to survive for days hiding in a cave. I smiled and told her that I needed to pick something up in the village pharmacy. *Farmacia!*

"*Machina?*" I was glad I remembered the word for car.

"*Si, si!*" Alessandro had a collection of vehicles, including a truck and his snazzy Audi RS5. The housekeeper pointed to the hanger with the keys to the vehicles. I noted two sets of keys for the Audi. Back in the room, I managed to find a space for my food in the tote. It was indeed a magic bag. I checked the railway schedules on my phone, slapped the baseball cap on my head and headed down to get the car.

Ornella waved as I left.

The gates opened and I turned right. I kept an eye on the rearview for anyone following me as I wove past farms, fields and curvy vineyards. Sure enough, after a mile or so, a dark sedan, large by Italian standards, appeared. I was prepared. I made a very sharp turn and shot down a hill, did a U-turn and parked behind a convenient stone wall. The sedan barrelled past, leaving clouds of dust in its wake. After a short wait, I shot out in the opposite direction, heading for my planned destination: the city of Asti.

Forty minutes later, I left the Audi in the station parking lot. I had just enough time to get the next train to Genoa.

Inside the station, I rushed down the platform to the ladies' room. I changed my appearance dramatically—blonde curls, travel hat, red top and platform boots, and oversized sunglasses—and teetered back to the waiting area to buy my tickets. Everyone in the station appeared to be totally focused on their phones, except for a grandmotherly type who was busy keeping two overactive children from being killed on the tracks. I hoped they'd be taking another train. At the small shop I bought a copy of *Vogue Italia* and a guide to Cinque Terre, also in Italian. I tucked the guide into the magazine. My main goal was to survey the people around me without appearing to do so. I peered down the tracks and checked the schedule on the board, and then strolled along the platform to find a bench with no one on it.

The train arrived on time and I hustled down the stairs, through the tunnel and up to the platform level and then slipped into the car. My heart rate had calmed by the time we arrived in Genoa.

I exited the train the second I could get through the door, searching for another restroom. The platform boots wobbled precariously as I hurried and I knew I had to ditch that part of my disguise. I needed my supply of one-euro coins. Inside a stall at the end, I changed into the dark top, the caramel-colored leather trench and the wedge sneakers. I swapped the blonde curls for the wig with the long copper braid and added the tweed poor boy cap to finish off the look. I drew on some heavy eyebrows with the eyeliner and added bright red lipstick. Good. I looked like someone entirely different and four inches shorter. I rolled up the red top and stuck it in the tote. The boots and the blonde wig went into the garbage can.

I hurried out the door and checked for my gate for the next train. The wedge sneakers were also quite wobbly and I hoped I wouldn't snap an ankle. I wondered if I was overdoing it. After all, could anyone have followed me? But recent history told me it was better to be safe than sorry.

On the next train, I wedged myself into the inner seat in the last row, close to the bathroom and the exit, both part of my plan. I could watch the other passengers and still escape quickly if I needed to. I didn't worry about people already on the train, but it was possible that the unseen people in that dark sedan had managed to follow me. While I could recognize the original O'Byrne villains, I had no way to know if they had accomplices here in Italy. I kept in mind their basic body shapes (what I thought of as the O'Byrne Bulk) as I scanned everyone boarding the train. A young mother with wild black curls and brilliant red lipstick seemed an unlikely villain, as did the stooped and white-haired couple who were slowly struggling down the aisle. What about the slender and stylish brunette, glued to her phone? The father with his teenaged son? I watched a pair of very pretty teenage girls. The blonde one seemed to ooze resentment at her seatmate with the perfect skin and the chestnut curls, who in turn appeared to be unaware of the daggers heading her way. None of them seemed dangerous. I kept a wary eye on a clump of wholesome-looking young tourists who were fascinated by everything and everyone on the train. Were they checking on me?

The elderly couple chose my section and fussed until they were settled in. I turned to my *Vogue Italia*. I didn't want to talk and reveal my very limited grasp of the Italian language. But so far, I felt safe.

Of course, I had no idea who else might be in the other cars. I was committed to Cinque Terre without a clear idea of how to find Esme and Signor Colibri, or even which of the five towns they might be in, if they were anywhere in the region. I had sent my two greatest allies in Italy on a wild-goose chase. I couldn't take a chance on aggravating Jack's head injury or triggering another heart attack for Alessandro. For purely selfish reasons I was glad they were safe at the *cooperativo*. I hoped no one was looking for a single woman, me.

The spectacular scenery seen from the train from Genoa to Cinque Terre was very distracting, but I couldn't be gazing at the gorgeous vistas. I needed to put together the pieces of one puzzle to conclude who was behind this. I had a sinking feeling and I sure hoped I was wrong. But right or wrong, I needed a plan. Once there, where to begin? Each town had a population under two thousand, with Manarola and Corniglia having just a few hundred. These tiny towns teemed with restaurants, bars, shops and tourists. I would count on the tourists for cover. And I'd have to hope the crowds weren't sheltering villains.

Chapter 22

Don't break in new shoes when traveling. Bad shoes on holidays have ruined many relationships.

I decided to start with Corniglia because that was where Esme had met the man I now suspected of being Sean Doyle in his favorite restaurant. It was my only lead. I was hoping someone in that restaurant or a nearby shop might recognize him from his "aged" reconstruction. Some of the staff could have worked there for years. They might even know where he lived. The five towns were very close so he could easily visit from any of the others, or even from a community outside the tourist area, like Levanto or La Spezia.

I'd brought a supply of tips for the restaurant and bar staff. It was a far from perfect plan but it was all I had.

Once I made the decision to start with Corniglia, I relaxed a bit. Just enough to survey the people on the train. I've always been interested in people and enjoyed watching them and wondering about their stories. Who were these people and where were they going? I assumed the white-haired couple dozing opposite me were off to visit grandchildren or maybe even great-grandchildren. Was the young mother with the audacious red lipstick planning to leave her rambunctious child with a friend while she met up with a lover? What about the jealous teenager? Would she make her friend pay for being prettier? And all those clean-cut students? Could they really be as wholesome as they looked? I have learned that people are often not what they seem. The train would be full of surprises, none of them for me, I hoped.

I went back to studying the maps concealed inside the *Vogue Italia* and worked on my strategy for Corniglia. Esme favored nice restaurants and good food. She would have been back to that place with Signor Colibri. Also, Corniglia was the smallest of the five towns and the hardest one to reach. It wouldn't take long to check it out. I sat back to soak in the dazzling views as the train raced along the Ligurian coast, the water sparkling and bright, each curve revealing a new view that could take your breath away. My overactive brain shot flashes of Esme's, Lola's and Glenda's faces into my consciousness. My knuckles were white as I gripped the magazine and tried to calm myself.

My elderly neighbors were awake at this point and staring at me. I smiled in what I hoped was an Italian way, although I suspected that a local would have simply ignored them.

They got up creakily as we pulled into Monterosso al Mare, the first of the towns and the one with the best beach, if memory served, although it was a bit early in the season for sunbathing. At least half the tourists on the train jostled toward the doors, spilling out as soon as the train stopped. In the confusion of people disembarking, I thought I saw a familiar hulking silhouette toward the back of the carriage. I couldn't be sure with all the movement. A crowd of chattering sunburned people pushed on, laughing and relaxed, perhaps from visiting one of the many beachside bars.

Corniglia was only about ten minutes further and the cluster of what I assumed were students started collecting their backpacks. I rose without warning, stuffed my *Vogue Italia* into my tote and skipped to the bathroom. Quickly I changed into the jean jacket and sandals and slapped the folding sunhat on my head. I popped the copper wig and the red sneakers into the tote as the train reached the station. A chattering wholesome-looking crowd waited outside the door. I opened the bathroom door to face them. I put my finger to my lips and then said in Italian, "*Mio ragazzo è cattivo! Pericoloso! Posso venire con voi?*" No one seemed to understand. I finally figured they were German, so I tried speaking English to them as Germans seem to pick up English easily. "My boyfriend is bad. Very dangerous. May I come with you?" I tried to look terrified.

That did the trick. They surrounded me protectively. As the train door released us, I was carried along by my new friends, following the arrows and the signs that said *Corniglia*. I wondered if they realized what awaited us in the approach to this gorgeous hilltop town. They looked fit enough, but the three hundred and eighty-two steps, the equivalent of twenty-two flights, would have most people puffing. I could have opted for the much easier road access but I worried I would be more exposed. With the switchbacks on the staircase and my eyes hidden behind my sunglasses, I could spot anyone on my trail.

My new friends clucked on in German around me and I struggled to keep up with them on the climb. They seemed to be in great shape, an inconvenience at that moment. Luckily I'd had plenty of exercise on this trip (mostly running away from bad guys) and I managed not to get left behind. At the top of the staircase, gasping for breath, I slipped away from the group and staggered into the restaurant I remembered so vividly. I recalled the bathroom being across the road and I broke into a run to get there. It was a tight space, but I managed to transform myself again, with the *mariniere*, the woven travel hat, and my denim jacket. I had pretty well exhausted my disguises. I emerged working hard at seeming relaxed. I approached the restaurant from the opposite direction, carefully checking my watch and glancing around as if I was expecting someone. I asked each passing server if they had seen my uncle, producing the aged photo of Sean Doyle. Not a single flicker of recognition. They all seemed busy and stressed and hurried away. I tried not to feel guilty at slowing them down. But my mission was important too. Lives were at stake.

Before long, a young waiter with a face that could have graced a film magazine made his way toward me, smiling in welcome.

Using my best Italian, I said I was waiting for a friend and indicated where I wanted to sit. The table behind a tree gave me a world-class view of the water on one side, the seductive curves of the vivid green vineyards on the other and the tortuous staircase just below. While still being inconspicuous, I could keep an eye out for the much less glamorous road in the back, where local buses arrived at the edge of the town and deliveries were managed.

I ordered a bottle of San Pellegrino and some bread arrived as if by magic, accompanied by a tantalizing fresh-from-the-oven scent. I chose a chocolate flan as it was well past lunch and I deserved a reward after the stairs. I sat back. I did my best to establish a rapport with any of the servers. My vantage point offered a chance to check out the other diners as well as climbers and clumps of people getting off the bus and strolling into the town. I wondered if the O'Byrnes would have the stamina to take the stairs if one or more of them had followed me. That glimpse of the hulking silhouette on the train still bothered me.

The waiter was attentive, almost flirtatious, and he spoke English reasonably well. When he brought my chocolate flan, I flashed the photo of Sean Doyle. "I am trying to find an old family friend. I know he loves this restaurant. Have you seen him recently?"

His eyes widened. "No, I am sorry, but I do not know this man."

"Oh, well. It was worth asking. Do you know this woman? She is his friend, and mine." I flashed the photo of Esme and me from my phone.

"No, signorina." I hoped he didn't get whiplash shaking his head that hard.

I shrugged amiably. "Never mind. I'm sure I'll find them. Could I have some more San Pellegrino please?"

I started on the chocolate flan, which was mouthwatering. I watched as my waiter headed away from the restaurant, out onto the street, and strode rapidly toward the narrow streets of the town. I left my half-eaten flan, my *Vogue Italia* and my jean jacket so no one would think I'd left without paying and rushed after him.

You cannot rush through Corniglia. The streets are crammed with boutiques, outdoor cafés and smart red patio umbrellas that can shade you but also impede your view. You need to dodge seductive racks and displays outside the storefronts, plus the outdoor seating for the bistros. Good for business, bad for me pursuing the waiter. I ignored the straw hats, the colorful tea towels and the heaping baskets of tangy lemon-scented soaps as I shouldered my way through the tourists.

All the rushing raised my body temperature. And it had gotten warmer. I'd figured it would be cool here on the clifftop village overlooking the sea, but I was wrong.

I got close enough to see the waiter slip into a boutique that was totally Esme's style with a lot of floaty scarves and bright linen dresses hanging outside the shop. My eye was caught by a spectacular coral mid-calf dress. Normally, I'd be captivated by this lovely merchandise, but this wasn't normally. Still, I pretended to be examining it while I spied. I checked the tag: the size was large and the price was fifty euros. I peered from behind the display to see the panicky waiter talking urgently to an angular woman with stylish, chin-length dark hair. Emotions were running high. Good! They both gestured wildly with their hands. If the bone structure was anything to go by, they were mother and son.

He ducked out again and raced back toward the restaurant. I had to decide: follow him or find out what the woman in the shop would do now. I stepped inside the shop with a group of cheerful English tourists. The dark-haired woman was talking excitedly on a cell phone by this time. I whispered to one of the English women, "I want to get that coral dress for my sister's thirtieth birthday and I don't want her to spot me." I handed her sixty-five euros and said, "That should cover the dress and VAT. I'll give you another ten if you can get it in a smaller size. That one's way too big for her." I glanced nervously at the door checking for the imaginary sister. Sure, I might end up minus a pile of euros, but I was out of options.

My new friend hustled outside, lifted the coral dress off the hanger and marched confidently to the sales counter. She waited until the call was done. She spoke English loudly to the saleswoman.

"Certainly, madam," was the response. The saleswoman disappeared behind a curtain to what must have been a storage area.

I leaned against the counter and lifted the phone, checking for the number of the last call. I called.

"No need to panic," said a familiar voice, speaking Italian.

"I won't if you don't," I said to my mother. "And don't even think about hanging up."

"What are you doing, Charlotte? Are you insane?" Esme preferred the lead in any drama.

"You need to tell me what is going on with you and your Signor Colibri."

"Charlotte, you have no idea of the danger you are in."

"Incorrect. I have firsthand experience with the O'Byrnes. I hold you responsible. They trashed our house and tried to set a fire. Did you know they burned Lola's house with Lola in it?"

She couldn't suppress her gasp.

I said, "So you'd better tell me what you are up to. I'll wait for you at–"

"Everything is not about you, Charlotte."

"This is!" But I was talking to dead air. Esme wouldn't be meeting me anywhere.

New plan needed.

The curtain jerked open and the saleswoman arrived with the coral dress held high. I slid the phone across the counter. I turned and admired a romantic-looking floppy straw hat. I purchased the hat and moved aside for the British woman, who paid for the dress. She gave me a nod as she headed out the door. Her friends followed and so did I. I accepted the package with thanks. She turned down the ten-euro tip. "Never mind, love, get something extra for your sister. I was happy to help."

I dropped the dress into my tote and looked in the window. The dark-haired woman was staring at her phone, her hand over her mouth.

At the next shop, I eased in, smiling shyly, and asked to try on a large, gauzy cream-colored scarf that could easily double as a shawl and a pair of sandals. "I need to change first, if that is okay. I opened the tote and showed the bag and the hat. "To see if everything will go together?"

The tiny dressing room was just a curtain across a corner in the back. When I emerged I was wearing the new sandals, the hat, the coral dress, plus the gauzy scarf artfully arranged around the neckline. The shopkeeper actually clapped her hands.

"*Bellissima!*"

I was pleased because I now looked nothing like myself when I'd arrived. I paid for the scarf, sandals and a new pair of white-framed sunglasses. I popped on the sunglasses and exited with my nose in the air, pushing my way through the throngs of tourists.

A stooped woman with scraggly white hair and a basket of lemon soap was approaching people and being waved away. She spotted me and made a beeline. The last thing I wanted was any attention from her or anyone, but I figured she was here every day, selling. I whipped out the picture of Sean Doyle. I tried to dig deep to remember my introductory Italian lessons.

"*Ai visto questo uomo?*" I said, meaning, Have you seen this man?

She scrunched up her face. "*L'americano.*"

"*Si. Dov'è habita?*"

But she shook her head. She didn't seem to know where he lived. "*Dov'è l'ai visto?*" At least she should know where she saw him.

She shrugged and looked away. I fished out a ten-euro note and waved it seductively. I asked the question again.

She shrugged. "*Alora, al negozio.*"

Of course, the grocery store! Even in fairy-tale perfect Corniglia, people have to eat. There must be regular food shopping and not just items to tantalize tourists. After a certain amount of drama, the woman pointed toward the next street and pocketed the cash at roughly the speed of light.

Turned out there were three grocery stores on what must have been the main street of Corniglia. Of course. But I figured that even the mythical Signor Colibri would need to buy food. And the glamorous Esme Adams wouldn't be surviving on cans of beans and take-out pizza.

I had no luck at the first store, where I bought a bottle of water. At the second shop, they weren't sure. The staff huddled together and studied Sean Doyle's photo until finally they all shrugged in unison. I purchased a chocolate hazelnut bar as thanks. I trudged along to the third store, wondering what I could buy that weighed less than water and wouldn't melt in my hand.

The first clerk shook his head dismissively. But a bright young woman behind the deli counter nodded enthusiastically. "*Si.*"

"Signor Colibri?" I suggested.

"*Si si! E molto gentile.*"

That was good. I was glad to hear that Sean Doyle was very kind. Probably some bank employees back in Montreal wouldn't agree. She continued rattling on about this *meraviglioso artista*, so unless I was mistaken our own special hummingbird was a wonderful artist. That was new.

I asked if he shopped in the store and if he carried his groceries home. Apparently that was quite funny. She gestured out the door toward the next two towns in the clifftop cluster. "*Galleria d'arte!*" She turned her attention to the grumbling customers who had been waiting during our two-language and many hand signals conversation. I headed off to try the next two towns and find the right art gallery.

My guide to Cinque Terre told me that people travel on the train or on the shuttle buses, but during tourist season, you can get a taxi near the train station if you are lucky. I caught a local shuttle bus to the train station and avoided the zillion stairs. But as I waited for the next train, a dusty cab wobbled in. I engaged him to take me to Riomaggiore. It was larger than Vernazza, which was in the other direction, and I thought more likely to have an art gallery. The furthest of the five towns, Riomaggiore, featured a cascade of multicolored houses, tightly packed with a pretty harbor at the bottom of the town. The streets were actually walkways between levels, much like a vineyard. I figured that the citizens of Riomaggiore must be in top condition if they were always climbing these hills.

I paid the driver from my dwindling stash of euros and began my search. I wended my way down the ancient stone steps toward the town center, attempting to stop anyone who looked local.

I showed Sean Doyle's photo to the first three women I spotted. I picked them because they seemed to be local rather than tourists. Too bad they skittered away. Crazy American was the theme in muttered Italian: *Pazza Americana*. Next I stopped a harried-looking man and waved the photo under his nose. My uncle, I said, "*Mio zio.*" I smiled brightly and tried not to look crazed. "*L'artista.*"

"*Ah, si. L'artista.*" So the word *artist* did the trick. Finally, he took my map and jabbed at a spot that seemed to be down near the water. "*Galleria.*"

At last, I had a place to go. I hurried along toward the art gallery, not allowing myself to be charmed by the many pots with bright flowers, geraniums perhaps, lining the steep stone staircases leading to apartments and their filigreed balconies, bursting with plants and furnished with small tables and chairs. I couldn't stop to admire the magenta bougainvillea blooms or the yellow, gold, soft gray, terra-cotta and brick-red houses, muted like the shades in an ice cream shop. This was no tour. But I understood why Sean Doyle would want to live here. Jean-Claude Dion had mentioned that Sean Doyle had an artistic side. Had the seductive views of the Ligurian Sea converted him from bank robber to artist?

My sandals were already giving me blisters and I limped along, hoping I wasn't going to have to go barefoot, when I spotted the *galleria*. I stepped in, slightly out of breath from rushing. But I got nothing but a curled lip and a scowl when I asked about Signor Colibri, *l'artista*, and showed the photo. I limped away and felt desperation washing over me. With no better plan I headed toward the harbor. Most of the people squeezing by were tourists. Locals had better things to do than elbow me out of the way. I was deciding whether to find a cab to the next village or try to get a boat ride when I spotted another gallery out of the corner of my eye. This one was on the left-hand side of the road. The proprietor nodded as I stepped in and turned back to his paperwork. He didn't sense a sale from sweaty, wild-eyed me. "Do you have anything by Signor Colibri?" I figured the gallery staff would speak English and I was right.

"Only one at the moment, signorina," he said.

My heart soared. "You have one?"

He beckoned me to a far wall and pointed. "Just one, I am afraid. We are waiting for a new series from him."

A new series. I stared at the large canvas that was stretched on a wooden frame. It captured the cascade of ancient, multicolored houses, the vivid flowers, the stone stairs, the essence of Riomaggiore. I could almost smell the sea air from it. Near the left edge, I spotted the sign for the Sentiero Azzuro and the path to Manarola. By the lower right corner, a tiny signature, *Colibri*, and above it, a brilliant butterfly. "I'll take it," I said, without asking the price.

He blinked.

I pulled out my credit card and waggled it. "But I want to meet the artist."

"Of course," he said, slipping the card from my hand. "Will shipping be a problem?" I took a quick photo of the artwork before we decided to take the canvas from its wooden frame and roll it up for a shipping tube. I would take that with me.

"Does he live nearby? I might want to buy more."

The eyebrow went up.

"Through your gallery, of course, since I found him here."

The proprietor pointed to the painting and a pale yellow house several levels higher on a curving street. "I will let him know you are coming."

"That won't be ne—" but apparently I was too late. He spoke rapidly in Italian before a worried look crossed his face. "So sorry, but he is not available today. Tomorrow perhaps?"

"Of course," I said with a false smile. As soon as the sale went through, I grabbed my mailing tube, which was long enough to be awkward, and hustled out.

My cell phone indicated I had a WhatsApp message from Ali. I took the time to glance at it as I trudged up the steep street and toward the steps to Signor Colibri's home. I hoped that it wasn't more bad news about Jean-Claude.

> *Charlotte: I am happy to tell you that Jean-Claude is recovering well and looking forward to getting home and writing again. Big news here in Montreal is that the O'Byrne sisters are being held by the police awaiting an extradition procedure for crimes committed in New York State. Apparently an unnamed source led police to make the connection. I'll keep you posted. There is also an unconfirmed report that DNA has identified Daniel O'Byrne as one of the bodies found in a fatal arson in Woodbridge, NY. Will keep you posted. Stay safe! Ali.*

Although I got a shot of adrenaline from this report on Jean-Claude and the O'Byrnes, I had to worry about whether he would uncover damaging information about Esme and me, not to mention Signor Colibri. But there'd be time to worry about that later. I was puffing when I spotted the house. I recognized it from the painting, a gorgeous soft yellow with a second-floor balcony, lined with potted plants. Bougainvillea climbed the walls.

As I tried to figure out how to access the house, I spotted two people, a man and a woman in Tilley hats, sporting backpacks. They ducked out of sight quickly. Had they been watching me?

"Got you now, Esme and Sean." I felt a surge of euphoria, until I heard a familiar voice behind me. A voice I should not have heard in Cinque Terre. The one person who could possibly have been behind all the trouble and turmoil. The person I'd been hoping it wasn't.

"Hello, Charlotte. I think we need to talk."

Chapter 23

Wherever you travel, things can go wrong. Always try to have a plan B.

It all dropped into place as I forced myself to smile at the woman in the sharp white shirt and the scarlet and gold Hermès scarf. My worst fears. Esme was always dashing around wearing jeans and a white shirt with one of her Hermès scarves, although not in picturesque Italian villages where it looked just plain wrong. I remembered when Esme bought that scarf and also the gorgeous plum leather cross-body bag that slashed across the white shirt. The bag had cost Esme nearly two thousand dollars, but when she damaged the bottom of it slightly, she'd passed it on and bought a new one.

Both items had gone to Glenda, along with stacks of pricy designer goods that Esme had tired of or damaged, trips that Esme had to bow out of at the last minute, unwanted gifts and certificates and even a perfectly good car when Esme decided she needed a Lexus.

Up close, Glenda and Esme didn't resemble each other at all, aside from both being roughly the same age, size and shape. Esme is and always has been beautiful. Glenda was quite attractive, but next to Esme, her eyes seemed too close together, her nose on the wide side and her teeth a bit too large. And the burgundy hair would never have done for Esme. Glenda looked like a normal if slightly eccentric person. Esme resembled a classic film star. I pasted a smile onto my unwilling face. "I am so glad you are all right. I've been worried sick and calling you. Sid is beside himself."

"Cut the BS," she said. "Where is she?"

"What?"

"Don't play games with me, Charlotte."

I shook my head. "I don't understand what you mean." I tried to think how I could attract enough attention to get help or get away. I seemed to have squandered every possible plan B.

"I mean Esme, as you know."

"Well, I've been chasing Esme all over Europe without any luck. I am thinking that I'll have to go to England next. She has a lot of friends there and probably more than one besotted man."

"Nice try. She's been here before and I am betting that she's here now."

A man emerged behind Glenda. He seemed to have no trouble continuing the conversation. His beefy, sloping shoulders screamed "O'Byrne." That bullet-shaped head was a dead giveaway for the males in the family and probably explained why the women stuck to big hair or puffy wigs. His travel vest with the many stuffed pockets would have looked clownish if Baby Bullets hadn't radiated such menace.

"And we both know who she's with, don't we?" he said.

I glanced back, but for once, there were no tourists on the steep streets of Riomaggiore, no housekeeper leaning over a balcony, no shopper struggling up the hill with bags. Where the hell was everyone? Where was Esme now?

"I have no idea," I said.

He sneered. "Do you think we'd believe you don't know who your father is?"

I jerked my head in what I hoped was a good facsimile of surprise. "My dead father?"

The sneer turned to a snort. "Yeah, right, dead. And that's why you are here so close to his house."

"He died in a plane crash twenty-six years ago." The catch in my voice was real. "I just learned about him and his criminal history and—"

"Enough with the crap." He raised his arm so I could see the gun he held. "Where is Shonnie Doyle?" The twisted narrowed eyes burned with hatred for the leader of the Hummingbird Gang.

This O'Byrne wouldn't hesitate to be rid of me. But he probably wouldn't kill me before he got what he came for: my parents. And whatever they had that belonged to Bobby Bullets.

I shook my head helplessly. "I have no idea what you're talking about."

Glenda bit her lip. "What if she's telling the truth?"

"Don't be an idiot," he snapped.

"No, listen, baby. It would be just like Esme to keep her only child in the dark. She's extremely duplicitous."

I perked up. "True. My mother is duplicitous."

"Talk English," he said. He hadn't taken those burning eyes off me. That gaze told me that I was toast whether I sold out my mother and Sean or not. He jabbed a finger at Glenda. "What brought her here if she doesn't know?"

"She's trying to find her mom and, don't laugh, baby, *save* her."

He did laugh. I shivered at the nasty sound. "Okay, then, where is your 'mom'? Don't give me any bullshit about England."

I straightened my spine. I didn't intend to die snivelling in front of these two. "No idea. I haven't tracked her down yet. I believe she'll go to England next. Wales, I imagine."

"I don't think she knows anyone in Wales," Glenda said, frowning.

He scowled. "Do you know everything about her? It's a work relationship, isn't it? She could have friends you don't know about."

"I *do* know everything about her. I booked her trips. I changed her tickets. I upgraded her bookings. I managed Sid. I dealt with the IRS and property managers and real estate agents. I booked her visits to her friends, everything from the flights to the car rentals or limo pickups. My whole life was about making damn sure that Esme Adams never suffered the slightest inconvenience." Glenda's resentment practically formed a black cloud around her. "What did I get? Hand-me-downs with stains or rips."

I dropped the awkward mailing tube and reached out to her. "Glenda, I always thought that you and Esme got along fabulously, although I know she can be a bit, um, self-focused."

Glenda threw back her head and laughed. "Self-focused? She is the most selfish person in the world."

Not completely true. My mother sacrificed for me when I was growing up and she still cared about me, in her own way. "I realize it would be, um, tough to work for her, but I believed you and Esme had it all sorted out and—"

"Save it. Where is she?"

He said, "Where is he?" at the same time.

"She has a friend somewhere around here. We visited years ago. I thought that I might recognize the place." I let a few tears gather in my eyes. It wasn't all that hard.

Glenda's laugh made my skin crawl. "That's just stupid. You're going to the places you think she might be. You have addresses. We've been following you across Europe."

I worked up a look of surprise.

She snorted. "Right, and you had no reason at all to be changing costumes like a trick-or-treater."

"I thought it was someone else. The people who trashed my house in

Woodbridge."

He gestured with the gun. "This is getting boring. Where are they?"

"I don't know. The police are looking for them. They have fingerprints."

"Where is your mother, you idiot."

I tried not to look at the weapon. Where were the swarms of tourists and the resentful locals? Who could help me? I said with what I hoped was great sincerity, "I told you. I keep hitting dead ends. I think they may have left."

"Nice try. If you don't want me to shoot you you'd better tell us."

I had no doubt he would shoot me one way or the other and maybe regardless of what I did, so I forced myself to shrug.

"You'd better figure it out," Glenda said.

Out of the corner of my eye I spotted a flock of touristy types ambling down the hill, taking selfies with the houses, balconies and steep flower-lined staircases in the background. Glenda and Baby Bullets had their backs to the path and hadn't seen them. Yet. Would they shoot these innocent bystanders? I couldn't imagine Glenda doing that, but Baby Bullets wouldn't think twice.

He noticed the small crowd coming and stuck the gun in my ribs. "We'll find a private place to talk."

"Walk toward the path," Glenda said, gesturing to the wooden sign that pointed the way to Manarola. I had always wanted to walk the Sentiero Azzurro, the rugged route with its breathtaking views of the azure sea, but not like this.

"It's closed," I said. "See? There's erosion and a danger of landslides."

"Sure, I see the signs"—she snickered—"and you know I always follow the rules." By now the useless tourists had vanished from view. There wasn't a single witness. And where were the police when you needed them?

Glenda and Baby Bullets pushed me forward and I scrambled over the barrier blocking the path, with them close behind me. I shuffled reluctantly along the trail. I had nowhere to go. You read about the taste of fear, but I was experiencing it now, sour and chilled.

"Again, the authorities have closed this part of the Sentiero Azzurro because of rockslides and unstable ground. People have died here, Glenda. We need to find a safer place to discuss our issues."

"Nice try," Glenda said.

Baby Bullets sneered. "Give me an effing break."

I could imagine the three of us tumbling into the azure sea or, worse, onto the jagged rocks on the coastline below.

I turned and stood my ground. "Glenda, you are Esme's friend."

Her face contorted. "Friend? I was her indentured servant."

"She paid you well and you could have quit any time."

She scoffed. "And have her badmouth me all over the industry? Publishing and author support is what I know. Anyway, she had no respect for me. She'd call in the middle of the night if she got an idea or had a complaint. Wake me on a Saturday morning at five thirty."

I knew it was true. "She's not the easiest, but this is—"

"This is *my* chance to be the one with the life, with someone who loves me. I'll buy the designer clothes and shoes and go everywhere I want. Me. Once we find Esme."

"Esme tried to be good to you, in her own way. Didn't she give you that gorgeous Hermès scarf you're wearing? That's worth—"

She scowled. "A hand-me-down. She didn't like the color. She can never offer anything without twisting the knife."

"Your bag is lovely. She gave that to you."

"Sure. She got a stain on the bottom. If I hadn't taken it, she would have tossed it in the garbage."

Oh, Esme. If only you weren't quite so much like yourself.

"After this I'll be able to buy whatever I want whenever I want it. Hermès scarves, even a Birkin bag."

"Look, Glenda. You could launch a harassment suit and not risk your freedom by harming or killing anyone. These days people are striking back if they've been badly treated. The courts and public opinion are backing them up." I chose not to mention that people had already been killed, like Lola, and harmed, like Jack. I also kept quiet about the generous salary, benefits and bonuses Glenda had always received. Not to mention the trips that Esme had chosen not to take at the last minute, when Glenda had seemed very happy to take her place in Australia or Rio.

"Killing any of you? All three of you are going to die," Baby Bullets said. "Only question is how much pain you'll experience."

I had been wondering why Baby Bullets was letting me talk so much, delaying the inevitable, but now I figured he was just reveling in his power to end my life.

Glenda said, "It was stupid of you to show up here, Charlotte. At least you'll die fast. It's on you if Esme has a long, slow time of it."

I was having trouble breathing as I processed this.

Baby Bullets wiped the sweat from his forehead with his sleeve. Without putting down his weapon, he slipped out of the vest, and smiled at me in a way you don't want to be smiled at. His piggy eyes glittered. He was a man who enjoyed his work. "Your knees, I think, first."

"Glenda, do you really think you've found love with this man? Did it occur to you that he might have sought you out because of your job and connection to Esme?"

"Shut up," he said.

Glenda stepped in front of him and leaned closer to me. Her face was tight with rage. "I am entitled to love and happiness. Robert loves me."

I had nothing to lose. "Glenda, you always did your homework. That's what made you so valuable. But you slipped up this time."

"What are you talking about?"

"Get out of the way, Glenda," Baby Bullets growled.

My knees wobbled, my heart thundered and my stomach clenched. Plus, my brain signaled what my death would look like, leaving me terrified and shaking on a crumbling path with the dry taste of dust in my mouth. I should have fallen sobbing to the ground and spilled everything I knew about Esme and Sean. But strangely enough, I had faced death before and, against all odds, was still alive. As they say, what doesn't kill you makes you stronger.

All these two cared about was getting me to talk. I pivoted and stared at the empty path ahead and their eyes followed my movement. With luck that would keep them from spotting the people creeping along the narrow treacherous path toward us. A man and a woman wearing Tilley hats were in the lead, others close behind them. I hoped against hope that Baby Bullets and Glenda wouldn't catch sight of them. Several others, likely locals mixed with tourists, inched closer. Did I spot a police uniform?

Glenda stood between me and Baby Bullets and his sleek black handgun.

"You know about his family, Glenda?"

She smirked. "They are powerful and effective."

"Sorry, Glenda. The Bobby Bullets gang are just second-rate mobbed-up thugs, in and out of maximum-security prisons. These are the people who set

Esme's friend Lola's house on fire with her in it and one of the brothers was stupid enough to die along with her. And really there's nothing left of them. The father is dying. The police have arrested the two sisters. They have fingerprints and other evidence linking them to arson and murder in New York. Oh, and there's still his wife and children. Did he mention them?" I made up that last bit, but what did I have to lose?

Lola's death didn't seem to bother Glenda, but the family was news to her. Shock washed over her face. "You are lying to save your life, Charlotte. Too late for that. If Esme was here, she'd say 'what a cliché.'"

"Well, if you're looking for a cliché, consider his girlfriend."

She jerked back.

"Glenda, he and his family are all over the internet. You just have to let yourself check."

Baby Bullets had had enough. "Cut the crap. Get the hell out of the way, Glenda."

"I can show you photos. Very lovey-dovey. Come on, Glenda. You can tell by looking at me I'm telling the truth. You think he'll need you once he's got Sean Doyle and Esme and the loot from the vault robbery?"

That was my last hope for breaking up this murderous team.

Baby Bullets elbowed his way in front of Glenda bellowing.

But I didn't plan to shut up. Or stand still. My knees were planning to move, and fast. I pivoted to face Baby Bullets and Glenda, while edging further away from the sheer drop. We were all in precarious positions. Glenda followed my move, her eyes burning.

I banked on Glenda's insecurity and tossed out a big lie. "The girlfriend is a model. The wife a former actress. Tall, blonde, glamorous, both of them much younger than you. He'll take that money and he'll head straight to Montreal and both his women. You're a smart girl, Glenda. How long do you think this thug will let you live with what you know?"

"Time for you both to die." He raised the gun again.

Glenda faced him, grief distorting her face. "What?"

He shrugged. "She's right. I can have any woman I want. Did you really think I'd stick with an old lump like you once I had what I wanted?"

"But you don't have what you want yet. You can't kill me until you do." I shouted, hoping my words would carry to the people edging along the path.

"I've got *you*," he smirked, "and I can make you do what I want."

With a howl, part anguish, part fury, Glenda lunged at Baby Bullets. The gun flew from his hand and he lurched backward, slipping at the eroded edge.

I kicked the gun along the path as far as I could.

Glenda shrieked and pounded at Baby Bullets' chest.

Cursing, he tried to push her away but she dodged, scratching his face and then kicking at his knees. His piggy eyes widened and his arms waved wildly as he struggled for balance. Then, seeming in slow motion, he slipped, tumbling backward, his long shriek blending with Glenda's wild screams.

Glenda stared in horror as he hit the rocks below. I sank to my knees, stunned. Glenda leaned over the cliff before whirling on me. "This is your fault. What if he dies?"

Behind her someone spoke. "No one could survive that fall."

Glenda whirled, eyes wide.

Esme stood watching, unmoved apparently by the horrific sight. An attractive and inoffensive-looking middle-aged man with a slight paunch, a weathered face and mischievous hazel eyes put his hand on her shoulder.

She said, "You brought it all on yourself, Glenda. That SOB is dead because he's a murdering villain, like everyone else in his family. He would have tossed you over after Charlotte if he'd lived to have the opportunity."

"Esme," I pleaded. "Not now. She's just seen . . ."

But Glenda was ready for a battle. "You used me and exploited me for years."

Esme wasn't having any of that. "I funded your college tuition because you couldn't afford it. I paid you well above the going rate for assistants. I covered your mother's medical bills. Of course, that was while you were still speaking to her. I gave you bonuses. What the hell did you want?"

"To be your equal!"

Esme snorted. "You were willing to betray me and murder Charlotte, who has always been kind to you. You are in no way my equal."

"Glenda." I stumbled to my feet, interrupting Esme. "This man took advantage of you. Come away from the edge. We will work everything out where it's safe."

Esme snorted. "Work it out? I don't think so."

Glenda paced, sputtering with rage. Esme had a point. She had always rewarded Glenda well, but Esme could ride roughshod over feelings.

Without warning, Glenda lunged toward my mother. I yelled, "There are three of us. Calm yourself."

Telling people to calm themselves never works. Glenda yanked the plum-colored bag from around her neck and swung it at Esme's head.

Sean Doyle stepped toward Glenda, his hands out to protect Esme. "Stop it." He hadn't even picked up the gun on the side of the path.

Glenda dodged sideways to get at Esme, lashing at her again with the bag. She slipped on the loose surface of the path. She wobbled and tipped back toward the edge.

Nearby, I heard voices raised in Italian. I thought they were shouting, "This area is off-limits. It is very dangerous." Then I heard a British voice insisting: "Please turn around at once. It is far too dangerous and this trail is closed. You must return."

"Help us," I yelled to the group inching on the path. "She is too close to the edge and she's hysterical. Someone has already gone over!"

At the sound of feet thudding closer, Glenda screamed, "Get away from me." She leaned further back, panic in her eyes.

"No!" I managed to grab the bag with one hand and Glenda's shirtsleeve with the other. "Hold on to me! I'll pull you back."

Sean joined me and latched on to Glenda's arm.

"Don't let her drag you over!" Esme grabbed my waist and yanked me back. I tugged on the bag, pleading with Glenda to lean toward me. The quality leather strap on the purse was strong but Glenda was in full-blown panic. We were all struggling on the edge of the steep cliff on a crumbling path that was no more than three feet wide.

"Get him away from me," she screamed.

"We're trying to help you. Everything will be all right." I yelled at Sean, "Move back!"

We heard voices raised in English and Italian. Without letting go, Sean shouted toward the people on the path, "Help her. Her husband already fell and–"

My grip on Glenda was slipping. I yelled, "Glenda, please, hold on."

I heard a flurry of steps, saw arms reaching out to grasp Glenda. One man looked like a police officer. Glenda's eyes widened at the sight of his uniform. He grabbed her right arm firmly. I was still holding on to the bag and her other arm. "Let me go," she yelled, pushing away, flailing wildly.

"Don't touch me. I want to die too. And it's all their—"

The final word was lost in an anguished cry as gravity won and Glenda cascaded toward the rocks below and her treacherous dead lover. The sound echoed in my mind. Whatever she had done or wanted to do to us, I'd cared about Glenda.

I collapsed onto the path and felt the shock as my head hit a rock.

Too many people gathered around on the narrow and dangerous path, including the agitated police officer and the worried British tourists attempting to take charge. A few locals kept squawking in alarm.

Sean called to the newcomers approaching, "Be careful! Go back! "*State attenti.*"

I crawled to the edge and peered down at the rocks and waves below. Glenda's crumpled body was half on the rocks and half in the water, floating, the bright scarlet and gold scarf fluttering around her. Esme dragged me back and wrapped her arms around me. She wailed, "*Sua madre è morta!*" Her mother is dead! That made no sense. Glenda was dead. My mother was right here—Esme, white-faced and dry-eyed held me tightly. "We have to do it this way," she whispered. "No choice."

"What? But Glenda is dead."

"Yes, and she brought it on herself. Just follow my lead."

I started to speak and Esme squeezed my arm to silence me. That has worked all my life. Her face was impassive as she snatched up Glenda's plum-colored bag from where it had fallen. Everyone else in the growing crowd seemed mesmerized by the horrific sight below the cliff. Where had all these people come from and where had they been when I needed them?

Esme opened the bag and felt around. "Her passport is here. And a car rental agreement." Esme stuffed them into her backpack. She took out her own passport and the soft leather wallet I had given her for her last birthday. She dropped them into Glenda's bag.

"Check that vest for ID, Shonnie." Sean Doyle bent over and picked up the khaki vest. He felt around in the various pockets and pulled out a wallet and a passport and tucked them back in again.

"O'Byrne, all right," he said. He slipped on the vest.

"Toss yours on the ground over there," Esme said in a voice too low for others to hear.

Sean Doyle kicked his wallet and passport further down the path.

The small crowd remained by the edge of the cliff, continuing to gawk at the two bodies below. The Italians were talking rapidly and waving their arms. The British man boomed instructions that no one paid attention to. Two Americans began to hug each other. No one took any notice of Esme and Sean. Or me.

Esme said, "I do love a good twist at the end."

I found myself shivering even in the heat. "Shouldn't we be doing something? Is there any way they could still be–?"

"No way in hell. But this could all work out for the best," Esme said, her face harder than I'd ever seen it.

"Work out how? She's dead. Dead!"

Sean Doyle spoke in a soft, almost musical voice. "She came here with Baby Bullets to kill us, to kill your own mother and you too. Her jealous behavior was the cause of her death."

"Did you know?" I asked Esme.

"I figured it out just in time to escape. She let something slip and gave herself away the last time we spoke. She wasn't as clever as she thought she was. I tried to keep you out of it, but you were too stubborn."

"Yes, but what do you mean 'work out'?"

Esme continued to whisper. "There are two dead Americans below. They will not be recognizable after that fall, but they match our general description. Everyone saw the three of us try to save her and they heard you pleading. Take this and keep it safe. Don't look at it now." I blinked as she dropped something into my pocket. "Just so you know, there's not much left to my estate. I've got what I need to go on with, but the Paris apartment will go to you and the condo in New York will be yours too. I imagine they'll sell for a reasonable price, although the French government will take a big bite out of the price. Use the flash drive however you want to. You are my literary executor, as you know."

My head was swimming. "But what are you talking about? I don't understand any of–"

Esme just shrugged and moved to stand next to Sean Doyle–I still couldn't think of him as my father–who was now explaining patiently to the police officer that, as far as they could tell, the dead woman was my mother and the man her partner. The partner had insisted on taking the trail and seemed to have dragged my poor mother and me along with him, recklessly.

He slipped and fell and the woman panicked and went over the cliff too." By now my teeth were chattering, no acting necessary. Esme turned back to me and patted my shoulder. "Their daughter is in shock, losing her family in that terrible way," Esme said with remarkably real-looking tears streaking her dusty cheeks. "She was very brave trying to save her mother. I was afraid she would be pulled over the edge too. She may even have a concussion from hitting her head. Look!"

Like a dope, I felt the hair on the side of my head. My hand came away bright red just before everything went dark.

When my eyes opened again, someone had wrapped a blanket around my shoulders.

An Italian woman kept saying, "*Poverina.*" Poor little thing.

Esme put her hand on the police officer's arm and said in passable Italian, "Is it possible for us to give our statements now? This tragedy has been extremely upsetting and we have a plane to catch."

Chapter 24

Don't be afraid to ask the right people for help if you get into a tough situation.

Time blurred. Was it minutes, hours or even days? However long, I was poked and prodded by a local doctor and fussed over by residents and tourists. Sean Doyle, now transformed into an amiably forgettable Canadian tourist named Robert O'Byrne, Jr., assisted by translating. Even in my stunned state, I wondered if he might be recognized by one of his neighbors. Of course, he looked different now, as did Esme in her role as Glenda, his American girlfriend. Sean dealt with the police. "Glenda" accepted sympathy for what she'd witnessed and dished some out too. Soon they were sent on their way with cheerful waves. Such nice people and after all, they had a plane to catch. Before they left, "Glenda" handed me the mailing tube with the painting.

"Be careful," I said as tears stung my eyes.

• • •

Hours later, still dazed, wrapped in a blanket and clutching the mailing tube, I watched as a white-faced Jack and a grief-stricken Alessandro barreled through the clinic door. Jack sputtered, "He drove that poor Abarth like it was Formula One."

"Please don't ask me to talk about what happened," I begged. "I just need to go home. But first I have to identify the bodies."

Alessandro caught his breath. Jack plunked next to me on the hard plastic seat. He held me and asked nothing.

Alessandro vanished briefly and then returned with coffee for the three of us. Apparently, there were no hard feelings about the borrowed Audi. "I have explained that I am your stepfather. I will identify her."

I shook my head.

He said, "It will be easier that way, Charlotte. They may not speak English."

My chin wobbled. "I need to say goodbye. And you didn't even know Sean, Signor Colibri."

Jack said, "I'm going with you."

In the end, despite my protests, we all went together. Alessandro squeezed my hand. Jack had his arm firmly around my shoulder. I held my breath, at the horror of the identification process and at not knowing what we would see.

As they drew back the sheet from Glenda's ravaged face, my knees buckled. Jack caught me in time. I struggled to speak.

Jack was smart enough to work it out. He'd known Esme since he was a child. He'd met Glenda several times. He could tell the difference between them. He wrapped me in his arms and we both turned away from Glenda's body. "I'll look after you," he whispered.

The attendant turned to Alessandro, who nodded slowly. I worried that someone would notice the relief washing over his haggard face as he realized that it wasn't Esme. Alessandro kept it together.

Next it was Baby Bullets. He had met the rocks head-on. I stared in shock, reminding myself that this man had been involved in all the attacks. He had been intent on killing Esme, Sean and me. And Glenda too as soon as it was convenient.

Alessandro said, "I never met this man."

I dug my fingernails into Jack's arm and said, "I am sorry, Alessandro. This was her companion. I only met him once." It was true enough if you didn't get too hung up on the names behind the pronouns.

I started to shake and Jack insisted on helping me from the room. If you asked me to describe anything after that, I couldn't. I didn't pay attention to the police, not even which of the many Italian police services they were. My statement might have been given by a robot, although no one seemed to find this surprising. I don't remember what the doctor told me to do or what he looked like. Glenda's betrayal had been traumatizing, but her death was even more so. I wanted to cover my ears to drown out the memory of her endless scream. Instead I fingered the memory stick that Esme had left in my pocket.

As Alessandro went to get the car and Jack hunted for coffees for the road, I stood in a hallway trying to get a grip. Esme charged past me, heading to confer with a pair of local officials. Sean paused next to me and looked down. I glanced up and gazed into his eyes, warm hazel with flecks of gold, exactly like mine.

"I'm so sorry, Seanna–Charlotte," he said, "for everything."

I opened my mouth and snapped it closed again. What could I say to that?

He squeezed my hand. "You were cheated out of a normal childhood and I was deprived of all the special moments when you were growing up. I can never make up for that. That is my greatest regret."

My throat was tight. I croaked out, "Why didn't you come for us?"

His face twisted. "It was too dangerous. Bobby Bullets killed everyone I was associated with, men who were like brothers to me. The O'Byrnes had criminal tentacles everywhere, even in the police and at the border crossings. You've seen how they managed to find us even after twenty-six years. No question they would have located you and Esme if I had ever shown up. I went to ground in Europe and chose to let Esme believe I was dead for a long time. Apparently not long enough," he said with a bitter smile. "This was a close call."

I shivered, flashing back to the gruesome events on the Sentiero Azzurro. Before I could say anything else, Esme swooshed past and Sean hurried after her, leaving me with even more to think about.

• • •

Tear tracks stained Ornella's face as we sat disconsolately around the huge round kitchen table. I thought the tears were more for Alessandro than Esme. Eventually, Ornella managed to pull herself together, dished up her special croquettes and urged me to eat.

Jack said, "Wow, what's in these? I can taste chicken and ricotta."

Alessandro, whose head had been in the clouds, said, "It's a typical Piedmontese dish. Ornella will have added sage leaves, onions, lemon juice, and parsley. She shaped that into croquettes, which are dipped in eggs and breadcrumbs."

"*Fantastico.*" Jack saluted Ornella.

For me, it tasted like sawdust, nothing to do with the immense skill of the cook.

Alessandro went back to staring off in the distance. Though he knew the truth, he also knew there'd never be a chance to reconnect with Esme.

No one objected when we headed to the guest house early along with a laptop borrowed from Alessandro.

I reached into my pocket to retrieve what Esme had placed there. I slid the memory stick into the laptop. I watched slack-jawed as Esme's final manuscript slowly opened.

Jack joined me in staring at the title page:

Not Who You Think I Am

There was nothing but the buzzing of a fly in the room as we let that sink in.

Finally, Jack said. "She knew she was going to disappear?"

"She couldn't have known what was going to happen. But she did know I was nearby. I called."

"And she knew the O'Byrnes were relentless."

"I believe she and Sean Doyle were planning to disappear when it all happened. Baby Bullets was getting too close."

"And Esme and Sean had nothing to do with the deaths?"

I shot him a sharp glance. "Nothing. They didn't cause either one of them to go over the edge. I can swear to that and there were other witnesses. I saw Esme and Sean leaving the house, probably heading to where a car was parked. They ducked out of sight just as Glenda and Baby Bullets arrived. They must have found out somehow where Sean's house was. Of course, the name Colibri would have meant something to Bobby Bullets. It's the same word in French and Italian, and he would have learned French growing in Montreal. I think Esme and Sean were about to leave. I made that phone call and that probably got them going. But Esme must have seen them forcing me onto the path. If I hadn't called, perhaps Glenda and Baby Bullets would still be alive and Esme and Sean would be off to a new and different life."

He squeezed my hand. "Glenda and Bobby caused their own deaths. And we were just lucky they didn't take you with them."

I inhaled and thought sadly about Lola. "So much devastation." Time to be strong. "I'd better call Pepper," I said.

"I'll do it. You're too distraught."

"What? I'm not distraught. Oh, right. I would be if Esme was dead. Sure."

Pepper did answer. I could hear her shouting from across the room.

Jack shouted back, "Listen to me, Pepper. Charlotte's mother died today in Italy. She fell to her death in a terrible, tragic accident. Her partner also died. Charlotte witnessed all of it. She's . . . in a bad way. Can you let everyone else in our group know? Including Lilith and Rose? We're coming home, but it will be good if Charlotte doesn't have to make those calls. People will need to give her some space. I'm worried about her."

Angry squawks emitted from the receiver.

"I know, Pepper. But we were trying to find Esme, who was not responding to anything." Jack managed to inject so much emotion into his voice that I knew it was real. "So we'll deal with whatever we have to when we get home. We hope to get out of Italy before the paparazzi show up once the police release Esme's name."

I sighed with relief when that was over. There was a good chance Pepper would throw the book at us, but I felt confident she knew we could never have killed Lola. There was no reason to think she was aware of the Hummingbird Gang or Esme's involvement in old crimes. Plus, Pepper had used the opportunity to nab those nasty O'Byrne sisters and collect a bit of glory.

My turn to make a tough call.

"Did I catch you at a bad time, Sid?"

"What do you think?"

"You'd better sit down."

I held the phone away from my ear. "If you're finished bellowing, I have to let you know that Esme died today in an accident in Italy along with her lover."

I'd never experienced silence from Sid before. "Sid?"

"Dead? But . . . What about the book?"

"Don't jerk me around, Sid. I lost my mother today and that's more important than the book."

Was that a whimper? Good.

"This is not a good-news story," I added. "But I do have the latest version of her final manuscript. And as her literary executor and her heir, I can ensure you get it."

"Is it finished?"

"You can read it and decide. You should also know that she, um, fired Glenda a while back, and so you'll be dealing with me from now on."

• • •

I had given my deposition and was hoping to return to Woodbridge. We had to wait to see if I would be needed at the inquest and, indeed, to learn when that inquest would be. I think Jack and I offered some comfort to Alessandro and Ornella. And *la dottoressa* could continue that.

Life was made somewhat easier because several reliable people, including a local police officer, had witnessed what happened. My deposition was enough to carry the day.

On our final visit to Riomaggiore to sign documents, I learned that Signor Colibri had left his lovely little yellow house to his brokenhearted housekeeper.

I felt confident that whatever Sean Doyle had taken from the heist would be safely in the wind with him and Esme.

It was time to move on.

Chapter 25

When you return, don't procrastinate on unpacking and laundry. Air out your suitcase and put it away for the next adventure.

Home at last! My heart soared as the cab pulled up in front of our yellow Victorian. It took a dip when I spotted Pepper, arms crossed, waiting in her vehicle. But before I could engage her, Lilith appeared with the dogs. She gathered me into a big hug as Truffle and Sweet Marie flung themselves at my ankles. "I think you'll be surprised by a few things," she said.

Jack's place was pretty much as we'd left it but my upstairs unit had been organized and practically sparkled. Nothing would bring back my ruined furniture and broken dishes, but Lilith had performed a miracle. Apparently she had help from her boyfriend, Seth, and Wendy, his mom, a happy former client. Ramona had also pitched in, and altogether they had recreated a home. A fantastic aroma of baking wafted from the kitchen. "Some of the furniture, including the sofa and dishes, came from Goodwill. I hope you don't mind," Lilith said. "You'll be renovating anyway and you can use the insurance money to get what you want when the reno's done. Jorge and his brothers from Jack's shop helped too. Jack put us in touch with them. They were reluctant to touch his apartment, but we all wanted to do something for you, especially after your huge loss. Um, the freezer's full of New York Super Fudge Chunk and Rose has made something special. You and Jack can fight over it."

I curled up on the new-to-me sofa and the dogs settled into my lap. I stroked their silky fur and felt some of my tension melt away. My hummingbird earrings felt just right.

Rose appeared from the kitchen with a plate of warm cinnamon buns. "I thought since you flew overnight, you might want breakfast." The cinnamon buns came with more hugs. Truffle and Sweet Marie, their black eyes gleaming, positioned themselves to steal a couple.

Lilith cleared her throat. "Some people want to come by to see you. I hope that's okay."

I could already hear Sally and Margaret chattering on the stairs. I had my mouth full of cinnamon bun when they appeared in the doorway. Sally burst into tears and Margaret looked even more somber than usual. The tough part for me was going to be faking grief.

Pepper followed them into the apartment and actually took the lead. She likes that kind of thing. "I want you to know that we are all here for you and we will be."

"Thank you."

"Given the circumstances, we won't be filing charges against you for obstruction or anything else. No action has been taken."

I blinked. I hadn't known that obstruction charges were possible.

"That's only right," Jack said flintily.

"Exactly," Margaret said. "No lawsuit against the police yet either on our side."

Pepper was reluctant to give up center stage. "By the way, those Canadians were part of a vicious Montreal gang headed by an elderly murderer who was released on compassionate leave. The two sisters have been apprehended and one brother's body was found at the fire site. The Montreal police tell me that the old man died just after his daughters were arrested. There's another son, but he's gone to ground somewhere in Europe. The Montreal police are confident they'll find him. I'm sure he'll get what's coming to him. We still don't know what the connection was with Woodbridge and the attack on your home and Lola's, but it will all come out in time."

I sure hope not, I thought.

But never mind. We were home, surrounded by friends and warm cuddly dogs and delicious treats. Tuesday nights would never be the same, but our cuts and bruises would heal and eventually the emotional trauma would fade. Our house would be renovated. Alessandro could get on with his life. Sid might calm down. Jack and I would have to return to Paris to dispose of the apartment in Batignolles once the estate was settled. We'd work in the *bateaux mouche* and the Musée d'Orsay and more. I'd sell the Manhattan condo and Regis would get an appropriate gift to thank him for his loyalty. Eventually Signor Colibri's painting of Riomaggiore would look amazing over our replacement sofa.

Jack and I would see what the future held for us and just possibly the phone would still ring on Tuesday nights.

Recipe

Chocolate Espresso Hazelnut Biscotti

These little twice-baked cookies capture the flavors of Piedmont and Ornella's kitchen and are perfect for dunking in your morning caffe latte.

3 large eggs
2 tablespoons instant espresso powder
2 teaspoons pure vanilla extract
2 cups unbleached flour
2 tablespoons good-quality cocoa
2 teaspoons baking powder
1 teaspoon salt
½ cup unsalted butter, room temperature
1 cup sugar, plus a few tablespoons more for sprinkling
1 cup blanched hazelnuts
4 ounces semisweet or bittersweet chocolate, coarsely chopped

Preheat oven to 325 degrees.

Place eggs in a bowl, add espresso powder and vanilla and beat well.

Whisk flour, cocoa, baking powder, and salt in a medium bowl. Using an electric mixer on medium speed, beat butter and sugar until light and creamy, about 2 minutes. Scrape down sides of bowl, then add egg mixture; beat just to incorporate.

Add dry ingredients and mix on low speed until blended.

Add hazelnuts and chocolate and mix to evenly distribute.

Divide dough into 4 loaves and place on parchment-lined baking sheets. Flatten loaves to about 1½ inches. Sprinkle loaves with extra sugar.

Bake loaves, rotating baking sheets front to back halfway through, until firm in the center and starting to crisp at the edges, 30–35 minutes. They will widen as they bake. Transfer baking sheets to wire racks; let loaves cool 15 minutes.

Transfer loaves to a cutting board. Using a serrated knife, slice ½ inch thick, at a slight angle. Arrange biscotti cut-side down on baking sheets and bake again, rotating baking sheets front to back halfway through, until dry and crisp, 30–35 minutes. Let cool and store airtight at room temperature. They will keep for about a week, but you might eat them all before then.

About the Author

Lapsed librarian and former mystery bookseller Mary Jane Maffini is the author of three and a half mystery series and two dozen short stories. Her Charlotte Adams professional organizer mysteries have been optioned for television. The series has been reissued by Beyond the Page Publishing and she is hard at work on some new Charlotte adventures.

There are six books in the Camilla MacPhee series set in Canada's capital, Ottawa, and two Fiona Silk comic capers take place in a quirky village in West Quebec.

As Victoria Abbott, Mary Jane collaborated on the five collector mysteries (Berkley Prime Crime) with her daughter, Victoria. Book Four, *The Marsh Madness*, won the 2015 Bony Blithe for "mysteries that make us smile."

In addition to the Crime Writers of Canada's Derrick Murdoch Award, Mary Jane holds three CWC Awards for short stories and an Agatha Award (Malice Domestic) for Best Short Story. *The Busy Woman's Guide to Murder* (Charlotte Adams Mystery #5) won the 2012 *Romantic Times* Award for Amateur Sleuth. She was also shortlisted for the Anthony Award for Best Short Story (Bouchercon), and *The Dead Don't Get Out Much* was nominated for the Barry Award for Humorous Mystery in 2006. Other CWC nominations include: Best First Novel for *Speak Ill of the Dead* and Best Novel for *Lament for a Lounge Lizard* and three other crime short stories.

You Light Up My Death, Camilla MacPhee Mystery #7, will be released in October 2022. Mary Jane lives and plots in Manotick, Ontario, with a cluster of mischievous dachshunds at her feet. Her husband sleeps with one eye open. You can read more about Mary Jane and her books and sign up for her newsletter at maryjanemaffini.com.

Made in the USA
Columbia, SC
07 November 2024

45916150R00143